FALLEN WARRIOR

FALLEN
WARRIOR

Dylann Rhea

Dream Seekers Press

Fallen Warrior (Storm Trilogy, Book Two)
Published by Dream Seekers Press

@2015, 2025 by Dylann Rhea
Cover design by: Dylann Rhea

Published 2025.
First edition Published 2015. Second edition 2025.

ISBN: 979-8-9899102-0-5

For
the readers.

PROLOGUE

Southwestern Germany
October 30, 1995

The faded hum of insects lingered outside the cabin's log walls. Chirping crickets created music for the dancing lightning bugs that flickered against the dead night sky. The trees stood silently, motionless, like grieving mourners at a funeral. The night, which should have been a joyous one, fell victim to the darkness.

A cool breeze blew in through the open window, swaying the curtains lightly. The sheer drapery brushed up against the back of the rocking chair where the new mother held her baby girl for the first time. Her blonde hair, damp still from giving birth, hung down one side of her face. Her gaze mesmerized by the tiny life fast asleep in her arms.

She breathed, softly, through a little button nose. Her

hand, a tiny little thing barely big enough to clasp one of her mothers' fingers. She was supposed to be safe in her arms, but her mother knew she wasn't. A bundle so new to the world, and yet, already burdened with things she couldn't comprehend.

Sharp words and hushed tones outside the bedroom reminded the woman of her reality. Reminded her of the mess she had created. The one she intended to fix for her baby, the only thing that mattered to her anymore.

The door creaked open. A tall, slender man slipped into the room, closing the argument behind him. He was young, like the woman, wearing a mournful expression he couldn't hide if he tried. "Helena," his voice broke through the distant noises. Gingerly, he stepped closer to the woman and her newborn. Her skin was pink, the slits of her eyes shut. He wished he didn't have to interrupt the blissful moment.

Helena hadn't lifted her gaze away from her sleeping child until he was standing beside her chair. Her soundless cry left a trail of tears down her cheeks. "It's time," he said. He kneeled beside her, taking her free hand in his. "It has to be now before it's too late."

"I know." Her words were nothing but a whisper. A fresh tear fell down the pathway the others had left. Helena's gaze pleaded to him, "Just give me another minute, Silas." He didn't respond. Instead, he watched as Helena said her last goodbyes to her daughter. She looked down admiringly at her, "It's not fair, what happened to you. You were supposed to be happy, with a loving family." Helena bit her lower lip to hold back any more tears. "And I'm sorry for what has happened. It's my job to protect you and make sure you're happy and loved, but..." She sucked in a deep breath and squeezed her eyes shut. A tear forced its way through the crack of her eye and Silas wiped it away before it could fall down her cheek like the rest had. "I messed up and you have to pay for my mistakes. It's not fair. And for that I am so sorry my baby girl." Silas squeezed Helena's hand tightly to reassure her she was doing the right thing, though it would be the most difficult decision she would ever make. She kissed the baby's forehead gently, "It's my responsibility to give you the best life you can possibly have. I'm giving you your best chance, but that doesn't mean I don't love you or you aren't wanted. Because you have no idea just how big my love for you is. I love you, Aurora. One day, I will see you again. I will hold you in my arms and tell you how much you mean to me." Her lips pressed against the baby's face one last time before placing her in Silas's arms.

"She'll be safe," he assured her before he rose to his feet with the bundle of pink blanket.

As Silas slipped out of the room, an older woman with deep wrinkles took his place, filling the void. The moment Aurora was out of Helena's sight, she burst into tears of grief, of anger, of guilt. The woman wrapped her tightly in her arms. She peeled Helena's hair from her face. "I—I can't do this," Helena said through sobs and heaping breaths. "I need her, she belongs with me. She should be with me." The woman didn't say anything. She only held her tighter and began to cry herself.

CHAPTER 1

June 30, 2014

The ground beneath the swing was nothing more than a patch of dirt now. Not like when Kaden and Megan were little. But summer nights the two would ride their bikes down to the park and go on the swings, just to be kids again. "Do you think we'll remember this?" Megan asked as she forced the swing as high as it would allow.

"What?" Kaden wondered. "Remember how to swing?" She traced a design in the patch of dirt beneath her feet with the tip of her toe. It consisted mostly of intertwining swirls that had no specific pattern, just elegant loops.

"No," Megan answered. "Remeber what it feels like to be young. You know," she lowered herself backward so she was horizontal to the swing before continuing, "when we get old and delusional."

"Who says we will even get that old?" Kaden said with a sharpness that came with the truth. "We could die in a car accident tomorrow."

Megan sat upright abruptly and jumped off the swing mid-air. "Sometimes I forget how much of a pessimist you are."

"I'm not a pessimist," Kaden corrected. Megan shot her a sideways glance before lifting herself off the ground. "I'm just being realistic."

In the distance, a long single howl rippled through the night air. It was a hollow thing, filled with sorrow or guilt or something Kaden couldn't quite put her finger on. She looked over her shoulder in the direction it came from. "Did you hear that?"

"Yeah," Megan waved her hand to disregard the noise. "It's probably just Mr. Volen's dog. Alright," she cracked her knuckles, "I'm going to superman this bitch." She darted into the swing, stomach down and held her hands out straight.

"It didn't sound like a dog," Kaden said as she eyed the empty street. "It sounded like a wolf," she added under her breath.

The low buzz from the street lamp grew louder as the light flickered on and off. Kaden got off the swing, making her way toward the street. In the dead night air there were only parked cars and street lamps glowing a shade between orange and yellow. There were no dogs, no woods nearby for a wild animal to come stalking out of.

Her attention lingered on the stillness for a moment,

until she was satisfied no dog would appear racing down the road looking for a victim. When she turned again to the swing set, she found it was empty. The swing swooshed back and forth like an echo. But no one was there. Megan was gone.

"Can anyone explain the difference between gems and crystals?" The college professor asked with enthusiasm to a sea of vacant faces. "Anyone?" She strolled out from behind the podium, her glasses lowered to the bridge of her nose. "Come on people," she sighed. "We're going on a field trip tomorrow and not one of you can tell me what the difference is?" The room remained still. Professor Manning used her index finger to move her wire rimmed glasses back up. "Kaden," she called. "How about you?"

Kaden jolted at the sound of her name. Her eyes flipped open wide from the dream back to the classroom and her professor. "I'm sorry, I didn't hear what the question was." She lied through her teeth. Usually, Professor Manning's muffled lectures floated through her thoughts in the background while Kaden focused on sparking her memory, unless she fell asleep. In basic Geology it was easier to focus, easier to shut down the critical part of her brain, easier to remember.

"The difference between gems and crystals?" she repeated from the top of her desk. She crossed her ankles together and swung them like a little kid.

"Gems are rare pieces of minerals," she answered. Her memory of geology from middle school was not something that had vanished like the night Megan disappeared. Earth science was one subject in school she found interesting and the reason she chose it. "Crystals are pure substances."

"Now, someone else give me an example of each one," she said. This time a few hands went up to answer her question. While students' voices replied, Kaden's thoughts wandered back to Megan and the night at the police station. She recalled the early morning glow of the sun rising from the back of the police car. The hospital staff that inspected her for any injuries. And everyone around her asking questions to determine who to contact. Countless hours passed by. Doctors, nurses, officers, and eventually the hospital's psychiatrist. It wasn't until then that she managed to remember her last moments with Megan and the rest remained a blank void.

Aside from a few cuts and bruises, Kaden's physical body was fine. What concerned the doctors was the severe concussion and memory loss. Something they thought would return in time, but three months later remained empty. Her therapist believed it to be dissociative amnesia. From Kaden's understanding, it meant she didn't want to remember the events that took place that weekend. Then she fell into a pit of anger and guilt. How selfish she was being. To Megan. To Megan's family, just to keep her mind safe. She used every spare moment, every class, every time she babysat, every waking second, she spent rifling through her memories for what happened.

All she could see, so crystal clear, was losing Megan at the pub. Standing in the middle of the street calling her name, but after that, there was nothing.

Everything was just gone. One minute she was calling Megan's name and the next, she was waking up in an alleyway. Her sister tried to remind her several times of her coming home for a brief period with a knife and a story about a trumpet player. But none of it made sense to Kaden. All she had was a silver cross necklace and a missing earring. The police kept the knife and necklace as evidence in their missing persons case. But that didn't bother her, as she could only see them covered in blood. Whose was it? How did she end up with it? Where did it come from? These were the questions that haunted her in the back of her mind day in and day out. The only source of relief she held onto was that the traces of blood on the items could not be identified by the police nor the hospital which meant it wasn't Megan's. But she was still missing.

"Alright," Professor Manning said. She leaned back in her desk chain as she munched on carrots. "Don't forget to prepare for tomorrow," she called after the students who had already begun to file out of the classroom. "Bring your worksheets and a snack! You will be graded on what you can find in Discovery Park."

Kaden lingered, collecting her book slowly. "Professor," she began. She walked carefully up to her desk. "I just wanted to thank you again for letting me join your summer course on such short notice."

She smiled widely before popping another carrot into her mouth, "No worries. I just hope everything is going well. I know you were having a hard time."

"Yeah," Kaden sighed. "Things are a little better, but I think taking this class has helped me," she explained. What she didn't say was that it prevented her from falling further into isolation and depression. Something her therapist encouraged.

"Well, I'm glad to hear it." Professor Manning started to organize her papers into a neat pile, "If you ever want to talk, I'm here."

"Thank you," Kaden replied as she left the room. The hallway bustled with students as Kaden flipped her phone open to discover two missed calls from Quinn. She quickly dialed her sister back, well aware of Quinn's new found anxiety.

"Kaden?" Quinn said with a hint of panic in her voice.

"Yeah, Quinn, it's me," she answered. "What did you want?"

"Why didn't you answer your phone?" she asked. "Your class gets out at two forty-five," she said quickly, "it's two fifty." Kaden dug through her purse for her bus pass as her sister continued to ask questions.

"I was talking to my professor, it was only five minutes," she reassured her.

"Five minutes is a long time, Kaden." Quinn paused. "When will you be home?"

Kaden thought for a moment realizing the extra five minutes she spent with her professor cost her the first bus. "Damn," she whispered under her breath. She double checked the time on her phone. "I'm supposed to meet the girls at the bus stop and watch them until their dad gets home. Um…" she thought about the rest of her schedule. "Ugh, I have that stupid kickboxing class after too."

"I signed you up for those for a reason," Quinn argued. "You never know when you're going to need to defend yourself. Besides, you took Joe down the other day." Kaden snorted to herself at the reminder. Quinn's boyfriend was a high school wrestler, but he was no match for a groin hit. "Megan's mom called again," Quinn added gingerly. Kaden's joy cut to a complete silence.

She sucked in a deep breath before saying anything else. "I'll be home around eight, I'll see you then." Then she hung up before Quinn could utter another word.

In the small entryway of the Anderson's house, Kaden tied her shoe laces. "How were the girls today?" Mr. Anderson asked as he searched through his wallet for money. She knew he didn't care for the actual answer, he only wanted to make polite small talk as he counted.

"They were..." She looked past him to the small kindergartner with her arms crossed and brows arched. It took three bowls of food to finally convince her to eat her dinner. "Good," she lied.

"Good. Good," he said. "Do you have change for a twenty?" he wondered with a ball of cash in his hand. Without answering she flipped open her bag. "So..." he began. "How's your mom?"

"She's fine," she answered, handing him a ten. "She's been pulling double shifts, but other than that, she's good."

"Good to hear," he half smiled. "We'll see you next week then."

"Bye, Kaden!" the youngest screamed loud enough

for the veins in her neck to bulge.

"Bye, guys," she waved.

Parked along the curb her mother waited. Ever since Kaden returned, her mother had been pulling double shifts to pay for her therapy, to contribute to kickboxing lessons, and the small tuition fee that came with community college. The Andersons and their children were Kaden's way of contributing. Of course, one of the girls was reason enough to quit.

"How was work?" her mother asked as Kaden slipped into the passenger seat. The car carried the aroma of a strong coffee, two shots of espresso. Loose strands of her mothers hair stuck out from all sides as her dayshift was transitioning to night.

"I will never know how teachers do it," she said as she shut the door to the cardboard box they called a car. "How was work for you?"

"Fine." The staleness in her mother's tone filled the space between them. "I have to be back in a few hours, so I'll be a few minutes late to pick you up."

"Okay," Kaden said. She watched as her mother took a sip of a steaming cup of coffee. "It won't be a problem."

Outside the car the city shifted from family neighborhoods to something more urban. The sun fell beyond the buildings making way for reds and greens and blues that filled the city's streets. The car came to a stop at a red light where a telephone pole plastered with missing pets and garage sale flyers old and new fought to be seen. One laminated poster reflected a smile Kaden had seen many times. Megan.

The moment the light turned green, Kaden's mother took off, not before Kaden caught a glimpse of Mrs. Hanes stapling a poster onto another telephone pole. "How has your therapy been?" her mother asked. "Do you like Dr. Grayson?"

The lingering feeling of guilt and shame curdled in Kaden's stomach. She swallowed it down before she answered. "She's nice," she said. "She wants to start something called guided imagery next week since I haven't recovered any memories from that night."

"And kickboxing?" she asked her. Her mother lifted her coffee again and took several big gulps. "How has that been?" It was as though she shifted from alcohol addiction to a caffeine one and Kaden wasn't sure which she preferred more.

"I hate it," Kaden admitted. "I have massive bruises on my legs from it. And I'm always sore." She shifted in her seat, lifting her pants past her calf to reveal the blueish purple stain which used to be her skin.

Her mother didn't take her eyes off the road to look. "Quinn's using most of her babysitting money to pay for those classes," she replied. "You should be happy you're learning something."

"I am glad," she said as she dropped her pants leg. "I just wish it didn't hurt so much."

The car slowed to a stop alongside the curb in front of the gym. "I'll pick you up across the street."

Kaden forced a smile. From the street, she could see most of the class was already present. It was filled mostly by women ranging between mid-twenties to late thirties. She didn't spend much time getting to know any of them, only the one woman she always seemed to partner up with.

The class warmed up with uppercuts and hooks, then practiced with punching bags. After that, they moved on to using pads where one partner held up targets for the other to hit. Through her time there, Kaden had learned high kicks, sidekicks, and roundhouse kicks. But what she found most entertaining were the mundane conversations that took place while learning how to defend oneself. "How has Quinn been?" Nancy asked as she high-kicked Kaden's forearm.

Kaden shook off the pain that rippled through her forearm. "She's been doing well," she told her. "How are the kids?"

Nancy cocked her head to the side with raised brows as she pondered the question. "Mary's been getting into trouble with her camp counselors again." She high-kicked a little harder. "I don't know what it is," she added. "She just does not want to listen."

"If it makes you feel any better, " Kaden offered, "the kids I watch aren't exactly amazing."

"I don't know what it is with kids these days," her breathing started to become short with each hit. "They just...Do. Not. Listen." Nancy nailed the pad protecting Kaden's hand.

"Alright!" the instructor called out. "Switch it up!"

Kaden gladly un-velcroed her hands. Her palms were finally able to breathe again once they met the cool gym air. She traded places with Nancy, rolling her neck around clockwise and then counter clockwise. "Ready?" she asked

Nancy.

Nancy nodded.

Kaden hit and then hit some more. The room fell away and suddenly it was just her and her target. Sweat built up, dripping off her forehead and falling from the crevasses of her collar bone. "For someone so small," Nancy's words were barely a thought in her mind. "You pack a lot of rage."

"What makes you say that?" she asked without bothering to remove her eyes from the pad. Most of the women in the class had stories. Some weren't afraid to tell theirs, while others, including Kaden, preferred to keep theirs close to the chest.

"You kick like you have someone in mind," she said. "And no one else has *that* many bruises."

"Well I don't," Kaden snapped. She sucked in her breath and released her anger into her punch instead of her words. "Have someone in mind, that is."

"Really?" Nancy wondered. "You don't have anyone in mind? Not a teacher or a parent or a boyfriend?"

The instructor turned off the music suddenly. Kaden stopped and when she did she realized just how out of breath she was. Her chest rose and fell almost so much she couldn't catch any fresh air. "Nope," she said sharply.

"I usually think of my husband," Nancy admitted.

A smile rose on Kaden's face before she made her way over to her gym bag and the bottle of cold water her throat craved. She popped the lid and chugged half of its contents down until she was satisfied. By then the women began separating into social circles which Kaden had no interest in. She shoved her belongings into her bag and waved her partner goodbye.

As she stepped out onto the dark street, her shoulder bumped into someone. "Sorry," she apologized before she could catch a glimpse of the person.

"No need to be sorry," he said, "lass." The sound of his accent crept into her eardrum. It was something familiar and strange. Like she wanted to turn and run but also stay at the same time. His hair was bleached and spiked while his face had a mousey quality. "The streets can be a dark place." A smile slithered across his face.

Kaden half smiled politely before she began to walk away. She stepped off the curb and onto the asphalt. On the back of her neck she could feel eyes watching her every move. Her footsteps quickened until she reached her mother's car. With her hand on the handle, she turned back to where the man was, only to find he was gone.

CHAPTER 11

Ireland, 1906

The halls of the Seelie Court danced with delicate tunes as somewhere within ear shot faerie musicians orchestrated piece after piece for the ball. Seelie Court gatherings were something of pleasure and delight. A mix of magical and regal as the guests expected nothing less. The Seelie Court of Ireland was where it all began. Emerald grass and rolling hills, cliffs that dropped to the sea, white caps and shoreline. The place in itself was magical. With dusk cresting against the meadows surrounding the Court, the celebration only seemed to grow more ravishing, more regal, more rambunctious.

The ballroom guests swept one another across the dance floor, less formal than it had started earlier in the evening. The King's posture mimicked the straight spine of his throne with a look of pain that matched such a position. The Queen, however, lingered among her fellow faeries, leaving her seat without a being to showcase.

Two young children zipped and weaved past guests, quickly dashing under tables, but not before the boy swiped two biscuits off the dessert table heading out the door. The little girl, dressed in her full, golden ballgown with her hair bound in a tight up-do, lagged behind her older brother. Just as quickly as they entered the ballroom, they disappeared towards the stables. "Finley!" she called out. "Wait for me!"

Her yearning to slow down only caused him to dart faster down the lush hillside in his velvet and gold swirled suit. "The heroic knight awaits no one!" he replied back to her.

"You are not a knight," she yelled. "You are my brother!" She lifted her dress to her knees to avoid any mud staining the hem of her dress.

"Not for long!" he shouted over his shoulder. "Soon I will be the best knight the entire Seelie Court has ever seen!" Finley flung the stable doors open to a pungent manure aroma. But he didn't notice. The excitement swirling through his body overcompensated anything that may have tarnished his mood. Restlessly, he waited for his sister. "Eva," he said, "if you move any slower I will toss a biscuit at your head."

"No you will not Finley," her tiny brow furrowed. "Those are for Shadow," she reminded him. As she approached the stables, she struggled to catch her breath.

"She'll eat it if it hits your head or not," he told her. "Besides," he said, tossing one in the air. "This one's for me."

Eva's once perfect brown locks slipped to one side of her head, leaving loose strands out of place. "Where did you find her again?" her fragile voice whispered against the stall doors.

"In the pasture... outside."

Eva gasped. *"Outside?"* The word came out as if it were a bitter thing. "But we're not supposed to go *outside.*" Her eyes grew in size at the thought. But Finley didn't notice. He only had eyes for the third stall on the right. He kept his footsteps light against the hay and dirt path toward the stall with Eva reluctantly behind him.

Finley summoned a nearby apple crate across the stable floor with a simple thought. It slid in front of the stall door so he and his sister could see her. The fragile black steed stood facing the opposite wall, the dark locks of her mane matted into knots. Her ribs stuck out on either side of her body, starved for food, water, attention. Parts of her looked as though she could fall at any given moment, yet she stood. "Isn't she beautiful?" Finley whispered. He put his hands on top of the ledge of the stall door.

"Why does she look like that?" Eva asked him.

Finley placed his chin on the back of his hands as he watched her. His horse. His Shadow. "Her owner was mean to her," he said absently.

"Why did you take her?" Eva wondered. "She's not *that* pretty."

"She needed a home," he said. Finley glanced over at Eva, a wicked smile beginning to form. "I already told you," he added. "I'm a heroic knight. I rescued her." He jumped off the crate to the ground, tossed a biscuit in the air and caught it. "Do you want to feed her?"

Eva gleamed. Her smile spread from ear to ear. She climbed off the apple crate while Finley unhinged Shadow's stall. He handed a biscuit to Eva before she waltzed in.

"Be careful," Finley warned. Shadow whined at her presence. "Slow, Eva."

Shadow moved uneasily, backing up as her whines grew louder with each footstep Eva took. In her own fear, Eva hurried toward the horse. "Eva, no!" Finley yelled. He took a quick step toward his little sister as Shadow bucked. A scream escaped Eva's mouth, a scream of terror and fear Finley had never heard before.

Within a blink of an eye, Finley's father pushed past him before the horse descended onto Eva. Everything moved quickly and slowly at the same time. Shadow flew up against the far end of the stall, her back hitting the wood with an agonizing thud. Eva was gone, out of Finley's sight all the while he stood between the stall door and his beloved horse.

"What were you thinking?" The deep bravado of his father's voice smacked him before he could understand what happened. The collar of his shirt was yanked so Finley stood under the lighting of the stable galley instead of the dim lighting of the stall. "Eva's safety is vital!"

Finley's gaze found Eva, a bundle of loose hair and golden mud stained gown with tears bubbling in her eyes, hiding unharmed behind a stack of crates. A wave of relief washed over him, but it didn't last long. "I–I'm–" his voice was broken up and he couldn't seem to get it right.

"You are what?" His fathers tongue was as sharp as

knives. "Can you not speak?"

"I–I…"

The color in his fathers face deepened to a kind of red Finley could only imagine. With one hasty step, his father had his upper arm in his grasp. "You think you are to be a knight?" he spat.

"Henry," someone spoke in the distance.

"It is more likely you will see the death of many for your disobedience."

"Henry." Only one person was permitted to call his father by his true name. The tone of her voice was not as sharp as his father's. It was stern and soft but deadly and threatening when need be.

The Queen stood at the threshold of the stable, the lighting from the ball in the distance like a firefly on a summer night. Her gown was golden and lace just as Eva's was. Just like Eva's, the hem of her dress carried traces of mud from the journey from the Court to the stable.

As soon as Finley's father's eyes fell upon his Queen, he released the grasp he had on Finley. "I should have never allowed you to keep that disgusting thing."

Blood filled Finley's mouth. The metallic taste was salty yet slightly sweet against his taste buds. He leaned forward against the ties that bound him to the chair and watched as his blood mingled with the old stains of crimson on the floor. His bloody salvia dangled between his mouth which came as a surprise since the last bit of water he consumed was days prior.

The piece that played from the record player was the same one from his childhood. From the ball and the cursed memory of Shadow being struck again by an angry man. Finley wasn't sure if Doyle knew about the memory, somehow, about the pain it brought him. He stood against the metal table, readjusting the iron knuckles burning his own flesh. As the skin bubbled along the parts where the iron met his knuckles, Doyle seemed unphased. Instead, he turned the music louder. "You know," he sighed. "I've always loved listening to music while torturing others. It gives the whole process a more, dramatic, flair. Don't you think?"

"I think," Finley spat the last of the blood onto the floor. "I think I'd rather have another round with those iron knuckles than chat with you about dramatic flair."

Doyle frowned. He pushed himself off the metal table and moved closer to Finley. "And here I thought we were friends." He paused, briefly, before the jagged raw iron split open the wound on his cheek again. The gashes were deep, his face bruised and swollen. At one point, Finley could have sworn parts of his teeth were showing through.

"Last I checked," Finley forced through the pain. "Friends don't tie each other to chairs." His skin burned, like a searing hot pain, like blistering skin after touching a hot tray. "Unless you're a *different* kind of friend." Doyle grasped Finley by his hair, lifting him so they were eye to eye.

He watched as blood oozed from Finley's fresh cut. Without a word, he released Finley's head which lolled back down to his view of the floor. Finley heard the clang of the iron knuckles hitting the metal table and the swoosh of the swinging doors as Doyle exited. "Was it something I said?" Finley asked through shallow breaths.

A shy pair of footsteps echoed in the room. Leila. Finley came to know her as the quiet faerie, the girl whose face he saw before he was brought back to the confines of his cell. She mended his wounds. She let Finley sip from her water bowl and spit out as much blood as he could before she wiped the gashes Doyle had made. The wounds always seemed to remain the same, beat red and swollen with infection. Blistering sores covered most of his body. Bruises and broken bones struggled to heal under the iron chains that held him down.

"I find it difficult to believe they don't have any peroxide in this place." Finley's lips screamed at him to stop talking. They too were cracked and thrusting for water. Leila remained silent. She proceeded to do her job as she had for the past three months. "I almost forgot," he said. Leila dabbed her rag on the bridge of his nose gently. "It's almost our three month anniversary, honey, what should we do? See a movie or maybe a play, perhaps?" She pressed against her cheek. Finley bit down against his teeth in pain. "My darling, if I didn't know any better, I'd say you're ignoring me. Did I do something wrong?"

"Leila!" Someone shouted from outside the doors. Leila flinched at the sound. She rose to her feet and hurried out before the guard had to call her name a second time. As she exited, a guard entered with Finley's iron chains to escort him back to his elegant royal suite decorated with rotting, moldy walls and filled with a single paper thin mattress.

The guards were all Dark fae, but not all of them were faeries. Some were creatures Finley had only read about in his bestiary. They were nasty looking. Some slimy and green skinned, others black as charcoal and dripping with a stench only the dead could stand. Some long haired, short haired, and no haired. Toothless rackety beasts with no manners or cares for the world.

As usual, the prison was overwhelming with conversations and shouts. Ear piercing screams of agony, of threats, and sometimes of pleasure. Most of the prisoners had been tortured for decades, some their whole life like Nicolai, Finley's cell mate.

"It was a bad day, huh?" the young boy asked from the corner he deemed the safest.

"Isn't every day a bad day here?" Finley asked as he lowered himself onto the mattress. His back ached as it hit the springs. It was no better than the floor except there were no rats roaming around.

"No," Nicolai replied as he crawled next to the bed so he could see Finley's face. "Not the days where we get...re...recr..."

"Recreational," he finished for the boy. Finley supposed the days he taught Nicolai weren't so bad. Or the hours in which he painted a picture of the outside world for him.

"Recreational," Nicolai repeated slowly. "Or when you aren't bleeding so much. Or when they decide to feed us. Those are good days. The days I hope for."

"I have to teach you how to hope for better things."

Finley opened his eyes to see the small boy watching him.

"Like what?" he wondered.

"Like escaping," Finley said.

"Shh," Nicolai pressed his fingers against his lips. "They might hear you and then we are both in trouble. I don't want to be taken to *the room* again." His big brown eyes widened with worry. The innocence that comes with a boy his age, still lingering at the surface. Nicolai was the puppy Finley had always wanted, but under different circumstances. Why Doyle had taken him, Finley didn't understand. He was an Acalica faerie and up until Finley had arrived had no idea what he was.

"Alright," Finley lowered his voice to appease the fear growing in Nicolai's eyes. "What about going back home to Bolivia? To your family?"

He pondered the question. "I guess I never thought of that," he said. "This is the only home I've ever known. What's it like?"

"Well," Finley sucked in a deep breath despite the pain it brought to his chest. "I've never been to Bolivia, but I hear it's a lovely place."

"No," he said. "To have a family. What's it like?"

Finley tilted his head to the side, "No one here has ever talked about it?"

Nicolai shook his head. "I've heard about a mother fu–"

"That's something different," Finley quickly replied. He sat up, using the wall to ease his aching muscles. "I imagine," he sighed. "It's having people who understand you," he said as he closed his eyes. "And love you for who you are. But it's when you lose them that you realize just how important they are."

Chapter III

The dinner Quinn had prepared had gone cold hours ago.

But there it was. Spaghetti with marinara sauce sitting in the center of the kitchen table with three bowls waiting to be filled. "Oh good," Quinn said, jumping from the comfort of the couch. "You're finally home! I made dinner, it's a little cold, but I can heat it up, just give me five minutes." She darted into the kitchen before Kaden or her mother could get a response out.

"You don't have to worry about me," their mother said as she flipped off her shoes. Her body slumped with every layer of clothing she took off. "I'm not hungry, I'm just going to go to bed."

Quinn stepped into the door frame of the kitchen

with a wooden spoon in her hand. "Are you sure?" Her face fell.

"Yeah." Their mother gradually forced her way up the stairs using the railing for support. It was the first time Kaden had seen her use the railing without being too consumed with alcohol in a decade.

Kaden slipped out of her shoes and dropped her gym bag by the stairs before entering the kitchen and slumping into a chair herself. "So," she said through a sigh. "How was your day?"

Quinn rummaged frantically through the cabinets, clanging and knocking pots and pans around. "It was good," she said. She wore a cheetah print apron over her clothes with a mismatched pair of socks on her feet. "I've been looking into a lot of different colleges. How about you? How was kickboxing?"

"It was—" her words were cut short when the doorbell rang. Her eyes darted to Quinn who in turn looked to Kaden. The two silently held one another's gaze asking without asking if they were expecting anyone. Quinn shook her head while Kaden shrugged. The doorbell rang again.

"Don't answer it," Quinn whispered. "They'll go away."

"The kitchen light is on," Kaden said as she gestured to the overhead light. "They know we're home."

"So what?" Quinn argued. She brought a spoonful of red sauce to her lips with the wooden spoon, winced and returned it to the pot. "We don't *have* to answer it."

Kaden bit her lower lip, wondering if the person behind the door was Megan or an officer that had news about Megan. Or if they had found out whose blood soaked her clothes, whose knife she carried when she roamed into the police station. Quinn's gaze pleaded not to answer it, but Kaden had to. She got up and unlocked the door when her heart sank further into her stomach. She wished she had listened to Quinn.

The dull porch light barely illuminated Mrs. Hanes's sullen face. She had lost so much weight since Megan's disappearance Kaden could hardly recognize the sunken features staring back at her. Dark circles under her eyes while her eyes themselves were beat red and puffy made her look more dead than alive. "Hi, Kaden." Her voice was nothing but a whisper with every word she breathed.

"Hi, Mrs. Hanes," Kaden whispered back. "How are you doing? Do you want to come inside?"

Megan's mom shook her head slightly, "No, that's alright. I just wanted to stop by and see how your therapy has been going. I know your appointment's tomorrow, but I was just hoping...that maybe...you remembered something. Anything." Her eyes widened with a distant hope as she looked at Kaden.

"I'm really sorry, Mrs. Hanes," Kaden began. She dropped her gaze, hoping to avoid witnessing Megan's mother's face fall from sorrow. "I haven't remembered anything. But my therapist wants to try something different soon," she offered. "She has a lot of faith it will work."

Mrs. Hanes nodded lightly. "If you remember anything, anything at all, please call me." She walked off the stoop without another glance as Kaden eased the door shut in her wake.

Kaden leaned her back against the door with a heavy sigh of relief. "I told you not to answer the door," Quinn said. "Are you okay?"

She sucked in a deep breath that she knew wouldn't relieve any of the guilt she felt inside her. "You're burning the spaghetti," she replied.

"Crap!" Quinn hurried back into the kitchen, but not before the smoke alarm went off.

"Megan's mom came by my house again last night." Kaden's sentence fell into the quiet four walls that made up Dr. Grayson's office. Dr. Grayson lounged across from her in her leather chair with her notepad in hand. While she seemed at ease in the space, Kaden leaned forward gripping the edge of the sofa.

"Did she?" Dr. Grayson asked. "Do you want to talk about it?"

"There's not much to say," Kaden lied. She snuck a glance at the clock on the wall. Its arms slowly ticked away for what felt like an eternity.

"Her visits must be affecting you if you brought it up," she said. It was easy for her. Sitting quietly in her chair listening to everyone's problems.

Deep down Kaden knew Dr. Grayson was right. She just didn't want to admit it. "Every time I see her," she paused. "There's something in her eyes. Like..."

"Sorrow?" Dr. Grayson finished for her.

"Hope," Kaden corrected. "Like maybe this time she sees me I will have remembered what happened. Where

Megan is, if she's even alive."

"That's a lot of pressure for someone. Especially someone who has suffered a traumatic ordeal." Dr. Grayson jotted something down in her notebook. "Nevertheless, you've made progress. Things like this take time."

Kaden's heart raced under her chest. She couldn't wrap her mind around how someone could remain so calm when it was infuriating. "Have I?" she wondered.

"Have you what?" Dr. Grayson asked. For the first time the whole session, Kaden and her eyes met. "Made progress?"

Kaden nodded.

"Kaden," she began. Dr. Grayson shifted in her seat, putting the notepad on the table beside her. "Every situation, every patient is unique. Some people recover quickly and others…"

"So I haven't, then."

"You suffered a severe concussion. It's not a race, these things take time." Dr. Grayson tried to persuade Kaden to believe her. But she couldn't. Her mind was a blank void and it ate away at her every day.

"It's been months and we haven't recovered any memories," she snapped. "We have made no progress. *I* have made no progress."

"I understand this can be frustrating," her therapist said. "But–"

"Frustrating?" Kaden repeated the word back to her. "Frustrating doesn't even begin to describe how I feel. When you have your best friend's mother knocking at your door nearly every night, wondering where her only daughter is, then you can talk to me about frustrating!" The anger rolled out of her easily, but she hadn't realized she had been yelling.

The room grew heavy, thick with tension. Kaden fell silent in her seat, her knuckles white from gripping the couch harder than she realized. "You see," Dr. Grayson said, pen in hand, notebook back on her lap. "That's progress. You may not realize this, but, you have a lot more things you need to work through as well. Besides your memory loss."

The clock above her therapist's head reached the ten o' clock mark. "I guess it will have to wait until next time," Kaden said with relief.

"Are you sure?" Dr. Grayson asked. "You are more than welcome to stay a while longer. My morning is—"

"I can't." Kaden grabbed her bag off the floor, "I have a field trip to Discovery Park today."

CHAPTER IV

"Guys," Professor Manning called, waving a handful of papers around. The shuttle bus from campus turned into the parking lot prompting the students for their adventure. "Make sure to take a sheet before you get off the bus," she announced over the budding conversations. "And don't do anything that will get me in trouble." When the bus came to a complete stop, the students jolted out of their seats, each grabbing a paper from the professor's hand. The sheet consisted of various earth elements with check boxes beside each one, though Kaden wasn't entirely sure they could all be found in Discovery Park.

Students split off into different groups in every direction. Finding the variety of rocks and minerals would have been easier with more than one set of eyes looking. But Kaden slipped her earbuds into her ears, hitting play on her chipped MP3 player instead. Conversations floated in and out of her attention, through the melody of her music. While her feet stayed focused on the path ahead, her mind wandered to her therapy session and the rage still boiling silently at the surface of her skin. Perhaps she *had* been making progress. After all, she was on a field trip for her college course. She was working and exercising like a normal human would. Maybe her life was falling into place after all. But there was a gnawing feeling deep inside her that told her it was all wrong.

With the sun beaming down on her, Kaden found herself wishing that her hair had stayed short. The bob cut wasn't something she would have chosen given the chance, but it would have beat the heat warming the back of her neck. She titled her head up to see where the canopy of trees separated for the path and the rays of sun poured through so easily. Kaden squinted at the blue sky and the big ball of fire that warmed her pale skin. Pale skin she had forgotten to sunscreen.

A group of her peers clogged the pathway up ahead of her, leaning over to examine something. She couldn't tell from her spotted vision if it was something from their list or someone's phone. Instead, she veered off the path and into the trees. The wooded area was dense with a full canopy to protect her fragile completion. There was tall grass and blossoming flowers. She kept walking further, letting the conversations of her peers fade and the music in her ears rise as the wildness grew.

Her brow stopped sweating. Twigs snapped underneath her feet instead of cackles from students. Kaden glanced over her list with the sun sneaking through the leaves above her. When she was satisfied with her distance she stopped. She glanced from her paper to the forest floor. There was too much debris and fresh green for her to see to the bottom of the forest bed. She squatted down, brushing bits of dirt and weeds out of the way for her to grab a rock she thought was on her list.

"What do you have there?" A voice asked from over her shoulder. She used her fingers to dig the specimen out from the earth it was plastered in.

"It's slate," she answered without looking back. Kaden laid her sheet of paper on her knee to check the box. "It's under the metamorphic rocks section," she added.

"You came all the way out here for a rock?" the voice asked. He sounded vaguely familiar, but with her earbuds in it was hard for her to place a name to the voice. She jotted down a few notes beside the box just in case she had to have more information to prove she had actually found it.

"What do you mean 'all the way out here'? The path is right…" Kaden turned slightly only to find the path was no longer visible. "Huh," she said to herself. "I must have walked further than I thought." As soon as the words fell from her mouth, the hairs on the back of her neck stood on end. Her heart skipped under her chest, beating fast while everything froze around her. "Were you following me?" She turned quickly to where the voice came from, only she was met with an empty forest.

"Did you fall on your head?" he retorted from a new vantage point. "This is my humble abode."

Kaden furrowed her brow, "What?" She shifted on

the balls of her feet to find herself face to face with a short, pale brown creature. Its stature was that of a small toddler with a rounded belly and rounded nose to match. Kaden threw herself backward onto her butt. She used the heels of her feet to kick herself further away from the little man. "What the hell?"

"I know I've gained some weight but you don't have to be rude about it." The grumpy thing's face scowled as he waddled with a bundle of sticks in his hands toward her.

Kaden reached for the thickest branch she could find and swung it in the beings direction. "Stay back!" she shouted. "Don't come any closer." Her rattled mind tried to analyze what her eyes were seeing. Her breath quickened and her chest tightened. "This is it, isn't it," she whispered to herself. "I've finally snapped and they'll send me away. I never thought it would happen. I really didn't. But they were right, I'm just like my mom." A blurry line of tears began to form at the bottom of her vision.

The rotund man stood awestruck as Kaden swung her weapon back and forth. "What on bloody earth are you talking about?"

"What was my messed up mind thinking when I created you?" she wondered. "I expected to see Megan, like I did at first, not–not some weird elf!"

The creature tossed his sticks to the ground, "Who are you calling an elf?!" He took a step toward Kaden, one of his hands balled into a fist. "The only reason I won't kick you is because you still owe me a favor and I wouldn't want to hurt you before I get it."

"Favor?" she asked. Kaden lowered her stick and

squinted at the thing more closely. "Why would I owe a figment of my imagination a favor?"

"You listen here, missy," he said with so much frustration in his voice that Kaden thought for a moment he might explode. "If you think that playing dumb will get you out of it, I can assure you, there will be severe consequences." She stared for a long moment, questioning why she would make up a yelling, grumpy elf and why he would argue about a favor.

The only thing she knew she had to do was find her way out of the woods and back to the path. To find her teacher and the bus until she could get to her mom or her therapist or both. Kaden lifted herself up, without paying the little thing any mind. *He is fake*, she told herself. She sucked in the warm summer air and began to walk in the opposite direction of the creature.

"Don't even think about it!" He ran up from behind her, using all his force to push her back down to the ground.

Her knees hit the ground first, the palms of her hands bracing herself before her face could hit the dirt. She waited there, tears welling in her eyes. *Am I so crazy that I am willing to knock myself down?*

The creature flipped her so her back was against the forest floor. He climbed on top of her, the weight of his body so real against her abdomen. Without fighting it, he gripped her forearm with his palm. His skin was clammy and soft like earth after rain. All Kaden could think about was when she would be well enough to pick herself off the forest floor again and crawl home.

But after a few moments of his skin touching hers, a green light illuminated her veins as did the little creatures. She watched as the light swirled under the surface of her skin, burning and tingling so much she wanted to rip herself away from him. "Stop!" she screamed as the sensation slithered its way up her arm. She pulled to get away, but he only gripped harder. "How—how does this feel real? What is this?"

The green light in her veins made its way up her arm through her neck, and to her mind. Kaden squeezed her eyes shut hoping it was all just a dream, a very bad dream. But images floated through her mind's eye, like a movie she had seen before. She found the face of a young man cradled in her arms. Her throat grew tight, but she didn't understand why. She felt the warmth of his blood on her hands, the stains they left.

Then she saw Megan.

Her Megan, a frail shivering body trapped in a cage.

The images moved slowly, almost backwards in time until they began to move rapidly and she absorbed them.

A dark warehouse transformed into a vivid, beautiful sanctuary where a woman with ruby red lips that matched her dress stood beside a throne.

A flash of sharp words between her and Quinn, something broken that she couldn't comprehend.

Moments in time lost, returned.

When Kaden opened her eyes, it all stopped. Her body shivered despite the warmth of the sun. Her eyes watered and lungs gasped for air. The forest spun, a blur of greens and browns. She flipped herself over, placing her palms against the solid ground. Her nailbeds dug into the earth while Theodore waddled into her peripheral vision.

She heaved and sobbed and couldn't stop the shaking. Megan was gone. Megan *had been* gone for months. Her dark curls and goofy laugh and chunky monkey ice cream. Her mother and father and her brother, broken. And Kaden couldn't stop the damn shaking. And Finley.

"I didn't mean to hurt you," Theodore whispered. He stepped closer to her. "Did it hurt that bad?" Theodore shuffled around for a moment, searching his surroundings. "Here," he said. He forced a green leaf in front of Kaden's face. "Use this."

Kaden didn't move. A part of her thought she wouldn't be able to move again.

Her cries died down to a soft sob a while later. She wasn't sure how much time passed, only that the sun had died down further behind the trees. Her palms ached from sticks and rocks that pocked at her skin. Her knees locked against the hard ground and her tears soaked the earth. "They're gone," she whimpered to Theodore. "Both of them."

"Who's gone?" Theodore asked wide-eyed.

Kaden turned around so she sat on the ground with her knees closer to her chest. A cool hand rested on her shoulder, the shock of it made her turn to Theodore. She had forgotten how small he really was. She had forgotten him.

She sniffled. "Megan," she answered through a whisper. "And Finley…they both…" A few straggling tears escaped the corners of her eyes.

"Pretty boy?" Theodore's voice jumped. "Pretty boys not dead."

Kaden watched her toes squirming in her sneakers. "Yes," she told him. "He is. I saw–" The words she wanted to say caught in her throat. Her eyes had seen Megan slit her own wrists. She had felt the warmth of Finley's blood on her own hands. Every inch of her skin crawled.

"That's impossible," Theodore said.

"No, it's not."

Theodore huffed and put his hands on his hips. "Now listen here, I heard from a friend who heard from a friend that Riley was bragging about him. About how he'd locked Finley up somewhere." Theodore leaned back a bit, "It's about time that boy got captured, maybe he'll learn a lesson or two."

"Theodore," she said, "I'm telling you, that's not true. I know he's dead."

"And I am telling *you*," he pointed his finger directly at Kaden. "He is alive! Riley is a faerie and faeries cannot lie. Or have you forgotten that too?"

Kaden's mouth made a fine line. "They must have misheard," she shook her head. "Thank you, Theodore, for giving me hope." Her blood soaked shirt flashed in her mind, the fluorescent lighting in the hospital, scrubbing her hands in the sink and watching as blood mixed with water. "I know he's gone. Megan, too." Kaden's stomach twisted into a knot. Her vision burned with memories of blood and pain and more blood. Her head felt woozy and for a moment she thought she might vomit or faint or both.

"Megan may be gone," he admitted with a shrug. "But Finley isn't. How do you know for sure he *is* really dead?"

"Because I killed him." The truth stung like a fresh wound. The words bitter against her taste buds. "I used an iron knife," she added. "The one he gave me. So, I know."

"Did you kill *him*? Or did you kill someone else?" Theodore didn't have eyebrows, or any other hair for that matter, but he used the muscles where eyebrows should have been and raised them.

"What?" She half pretended to be interested in the words coming out of his mouth. The music from her earbuds played a song quietly in the background from the comfort of the ground where they had fallen. Everything felt worse than it had before. Broken into pieces she thought would never mend.

"Well, you could have killed another, masked in an illusion to look like Finley. If no one specifically declared his death, he could be alive."

Kaden's brow furrowed. She followed Theodore's line of thinking easily. Faeries could not lie. And words had a funny way of being bent and twisted against their tongues. "No...maybe...I don't know. I didn't listen to the specific words being spoken, I had a dead body in my lap and one in a cage."

"You see! So you don't know." The gnome crossed his arms over his chest with a quick nod. "My sources know what they're talking about, trust me. Gnomes know."

She shook her head slightly, conjuring the memories

she once craved. Looking at them ripped a different part of her each time. When she closed her eyes, the cool summer breeze washed over her like the dampness of the warehouse. There had been two Finley's that night. One in front of her. One on the balcony above her. Then the eyes. The purple eyes that flashed with magic and mayhem. The purple eyes that caused fear and anger to course through her body. Enough of it to make her snap and stab the thing that was her friend.

The memory brought back the rage to her cheeks. Her muscles tightened and her teeth clenched at the thought of Doyle. "I saw," she began, still with her eyes closed. "I saw a flicker of purple eyes. It was Doyle. It must have been, that's why I killed him. He said it wasn't the trick I thought it was–"

Her eyes flashed open. The forest was still as another brush of wind passed through the trees.

"There you go," Theodore smiled. His grin was something of a crooked thing with few teeth. "You did not kill him, you only thought you did."

Theodore shuffled his little feet toward the dirt hole he called home, leaving Kaden on the ground a few feet away, her emotions swirling into two different directions. Megan was dead. Dead. But Finley was alive. She felt hollow and yet somehow anxious to move. "So then, who did I kill?" The words sounded awful coming off her tongue. She *had* killed. There always seemed to be blood dripping from her hands.

"I don't know *everything*," Theodore replied without turning to face her.

She bit down on her lower lip, hard. Doyle had killed Megan and captured Finley. Before that, Keeley had been taken prisoner too, but by the Light fae instead of the Dark. A world of fae hidden, but just as destructive as her own. Then she remembered, remembered what Finley had told her. She was not Kaden Storm. Her mother was not her birthmother. Her sister, not her sister. The blood in her veins, something of a mystery.

"How do you know for sure Finley's still alive?" Kaden asked suddenly. "It could be a trick."

"Because, like the rest of the faeries, they are nothing more than idiots with big mouths." He turned then, his eyes big and brown as the space surrounding him, Kaden could see why a creature like Theodore blended in so well without being seen. "How could you not remember?"

"Doyle," she told him. "He erased my memory so I couldn't remember what happened."

"Ah," he said. "Well, it's a good thing you owed me a favor."

Kaden's lip lifted into a smile, then fell again. "This is exactly how I pictured my memory coming back. You and me, alone in the woods."

"You're welcome."

"Why did it work?" she asked him. "When you grabbed my arm?"

"Favors or deals that are bound cannot be unbound. Whatever Doyle did to you wouldn't be able to penetrate such a bond. I am sorry to hear about your friend," he said with a shrug. "You'll make new ones."

"No," she said flatly. "Not like that. Not like us. You

can't just replace people."

Theodore let out a sigh, "I've lived a very long time," he began. "Friends have come and gone. One day I will be the one to go, as will you. Take a flower for example." He plucked a small daisy from beside his home and raised it to Kaden. "If one flower wilts and dies that does not mean the other flowers around it must do the same. So we remove the flower from the garden, but the memory of its beauty still remains."

The sun's golden glow made the daisy in Theodore's hand almost magical. He handed it to her and she took it. She twirled the stem in her fingers and watched petals spin at her command, backwards then forwards. "Finley once told me faeries could hear their names being called," she said to herself. Kaden stopped the flower, staring into its yellow center. "Do you think he would be able to hear me?"

Theodore pondered the question only for a moment. "I know I may look brilliant, and don't get me wrong, I am. But do I look like I know *everything*?"

"You're always saying you *do* know everything," she argued.

"*Almost* everything," he corrected quickly. "You should really learn to listen more."

Kaden lowered the flower onto the forest floor. She thought about how without roots to grow it would die. She thought about the dying sun falling fast beyond the trees where she couldn't see. She thought about how she couldn't save Megan. How she failed. "I need to save him," she said suddenly.

"Well," Theodore huffed. "Good luck to you then."

He turned away from her, back to his pile of sticks.

She rose to her feet, the ground seeming unsteady at first. Kaden wiped the bits of debris from her clothes. "Actually," she began. Theodore half turned toward her. "I'm going to need another favor. Are you interested?"

He squinted up at her, curiosity gleaming in his eyes. "That depends," he said. "What do you want? Because whatever it is, I will need an equal favor in return."

"Can gnomes' portals travel through realms without being detected?" she asked him.

"...Yes," he hesitated. "Why?"

"Because we're going to break Keeley out of the Seelie Court."

CHAPTER V

Ireland, 1920

"Brother! You will never guess where mother is taking us!" Finley forced the heavy doors of the library open. Normally, he would never be caught dead in the Seelie Court's hall of books, old and new. The walls were covered floor to ceiling with literature, shelves and ladders, balconies and towering glass windows at the far end to let in the light. Even the dome ceiling had elaborate gold coffering which always seemed to give Finley a headache when he glanced up at the artistry.

To Finley's mother, art was the most sacred gift people had, connection to one another. But Finley never considered books to be art. To him, they were merely pages with words that teachers used for lessons.

"Pas maintenant," Thierry replied from behind the lavish desk facing the east side of the gardens. It was consumed with gold trinkets for studying the stars.

"Did you say something?" Finley asked. "I couldn't understand you behind that book."

Theirry slammed the book in his hands shut. The sound it made echoed throughout the rows of shelves. "If you must know," he said. "I'm practicing my French for the festivities next month, something *you* are too childish to understand."

"Just because you're twenty one doesn't mean you can't remove that stick from your arse," Finley said from across the desk. Theirry threw the nearest book at his brother's head, but Finley dodged it easily. "While you're in here with your fancy books, I'm learning to become a knight. Nothing can hurt me," he teased. "So, go on, guess."

Theirry scowled. "I have no desire to play games, Finley." He stood from his chair and waltzed toward the wall of books to his left. "Perhaps," he said as he reached for another. "You can play with Eva."

Finley scrunched his brows together, "Eva only wants to play tea party," he argued. "And I'm eleven. I'm too old to play an imaginary game with my little sister."

"Was it not just yesterday you had an imaginary sword fight against a two-headed beast in the garden?" Theirry let out a gentle snort for his own amusement.

"You are missing the point, brother," Finley replied with a dramatic sigh. "We are going to the first rodeo ever in Ireland! With horses just like Shadow! Can you believe it? You, me, mother, and Eva."

"I can't go," Theirry said as he climbed up a golden rimmed ladder.

Finley jolted over to the ladder and stood under it.

46

"Why not?" he asked as he watched his brother scroll through the spines of each book carefully.

"Father is taking me to another meeting with him. I have much to brush up on before then."

"I have not even told you when we are to go," Finley shot back. He lifted himself up on the first step of the ladder.

"Stop that," Thierry told him as Finley began to tug at the fabric of his pants. "You are too old for such foolishness. It does not matter when you will go. There's not enough time in the day for me to study." He wiggled his leg free of Finley's grasp before sliding back down with two new works in his hand. "You really should respect your place in the household."

Finley glanced around, confused. "Like how?"

"For starters," Theirry began, "you should respect father more."

He marched over to the delicate couch in the seating area and plopped himself down. "Maybe I'll start respecting him when he starts respecting me," he huffed. "I don't see why you can't come. All you do is hide behind your books."

"Because," Thierry sighed. "I have my duties."

"Why do you have to have an answer for everything?" Finley asked him.

Theirry flipped through loose sheets of parchment on the desk. "The studying I do is the same as the studying you do," he explained.

"I don't study," Finley said, appalled.

Thierry glanced up, his gaze serious as it always seemed to be. "You study war," he said. "You study physical combat, don't you?"

"Because I have to," Finley told him.

"As I have to study history, languages, art, and geography. My job is to be a good mate for a future Seelie Queen."

Finley sat up on his knees, "Shouldn't I know that stuff too?" he asked.

Thierry looked back to his work ahead of him. "You must train," he said flatly. "Perhaps when you're older you might find pleasure in reading and history."

"Can't you teach me?" Finley jumped up off the couch to the great big mahogany desk where his brother took his seat again.

"What?" Thierry asked.

"You can practice by teaching me!" Finley shouted. His voice carried throughout the gallery of texts.

"Finley," he began with doubt hidden in his voice. "I don't think—"

"Pardon mon Francias," Finley said before his brother could finish his sentence. He raised his chin a little higher, proud of himself for having remembered some of what his French teacher had taught him. His interests laid more closely with the curse words he could teach his peers.

A slight smile curled his brother's lip, "You have much to learn," he told him.

Finley smiled wide, "Merci."

A faint brush of coarse hair swept across the bottom of Finley's bare foot. It sent a shiver down his spine and roused him from his sleep. He had gotten used to the cell rats wandering around, looking better fed than any of the prisoners. Still, this particular rat had one eye which prompted Finley to name him Polyphemus after Poseidon's cyclops son from the Odyssey, something Nicolai knew nothing about.

He shifted from the stiff position he had taken on the floor with his back against the iron bed frame. His muscles ached with each movement and the stiffness in his bones begged him to stop, but if he did, he knew the pain would only be worse. "Finley?" Nicolai said through a yawn, his sleepy eyes still closed.

"Yeah?" he whispered. Finley stroked the back of Polyphemus's body, but the creature hissed as it scurried away.

"Do you think you could teach me how to use my powers one day?"

Finley hesitated. He was a fighter. A knight. Not a teacher. Had he been a teacher he would not have ended up on a cold hard floor with chains around his neck. Had he been a teacher he could help Nicolai learn the ways of his kind. But he wasn't.

"I'm not an Acalica faerie," Finley said plainly. "My abilities are different from yours."

"Really?" He sat up, the sleep in the edges of his eyes still crisp. Despite the sound of his voice crackling with excitement or intrigue or both, Nicolai appeared so fragile to Finley. The boy was always tired, always hungry, though Finley wasn't sure he even realized that himself. On occasion they were allowed to roam the first floor, chained and served some slop or another to keep them from eating each other. Sometimes that didn't work.

"You can do a lot that I can't," he explained as he scratched the blistered skin that cursed his neck. The iron chain itched and burned and boiled layers of flesh. Finley wanted nothing more than to rip it off or , at least, scratch until there was nothing left *to* scratch.

"Like what?" Nicolai asked as he himself began to scratch.

"You can influence rain and hail," Finley said. He knew only from studying his bestiary backwards and forwards until every bit of it was pounded into his brain. "Frost too. I can't do stuff like that."

"Wow!" he exclaimed. His nails proceeded to claw into his own skin deeper. "That sounds amazing! But...what are those things?" Finley glanced over at him. He was so young and yet so sheltered in such a hideous place.

He half smiled, a weak thing when the clatter of a thousand iron chains erupted. Finley got up and snuck a peek outside his cell to where a few Dark fae dragged the long leash. "Maybe I'll tell you another time," he said. He had counted five days. Five days was the longest amount of time the Dark fae would go without feeding them. Five days or, they would begin eating each other.

The guards matched the broken-down prison perfectly. Some of the Dark fae looked as human as Finley, but bulkier with crooked scar. They wore various chains made from different materials hanging off their black clothes. It made it easier for the guards to strike a prisoner down for misbehaving, which Finley had learned from experience.

Each time the prisoners were escorted to the cafeteria, the Dark faeries connected them all together, collar to collar to what Finley learned was a long leash. It stifled prisoners' movements and prevented them from using their abilities.

When the guards got to their cell, they attached Finley ahead of Nicolai and behind William, a hairy face with a snout for a nose. The fae chain was led down two sets of stair cases, past several torture rooms, and into a large space used for the cafeteria.

The room was dingy like the rest of the building. Half the lights in the room worked while the other half flickered on and off. It smelled like urine just as Finley remembered from the first time he woke up there, but with a hint of burnt meat. The smell made him question what was put into the food they ate. Not that it mattered. He would eat it anyway.

The line followed the path given to them by the guards. It went in front of the long table which already had the food, then hooked around to whichever table the line followed. "What are we having today?" Nicolai whispered to Finley.

"What we have every time they feed us. The stale biscuits and mystery meat." He scanned the plates before his turn to pick so he could grab the best looking one for Nicolai, then he would switch their plates at the table. He watched as servants added plates to the counter and was surprised to see Leila as one of them. In the past few months he had only seen her in the torture room washing away some of the pain from his round with whichever Dark fae's turn it was. She was silent. Always silent. But now her cheeks were flushed red as she conversed with one of the other servants. Their words were sharp, Finley could tell, but their whispers were too impossible to hear with all the grunts and bitter arguments between the other prisoners.

He leaned as close to her as he could. Buried deep in the grumbles and groans he caught a delicately harsh word. Finley turned quickly to Nicolai, "Why didn't you tell me Leila was French?"

Nicolai shifted his gaze off the table of food up to Finley, his brow furrowed. "I didn't know that. I could never understand her."

Finley felt a tug from William as he moved forward. It was either move or be dragged. "Come one, Treasach," he snapped. William was a particular fae that Finley had never encountered before he arrived. He knew everything there was to know about Bugganes, almost always harsh beings which resembled a cross between a mole and an ant eater. His demeanor was something Finley had grown accustomed to. He took his plate quickly as did Nicolai before they were ushered along to their table.

At each meal they always sat next to the same group of fae which made it easier for Finley to gather every bit and piece of story he could manage from the others. They all had very similar tales, none of them able to recall where the prison was located.

Conversation was few and far between as long as the guards they had were decent. One guard in particular entered the cafeteria when there was no one to be tortured or maimed. He was the type to make prisoners flinch and cower when he walked by. Just his presence caused everyone to quiet their voices from the little bit of conversation they could sneak out.

Nicolai pretended his fingers were the legs of a long spider and used them to crawl over to Finley's plate and snatch his stale bread while Finley poked at his meat. He had tasted many different foods in his lifetime, but he had never eaten whatever meat they served. He was afraid to even guess.

A scuffle from the other side of the room drew every inmate's attention. An appalling fae with a busted nose seemed to be trying to steal someone else's food off their plate. Nicolai glanced over at Finley with fear in his eyes. It didn't take long before the one guard everyone feared had him dangling by his feet in the air and anyone attached to his chain choked along with him. The guard didn't utter a word, only grinned. He unlocked him from his chain and dragged him kicking from the room. With the blood thirsty guard gone, the inmates were able to breathe a little more easily. "Probably taking him to solitary," Hugo murmured under his breath to his fellow prisoners.

"Well they're not taking him to a day spa," William said through his chewing.

"Maybe they're just taking him to the torture room," Finley suggested and hated the way he said *just*. He tried to hide the movement of his mouth behind his hands.

"They only bring fae there that they want information from," Hugo said. He made it a point to speak downwards at the table to avoid being seen.

"Him and the other guy will be the only two in there until they take him outside," William added. William snuck a glance around the room to find the nearest guard to him.

"What other guy?" Finley asked discreetly.

Hugo shot Finley a quick glance. "Nobody knows his name," he answered. "He's been in solitary since the beginning. Rumor has it he tried to escape and got caught."

"So why didn't they just kill him?" Finley noticed Nicolai curl into himself as his eyes scanned the room like a hawk for guards. He never liked it when Finley talked to the others.

"No clue," William said.

Finley counted the guards, checking to make sure each one was still at their designated post. "What will they do with the other guy?"

Both Hugo and William exchanged a quick glance, "Send him to the crow."

Finley's brow furrowed. "The crow?" Nicolai took Finley's elbow in his hand and squeezed but it was too late.

An iron rod smashed the bones in Finely's left hand, pinning it to the table and sending rippling pain up his arm. The guard had Finley's head against the table in seconds. "There is no talking allowed," he threatened so close to Finley's ear he felt the warmth of his breath. It smelled of rotten egg, hot garbage, and death. "Next time I catch you," he warned, "you're going to wish you were never born."

"I already wish I was never born," Finley said. "You might want to invest in a mint though." The guard lifted the rod again, smacking it across the back of Finley's head. The strike sent a mind numbing pain scattering throughout his head. His vision blurred the cafeteria's dinginess away.

"You ought to respect us more, fool."

CHAPTER VI

Kaden hadn't missed the roller coaster ride of Thoedore's portals. Her stomach jumped into her lungs all the while her insides twisted into a knot. Luckily, Theodore was able to land them in the approximate area she had in mind. The first time Kaden had been to the Seelie Court there were gargoyle guards and faerie knights, stone walls and long halls. But with Theodore, she could bypass all of it, landing directly in the dungeon. As far as she knew, there was only one guard in the dungeon, one exit, two if she counted Theodore.

Without the iron dagger Finley had given her, she had no way to defend herself against a faerie. Only the new set of skills she had picked up from kickboxing which wasn't enough to take out someone with magic.

As she swirled down the dirt tunnel, her emotions

cast her in a dark storm. Everything felt like it was pressurized in a bottle. Anger, heartbreak, guilt. It all threatened her just below the surface. Boiling and brewing, fighting for her attention. All she could see in her mind's eye was Megan. Despite the kind words Theodore had offered her, Kaden knew what had happened was her own doing. But she buried it down. She couldn't cry, wouldn't cry. Not yet. Not when she had a chance to save someone. Her friend.

The portal curved sharply left, then right. She knew she needed Keeley if she was going to save Finley. Keeley was a faerie and far better equipped to help her rescue Finley than Theodore. That and she had no choice in the matter. Theodore requested favors and Kaden wasn't sure what that looked like. Even if Keeley didn't seem too fond of her. She needed her.

"Get ready!" Theodore cheered with the delightful glee of a child. Though doing this got him a favor, Kaden had a feeling he enjoyed the adventure. "Wee!"

The portal spat them out in the damp cellar of the Seelie Court. Its walls, faded brick from time and fixed with iron confinements. Kaden sat still as she waited for her vision to stop swirling. When the room came into focus, she saw a glimpse of the guards desk down the row of cells. The only noise the portal made was the thud of Theodore's round body hitting the ground. Everything else was still.

Keeley scowled over at Kaden and her ridiculous companion who faced the wrong way. Her hair was as long as Kaden remembered, white and silver with a red feather entwined in it. The crimson band of paint she had once worn across her eyes faded to nothing more than a memory. "Is this an attempt at my rescue?" Keeley scoffed. "You and a hairless gnome?"

Kaden rose to her feet, swiping the bits of dirt from her knees. A rustling came from the far side of the cells where the dungeon stairs waited. As soon as she found her equilibrium, she held her stance that she had learned to defend herself. "Kaden?" someone asked. The voice was familiar, but she still clenched her hands into fists in front of her while Theodore struggled to get off the floor.

"There's no need for *whatever* that is," Keeley told her. She pushed herself off the brick wall she leaned against and walked over to the front of the cell. "The new guard is...well, new."

A dirty blonde boy wearing a helmet too sizes too big stepped into Kaden's line of vision. "Kaden!" he gleaned. "Look!" The boy pointed to his towering helmet with pride, "They made me the new guard!" The grin spreading across Blaine's face faded slowly, dropping to a confused express. His face scrunched together as he registered Kaden in the dungeon. "Wait," he said. Keeley rolled her eyes and turned her back on the boy. "You're not supposed to be here." He glanced from Kaden to Theodore and back again. "I think I'm supposed to report this since you're a fugitive."

"Prodigy," Keeley scoffed. "Is he not?"

Kaden lowered her fists back to her sides as the relief of seeing Blaine washed over her.

"Soooo," Theodore said with his feet finally on the damp floor. "This is what the dungeon looks like." He spun slowly in a circle with his hands placed on his hips. "You know," he began. "I had a friend—"

"We don't have time for stories, Theodore," Kaden said before he could ramble on.

Theodore took a step away from Kaden and looked her up and down. "Well," he said. "Aren't you in a mood?" Kaden shot him a sharp glare.

"Where's Finley?" Keeley asked, breaking the exchange between the two. She edged closer to the iron bars, sure not to touch them. "Did he send you?"

"I'm almost positive I'm supposed to tell someone about this," Blaine mumbled. He looked from Keeley to Kaden and occasionally down to Theodore who was too busy being nosy about the structure of the Seelie Court to pay attention.

"Blaine," Kaden said calmly. She caught his eye and smiled weakly, grateful he was just the boy from the village and not a garrison of knights. "You can't tell anyone we're here," she pleaded. "Finley's been taken."

The boy's eyes widened in horror.

Keeley took the iron bars in her hands despite the burning it did to her palms. "What?" Keeley asked quickly. "How? Where? Blaine let me out of here you imp." She released her grasp on the iron, glancing down to find blisters.

"I don't know," Kaden replied. "I just found out myself." She made her way over to Keeley who was struggling to get out of her cell. Blaine stood like a statue frozen in his spot, unsure of what he was supposed to do. "A Dark fae took him," she explained. "His name is Riley. And I need Keeley to help me find him." Her eyes begged

Blaine, pleading for some redemption. She hoped the love he had for Finley was stronger than the loyalty he had for the Court. Kaden looked away from him to Keeley. "I'm just glad you're still alive," she told Keeley. "I wasn't sure if the Queen had done anything to you. Especially since Finely and I got out."

"Not for lack of trying…" Keeley mumbled under her breath. Kaden's shoulders fell as did the edges of her mouth, yet another person she had put in harm's way. "I was sentenced to be executed." Keeley's expression was stone. Her eyes, as cold as a killer. "Cadell managed to sway the Queen's decision."

Kaden furrowed her brows at the name. "Cadell," she repeated. Her mind replayed the events at the Seelie Court when she had first stepped foot among its grand walls. *Cadell.* "He was the one with the staff? Her Seer?" she questioned, but she didn't need Keeley or Blaine to reply. His silence had been deafening. The horns at the top of his temple were a magnificent yet terrifying sight. "How?" she wondered.

"A vision of course. The only thing the Queen seems to rely on anymore. He saw that I would rise during the great destruction. So, she decided to keep me down here until that time comes." Keeley scoffed to herself. "After all I've done for that wicked wench."

The great destruction.

The vision Cadell had when she met the Queen.

Darkness on the horizon.

The Queen had wondered, feared even, that Kaden would cause such a disastrous event. Perhaps she was right.

Kaden glanced up at Keeley. "We need to get you out of here," she said. She glanced over to Blaine who had remained awe struck by the events unfolding in front of him. "Blaine," she called his name to snap him out of the trance he seemed to be in. His eyes met hers and he swallowed hard. "I know you have a responsibility to the Seelie Court," she began. "But Finley's in trouble."

Blaine looked back and forth between Kaden and Keeley, one hand on the sword's hilt and the other clenching the keys to Keeley's cell. "But...I..."

Kaden inched forward. "Blaine. You're either helping us or not."

"No pressure, boy," Theodore whispered from behind Kaden's leg.

Blaine shifted uneasily. "Well..." He let out a sigh, dropping his hand off his sword. "If Finley's in trouble..." The little soldier boy flipped through the keys dangling off the giant ring. "Mother is going to be so angry."

"I'm sure your mother will be proud you're helping a friend," Kaden reassured him. He unlocked Keeley's cell, a high pitched creek rippling throughout the dungeon. She stretched her arms out like a cat waking from a long nap.

"You cannot fathom how long I have been waiting for release." She twisted her body to crack her back while Blaine skipped sideways back over to the guards desk. "I remember when I thought being stuck in a cell by myself would be horrid, then they sent *him* down with his pan pipe." Kaden hid a faint smile. "He won't stop playing that devil's instrument," she whispered to Kaden with the utmost seriousness.

"Hang on," Blaine said from behind the desk. He scoured through the hidden compartments, "I just need my pipe and I'll leave the keys, I don't want to be rude."

Kaden hesitated briefly before speaking, "You're coming too?" she asked gently.

"Well of course!" Blaine answered. "Finley's in trouble and if I stay here, who knows what the Queen will do to me for letting the Silver Fox out of her cage."

"Silver Fox?" Theodore repeated.

Blaine grinned, "It's the nickname I gave Keeley, isn't it brilliant?"

Kaden pinched the bridge of her nose, "That's not what that means, Blaine."

"Someone give me an arrow so I may end him quickly," Keeley said. She sucked in a deep breath of the moist air, "Get me my sai swords from the cabinet along with my bow and arrow," she ordered.

"Umm," Theodore chimed in, waddling into Kaden's view. "Kaden, a moment please." He wiggled his child-like finger, instructing her to follow him further down the dungeon's corridor. She lowered herself so she was at his eye level. "We said we would be retrieving one prisoner. Now we have two."

Kaden glanced over her shoulder as Keeley and Blaine began bickering over something. "We don't exactly have a choice in the matter. If we leave Blaine behind he'll be forced to talk and I can't have a whole army chasing us. The Queen will not tolerate any of this including you."

Theodore scrunched his face up at her. "I have no obligation to bring two filthy faeries through my portal," he argued back. "Just one. So, will it be the Silver Fox or Peter Piper over there?"

She stood up straight, "I'm not choosing. We're taking both, we have a deal," she reminded him with a sharp tone. Theodore's expression grew grim. A twisted smile curled his lip and his eyes narrowed slightly. "We have *two* deals, to be exact, and I expect you to provide me with an equal favor."

"And I will," she told him. "But we are taking both. It's non-negotiable. If Blaine stays behind, we're screwed. And you don't want the Queen knowing a gnome is capable of entering her dungeon without being noticed, do you?"

Theodore squinted. "Fine," he agreed. "We take both, but don't forget, equal favor in exchange."

"I won't," she promised.

"Are you two finished?" Keeley asked impatiently. She secured her sai sword in her belt, one on either side, with her bow strung across her chest. "It isn't wise to linger."

"Don't get your panties in a twist," Theodore snapped. "Damn faeries," he mumbled as he shook his head. Theodore began to trace the ground with his foot, creating a portal back to Discovery Park.

Blaine leaned close to Keeley, "What are panties?" he whispered.

Keeley clenched her jaw tight.

"Oh God," Kaden cursed herself.

"What!?" Blaine asked from behind her. "Is it the panties?"

She held his gaze for a moment, "What? No. I'm supposed to be on a field trip right now." Kaden slapped her palm against her forehead. Then she remembered all the loose ends she needed to tie up before she could go after Finley.

"How was the field?" Blaine asked her. Keeley grabbed his helmet, tossing it with a clank to the floor.

"Never mind," Kaden brushed him off.

"Human world here we come!" Blaine shouted.

The dungeon floor cracked as the ground began to sink in on itself. The dark hole swirled into a whirlwind and before she knew it, Theodore jumped in.

Kaden's hair danced around her face as she watched it in all its magical glory. She looked over to Keeley, "After you," she said. Keeley took the plunge with Blaine on her heels. Kaden hesitated a moment longer before she could bring herself to jump in after them, back to her world.

"Wow!" Blaine's voice echoed through the woods, in full bloom, that surrounded Theodore's home. Discovery Park seemed plain to Kaden compared to the lush rainforest of the Seelie Court. "Look at these trees! And the leaves! They're so…green." Kaden wasn't sure if Blaine had landed fully before he darted from tree to tree, bark to bark, feeling their texture under his hand.

"Blaine," Keeley said through the irritation rising up inside of her. "They're exactly like the ones we have."

"No they aren't," he said with his ear pressed up against one's trunk. "These are human. Can you hear them?"

Kaden looked at the thin line of sun left in the sky. "Keep your voices down," she whispered. "You both have to stay hidden here."

"Excuse me?" Keeley snapped her head to face Kaden.

"I beg your pardon," Theodore questioned at the same time as Keeley.

"You can't walk around in those outfits with pointed ears," she told Keeley. "Trust me, I have a plan."

"*You* have a plan?" Keeley crossed her arms over her chest. She was taller than Kaden, even as she stood with her weight leaning on one leg. "Do you mind sharing with the rest of us or are you planning to just order us around?"

"You're in my world, now," Kaden reminded her. "Until we are in your realm of your expertise, I'm in charge." She flipped out her phone from her back pocket. Relief washed over her when she found no missed calls or messages from her sister. "I'll get you clothes from my house," she explained, tucking her phone into her back pocket. "Then I'm going to the police station."

Keeley tilted her head curiously, "What's at the police station?"

"Finley's necklace and knife," Kaden answered evenly.

"Fine," Keeley agreed. She sucked in a deep breath of city air, frowning slightly. "I'll make sure Blaine doesn't get us seen."

"Hey!" Blaine yelled from a tree limb.

Kaden pressed her index finger to her lips but then wondered if Blaine knew what the gesture meant. "I'll be back by nightfall," she told them. "I promise."

"And what about me?" Theodore tapped his foot. "What am I supposed to do with two faeries hanging about?"

Kaden shrugged, "Maybe *you'll* learn a thing or two about them that you'll enjoy."

Theodore squinted. "I doubt it."

Kaden turned away from them when Keeley called after her, "Hey," she said. The word sounded odd coming from her, but Kaden turned back. "The longer you're gone, the better the chance Blaine won't be alive when you get back."

"I heard that!" Blaine said. "I'll have you know I have the authority to kill you for escaping."

Keeley rolled her eyes, "I didn't escape, you twat. You let me out."

"The Seelie Court doesn't know that," Blaine teased.

Theodore looked from them to Kaden, "I'm going to need ear plugs before my ears bleed from this stupidity."

As Kaden emerged from the path she made for herself, she ran into someone with a blank sheet of paper in their hands. They didn't seem familiar to her, but she recognized the paper she had held in her hands not a half an hour earlier. "Did you find anything?" he asked her.

She glanced at the desperation in the boy's eyes, "Oh...uh.. Not much." She shrugged. His attention fell back to his paper as he began to wander away. "Hey," she said, hurrying up to walk beside him. "Do you know if we're leaving soon?"

His focus remained on the blank checkboxes before him. "In about five minutes," he replied. "I've been looking for someone with answers."

"Why?" she asked.

"Why?" he repeated. He looked over at her with a furrowed brow. "This is a graded assignment."

"Right."

He drew his attention back to the path they found themselves on when they rounded a corner to a larger group of students. "Hey, guys! Wait up!" The boy darted ahead, blending easily into the crowd headed for the bus. They morphed into a blob of people, simple people with simple lives. They all held the same piece of paper in their hand. Kaden reached into her back pocket and found the same one folded twice. In her silence, she unfolded hers. There was one answer. And it wasn't on her paper.

She crumpled it up into a ball. It felt as if all her anger went into that small act but there was so much buried. She was a pit of crooked thoughts and endless feelings.

Megan was gone.

Not away. Not taken. Gone.

Her stomach heaved and twisted until she found herself vomiting bile into the nearest bushes. After, her mouth was dry and tasted like acid. As her stomach settled, she wiped her mouth with the sleeve of her shirt.

Without thinking about the movement of her feet, she made her way to the bus, to the chattering of her peers, and the pile of papers being handed to her professor. Kaden walked past her without a word to a window seat.

The dry summer air stifled the bus as it sat all afternoon in the sun. But the window where Kaden pressed her forehead was slightly cooler. It calmed her like when she was a child sick with the flu and her mom brought her a cold towel for her head. No, not her mom. Someone else's mom.

A thin line of tears formed in her vision, blurring the yellow and orange glow of the setting sun. Her nose began to run, despite her trying not to show it. She used the sleeve of her shirt again to contain her bodily fluids. All she could think about was how desperate she had been to save Megan, how hard Finley had tried to help her. How he came back to save her.

Months of not knowing. Months of waiting and wondering. Months of time lost and so was Megan. Kaden finally knew the truth and she wished she hadn't.

The lights were on when she got home. Standing from the sidewalk, she could see the outline of Quinn moving around inside. The last time she had been there, she knew nothing. But everything was different. The fae world was real. Her mother's mind was consumed with truths while everyone believed she was unstable.

She clutched the key in her hand so tightly it began to imprint its pattern against her palm. She took the steps one at a time. The first was where she tripped going up the steps and scraped her knee once. The second where she liked to sit on summer nights when the air was clear and carried a breeze. The third, where she took her first day of school photos. Somehow the house just wasn't the same.

The front door swung open before she even got to put her hand on the knob. "Hey," Quinn smiled as she slipped her sneaker over her heel. Kaden watched as her smile fell. "Are you okay?" her brow furrowed.

Kaden lifted one edge of her mouth into a weak smile. "I'm fine," she lied. "Just drained from the sun." She slipped inside past her sister. "Is mom home?"

Quinn studied her as she entered. "It looks like you've been crying," she suspected. Quinn took Kaden by the elbow and turned her sharply so she could examine her face. "Did something happen?"

Kaden glanced down at Quinn's hand gripping her funny bone. "No," she sighed. When she met her gaze she found years of memories. "It's probably just my allergies, I was out there for a while." Kaden took her sister's hand and squeezed it. "Nothing a little medicine can't cure."

Quinn nodded, despite doubt lingering in her expression. "I was going for a jog," she said as she dropped her grip. "You want to come?"

She could say yes. She could go and forget again. But she knew she wouldn't.

"I can't," she said. "But you go."

"Are you sure?" she asked. She took her foot in her hand to stretch her quid. "I might stop at Joe's and watch old movies or play video games."

Kaden shook her head, "I have some stuff I have to take care of," she explained.

"Sounds serious," Quinn teased. A smile stretched across her face. Dimples peeked out on either side of her cheeks.

Kaden couldn't help it. She took Quinn in her arms and squeezed her tighter than she ever had before.

"Are you sure you're okay?" Quinn asked her.

Kaden let her go. "Yeah," she sighed. She released Quinn from her grasp. "Don't worry about me so much."

"I'm sorry," she said. "It's in my genetic makeup to worry." Quinn shook Kaden by the shoulders. "I'll see you later." Then she was gone.

Kaden watched her jog to the street and disappear down the road.

When she turned to the kitchen, the evening light was fading from deep orange to hues of purple. Kaden leaned on the kitchen archway with one shoulder. All she could see on the table were bright red letters with numbers and final notices. "Hey, Mom," she said gently.

Her mother didn't turn around as she punched numbers into her calculator. "Hey," she replied.

Kaden pushed herself off the archway and took the seat adjacent to her mother. She sat away from the back of the chair. Her mother's hair sprawled out in different directions. The crows feet at the corners of her eyes, cracked and crawling further and further. "I'm sorry," Kaden said softly. Her voice felt like a whisper or something softer. She fiddled with the ring on her finger.

"For what?" her mother wondered.

Kaden sucked in a breath and let it out. "For what you had to live through alone." The pen her mother was using stopped short. "No one believed you," she said, fighting to hold back tears from welling in her eyes. "I didn't believe you...but you were right."

Her mother's hand began to tremble. Kaden reached out and took it. When she finally looked up, her eyes were filled with tears. The kitchen filled with the sound of their soft cries. "I remember," Kaden managed. "I remember what happened to Megan." She squeezed her eyes. "And I know—I know I'm not—your daughter," she heaved her words out before they got caught in her throat and they stayed there. "But she's out there somewhere."

Kaden's mother took her other hand and then squeezed, holding onto one another for dear life.

"I can't–I can't stay here," she continued. "There's someone I have to help. But I promise you," Kaden caught her mother's red and swollen eyes. "I will find her. I will find your daughter. I will find out what happened. And I will bring her home."

Her mother pulled her close. So close, Kaden wasn't sure what parts were her and which were her mothers. Their tears blended. Their hearts followed the same beat for the first time. For the first time, Kaden saw her. And she didn't want to let go.

When they pulled away, her mother used her thumb to wipe Kaden's tears from under her eyes. "What do you need me to do?" she asked her.

CHAPTER VII

With her head tilted higher than normal, Kaden's mom waltzed through the police station doors with a sense of confidence Kaden had never seen before. She marched directly up to the front desk as though her presence was an honor. The station had been ground zero for Megan's missing person's case. The overhead lighting seemed brighter than it had when Kaden stumbled inside the first time, causing her a slight headache at the base of her temple. Her chest tightened with each moment that passed by. Each step closer to the front desk sent warning signals to Kaden's brain, but she didn't listen.

Sweat dampened her palms as she stood beside her mother. She swallowed the lump forming in her throat. Kaden's minor experience when dealing with a rescue plan was always supported by Finley. Someone with magic and a certain charm she couldn't deny. Her mother's type of charm was more harsh rather than cunning. It didn't help that they were planning on stealing from the police station.

"Excuse me," her mother called to the officer politely. "I would like to speak with the Detective working on the Megan Hanes case. Detective Smith, I believe."

"Is he expecting you?" the officer asked without shifting her gaze from her screen.

"No."

Without looking, the officer pulled out a clipboard with a pen attached to it and slid it over the counter. "You'll need to fill this out," she said.

Her mother took the clipboard bitterly, her lips turning into a fine line. "My daughter believes she remembers some information," she added. "Being the only witness, I would think Detective Smith would be eager to see Kaden since she's vital to his case."

The office's gaze shifted off her computer screen to find Kaden who tried her best to look fragile, though she didn't have to try that hard. "I'll let him know you're here," she told them. She stood from the desk and took the clipboard back. "You can have a seat while you wait," she added with a nod towards the few chairs in the lobby. The officer disappeared into the back offices of the building leaving them alone.

Kaden headed toward the row of empty seats. "Stay here," her mother said before she got too far. Her mother's deep brown eyes glanced at her out of her peripheral vision. "They'll take longer if we sit."

She followed her mothers lead. The station was quiet

aside from a few soft conversations taking place somewhere Kaden couldn't see. It smelled of coffee with a hint of mint like chewing gum. "Are you sure this is going to work?" She leaned closer to her mother who clutched her purse to her side.

"Trust me."

She did.

"Mrs. Storm." Detective Smith appeared around the corner of the hallway. His red tie was askew where it should have been tight. The clean white shirt he wore was wrinkled and hiding a hint of sweat stains under his arms.

"Ms. Storm," she corrected him.

Kaden hid the slight curl of her lip.

Detective Smith nodded politely, "Please," he gestured for them to follow him. "We can talk in my office."

The plan was unfolding nicely. Their steps followed behind the detective against ugly frayed carpeting. They passed closed doors and an array of desks open to the public eye. A few officers lingered with their own obligations, none of them looked up.

Detective Smith held the door open to a musky smelling room where a picture frame of two toothless girls grinned widely. "Please," he began. "Have a seat."

Kaden and her mother took the seats across from him as he sat behind an oak desk where piles of papers and a mug of half-drunk coffee rested. "Officer Jones informed me you believe you have recovered some memories from the night of the disappearance."

"Yes, she has," her mother said with her purse in her lap. "Go on, Kaden."

Heat rushed to Kaden's cheeks. She swallowed any bit of fear she felt before she spoke. "After I made the phone call to the police that night," she told him. "I found Megan."

The detective shot her quick glance. "Found her?" he repeated. His brow furrowed, making the wrinkles on his forehead deepen. "In the report, you claimed she had been taken."

Kaden nodded in agreement. "Yes." She sat up closer to his desk, the tips of her fingers touching the oak. "I meant after that," she corrected. "She was in a warehouse, not far from the docks."

One of Detective Smith's eyes squinted. Without taking his attention off of her, he reached for a notepad and a pen. "What warehouse was this?"

Thorndyke.

"I don't remember," she lied. It grew easier with each one that slipped off her tongue.

He studied her for a moment. "Do you remember anything else?" he wondered.

She stared beyond Detective Smith into the empty space that filled the rest of his office. She could almost see Megan standing there. Kaden swallowed. "I remember blood," she told him. She twisted the ring on her finger. "And a cage."

Detective Smith's head cocked to the side slightly. "A cage?" he asked. "What kind of cage?"

"Like a big cage," she shrugged. Kaden exchanged a glance with her mother. It was working. Slowly she began to watch as doubt slipped across his expression.

"Do you recall if anyone was there?" he questioned.

"No."

"Were you alone?"

"I don't know."

Detective Smith lowered his pen back into the pile of mayhem before him. The office sat in silence. The hands of a clock ticked by somewhere Kaden couldn't see. The phone on his desk rang. He laced his fingers together as a faint sigh escaped his lungs. "Have you spoken to your therapist about this new memory?" Detective Smith asked.

"No."

His lip flinched. "Thank you for coming in," he said, then he turned to her mother.. "I think it's best if Kaden speaks to her therapist so we can confirm the memory is real."

Her mother didn't miss a beat. "Excuse me?" Her question was a fine line, sharp in tone with a hint of challenge. "She has spent months trying to help you," she added. "She's been straining herself and now she has new information and you want me to take her to her therapist?" Her mother sat away from the back of the chair, her knuckles turned white from the grip on her purse. "Which the department doesn't pay for by the way."

Detective Smith raised his hands in an attempt to ease the tension swelling in the room. "Mrs. Storm," he began.

"Ms. Storm."

He nodded. "Ms. Storm," he corrected. "May we speak in private?"

A tight smile formed on her mother's lips as she turned toward Kaden. "Kaden," she said. "Why don't you get some water from the fountain outside while I have a word with Detective Smith."

Kaden nodded and slipped out the door.

She made her way down the hallway, her mother's voice fading in the distance. Each step was calculated, not too fast and not too slow. She found a sign against one of the plain walls: *Restroom. Booking. Interview.* But there was no sign for an evidence room. Kaden swallowed a curse. Ahead of her was the water fountain nestled in between each restroom door. She snuck a glance over her shoulder, but there was no one.

The end of the hall split into two directions. To the left, a set of chairs waited outside one of the interview rooms. To the right, a door with a sign that indicated there were stairs. Kaden peered around her immediate area where the lights had a slightly more orange tint to them than the front desks. She casually made her way toward the stairwell, looking through the glass window. A set of short steps, a landing, followed by another set of short steps. But at the landing a sign pointed down. *Evidence Lockup.*

She winced as she pushed the door open, hoping an alarm wouldn't be triggered. When it didn't, she looked over the railing to make sure no one was below and scurried down the steps.

When she reached the bottom, she found a door with another glass window. But this time, she found not only was there an officer inside, but the door required a security code. "Of course," she angrily whispered to herself. The handle was in arms reach. The cage that held clues not ten feet away. All she wanted to do was reach out and tug it open. If only Finley weren't the one she was trying to save.

The muscles in her calves tightened, eager to kick the door down and get what she needed. Her jaw locked. She let out a sigh and then she turned away.

At the top of the stairwell, she forced the door open roughly without looking. An officer stood at the fountain filling a cup of water and looked up. His brow furrowed when he saw her. Blood pumped faster in her veins, as her heart rate jumped.

"You're not allowed down there," he frowned. "That's a restricted area."

She made a snap decision. She pulled up every bit of every emotion she could grasp. She sucked in sharp breaths, allowing her chest to rise and fall quickly, making her words come out in heaves. "I'm sorry," she told him. A thin line of tears began to form at the rim of her eyes. "I was on my way to the bathroom when I heard this lady yelling. I was so scared, I didn't know if she had a weapon or not and—and I thought this was an exit–so I—I'm so sorry."

The officer glanced over his shoulder quietly. For a beat, her mother's voice filled the space between them. Rambling and raving, her mother's specialty.

"I just wanted to report my...stolen bike," she added.

"Alright," he said. He stopped filling the cup of water and handed it to her. "Just calm down. Here," he gestured for her to take a seat in the narrow hallway with the interview rooms. "Wait here a minute and catch your breath."

Kaden nodded and followed him. "Thank you," she offered. The seat was lumpy and worn, but she sank into it easily.

The radio on the officer's belt crackled to life with indistinguishable words. "I'll go see what's going on," he told her. "Just wait here."

Again, she nodded. Her shaky hand took a sip of the water he had given her as she watched him head back down the hallway. As soon as he was gone, she stood up. She headed further down the interview hallway in search of the real emergency exit. The further away she got, the more angry she became.

Night had fallen. The time she spent trying to get Finley's knife and necklace, wasted. She poured the rest of the cup's contents into a nearby plant before entering another hallway. Hallway after hallway, the station was nothing but hallways and locked doors and she hoped she was headed for a back exit.

She passed by an open conference room door, the cool air conditioning a relief from the summer heat. Her steps slowed as she looked inside.

A board covered in a large map of Seattle, lined with red string, and photos of girls in all stages of life stared back at her. Kaden took a step backward to stand in the threshold. The room was empty. Quiet. Several boxes rested on the conference table, marked with numbers and names Kaden didn't recognize.

Her eyes swept across the labels.

The cool chill of the air prickled her skin when she stepped inside. The distant sounds of the office, far, far away.

She traced her finger along the table.

Kim, Ann.

Franklin, Penelope.

Cruz, Lola.

Hanes, Megan.

Kaden froze. She followed the curves and letters of her name over and over again. She rested the palm of her hand against the top of the box and sucked in a deep breath before lifting the lid.

She found her sweatshirt covered in blood in an evidence bag. The sight of it was like a punch to the gut. Underneath, she found the iron blade Finley had gifted her, stained with traces of crimson. She took it out of the bag and slipped it against her back under her clothes. The iron against her skin felt like nothing. There was no pain or burning. She wasn't a faerie, but the question lingered at the back of her mind. What was she?

Hidden in the corner of the box, she caught a glimpse of the silver necklace. Kaden slipped it out of the bag and into her pocket. She covered the lid back exactly as she had found it. But before she could leave, she stood motionlessly, her gaze drawn to the board that placed the missing girls.

She spotted Megan's easily. It was her high school graduation photo. Part of her wanted to take it down. She wanted to take all of it down. Instead, she pulled away, slipping out of the room and headed toward the exit.

The driver's door swung open, courtesy of Kaden's

mom. "Did you get what you needed?" she asked quickly. She plopped herself in the seat and started the engine.

"Yeah." Kaden revealed the items she took. "Detective Smith left the evidence box in the conference room. Did he suspect anything?"

"Please," she snorted. "Men don't know how to deal with over-excitable women. He thinks I'm taking you to your therapist tomorrow." The car pulled away from the curb into traffic. "But if he looks in the evidence box, he'll show up tonight." The city lights blended together against the dark hues of blue making way for distant stars, though light pollution made it impossible to see beyond two or three. The moon was the only light in the night sky she could see clearly. "Where did you need me to drop you off?" she asked.

Urban life flashed by her window as her mother drove. Kaden watched it all. "Discovery Park," she said. She pulled out the silver necklace from her pocket, tracing her thumb against its pattern. "Hey Mom?" she asked suddenly.

"Yeah?" her mother glanced over to the passenger seat briefly before returning her eyes to the road.

"What will you tell Quinn?" Kaden asked hesitantly.

The question filled the car with a sad kind of silence. The kind that follows bad news. Kaden wasn't sure if her mother was struggling to find the right words, or if she didn't know herself. "The same thing I'm going to tell the officers," she answered, breaking the silence. "That you never came home after we went to the station." Kaden's finger looped around a swirl in the design of the necklace, the blood dried and caked into the crevasses. "Don't worry," her mother added. "I'll get her through this."

"Yeah," she replied quietly. Kaden looked over to her mother, "I know you will."

Her mother smiled weakly. "I promise," she held her gaze. Kaden returned the smile. She thought she could see the shimmer of a tear forming in her mother's eye before she turned away. "Leave your credit card," she said suddenly as she cleared her throat.

"What?" Kaden asked her. "But I'm going to need—"

"You can't use it," she informed her. "The cops will be able to track your purchases, it's in all the documentaries. I have cash for you."

A faint laugh escaped Kaden at how ridiculous everything was. Then her mother started to laugh. Suddenly the car was lighter. "Right," Kaden said as her laughter stopped.

The car slowed as her mother pulled up to the park's entrance. Fireflies sparkled in the night as a gentle wind passed through the open windows. Her mother put the car in park and turned toward her.

They sat there for a moment without saying anything. Then Kaden's mother leaned over the center console and hugged her. Kaden pulled her in tightly. Her perfume was sweet and floral, like a garden in spring. She breathed as much of it in as she could. "Promise me," her mother said in Kaden's ear, "you'll be careful."

"I promise." She gave her mother one last squeeze before she exited the car and headed into the park. Kaden didn't want to turn around and wave like she had done the first day of kindergarten, because she didn't know if she was coming back.

CHAPTER VIII

Departure Day
Ireland, 1934

Departure Day was supposed to be the single most important event in Finley's life. The twelfth birthday of any son born after the first, was the day they became a knight in the eyes of the Seelie Court. The event took place from the moment the sun rose over the emerald green hills. There was music and laughter, games and food around every corner. Royals from other Seelie Courts travelled to bear witness the monumental celebration as Finley would take the position as apprentice to the knight commander for another Seelie Court. It was the day that separated Finley from his brother and sister.

Faerie royals needed daughters to inherit their mother's crown which left sons like Thierry and Finley to other obligations. First born sons like Thierry were chosen to marry first born daughters. An arranged marriage set up by parents with little to do with love and more to do with status. Second born sons, and any son thereafter, fit into different roles in the Court.

The morning started with ceremony; a sword that graced both of Finley's shoulders by his mother the Queen. Light cascaded through the stained glass windows of the sacred hall and with a little magic, burnt orange and yellow leaves fell from above. The day was exactly as Finley had pictured since he could remember. But his favorite part would come at night. The supper was hand picked by him and the moment he learned that bit of information, Finley kept a secret list of things he expected to have. It was all of his favorites, from colcannon made with kale and cabbage to stew which mixed all his favorites in one bowl; lamb, onions, parsley, and more potato. The aromas danced across the grand hall alongside the fae who celebrated Finley's accomplishment.

Finley swung Eva in a circle as they glided across the dance floor. "Slow down, Finley, I'm getting dizzy!"

"Then we must go faster until your eyes see clearly." He spun her faster, a grin stretching across his face as his feet picked up speed.

"I'm going to fall over, Finley!"

He grabbed his sister, tight around her waist. "Don't worry," he told her. "I won't let go. I promise."

The two swung so fast that Finley lost his balance. The inertia sent the both of them flying off the dance floor and into the crowd of chatting faeries. Eva bumped into Thierry's back while Finley, regrettably, slammed into his father.

They stumbled with blurred vision as their eyes attempted to adjust to the stillness at which they landed. Thierry hid a half amused smile at them, but was quickly washed away as he was pulled back into his conversation.

The sharp glare Finley's father gave him pierced through him. It was the same expression he had faced many times. Each time, Finley wanted nothing more than to return the look.

"Forgive my son," he apologized to the King of the some part of France Finley couldn't remember. "He still doesn't know when to obey his elders."

"Pardon me, Father," Finley began politely. His vision returned to see his father with complete clarity. "But I don't recall you giving me orders to obey today."

His father's expression twisted. Red rose to his cheeks as a vein in the temple of his forehead began to bulge. But Finley knew he would not break character in front of another Seelie King. He glanced up with a coy smile. Under different circumstances, he would be lashed, but he didn't need to worry since it was his last day with him.

"Your son has quite the tongue," the King said to Finley's father. "Rather humorous, isn't it, your Majesty."

"My son believes so." His father turned away from him sharply. "Thierry is very fond of your young Juliette…"

Finley rolled his eyes hearing another attempt at Thierry's betrothal. It almost made him want to vomit.

"Sir Treasach," someone said from behind him.

Finley dusted his velvet coat and trousers for any remaining debris they may have seen during the jousting earlier in the day.

"Sir Treasach," they said again with more effort.

Finley looked up to find one of his mother's hand maidens. Her eyes were set on him, but he glanced over to Thierry who paid no mind. When he looked back she was still staring at him. He pointed to himself, "Me?"

She bowed her head slightly. "Her Majesty the Queen requests that it is time you gather your belongings for your departure."

"Thank you, Tamara."

Eva hurried over, grabbing Finley's elbow. "She called you Sir," she squealed. "My brother Sir Treasach."

"You already have a brother, Sir Treasach," he corrected.

"Now I have two," she smiled.

"Well, I must go and see to my things," he said.

He moved to walk away when Eva pulled his elbow back. "Why can't I come with you?" she asked him. Her face fell so her eyes resembled puppy dogs.

"A knight needs to be free to pack his under garments himself." Eva released him from her grip. "And soon they will be bringing out dessert and I need you to save some for me."

Eva's eyes widened as she scanned the grand hall for any traces of sweets and magic, "Don't worry," she whispered. "I'll find it."

Clambering through hundreds of friendly congratulations, handshakes, and hugs, Finley fought his way to the exit. Red lips stained his cheek from Royal Seelie women he was forced to wipe away when they weren't looking. When he finally broke free, he found himself in the solitude of the hallway that guards and maids used. It was a narrow path with little light, but it was much easier to use than the ones stuffed with faeries he didn't know and didn't intend to meet.

The music from the grand hall echoed down the chambers, bouncing off the architecture and stone. The floors beneath his feet were stone and never were good for Finley and Eva to glide down on their knees which he learned the hard way. But the marble outside the grand hall had just enough slip and space. The only reason he and Eva were forced to stop was when Finley accidentally hit an antique table with a hand painted clay vase. The sound it made when it hit the floor echoes in her ear each time he passes by it. Though it was fixed, he could never look at it the same way.

He found the doors to his chambers open, most of his things already packed with the help of his mother. Only a few mementos were left which he hated. He had to choose which would come with him and which would forever be left behind.

His twelve knight figurines atop their horses waited along the far window sill. He bunched them up in his hands, their swords prickling his skin as he buried them into one of his luggage bags.

Beside it, he saw a small box wrapped up with a note attached.

A gift for my son on Departure Day. Signed *His Majesty the King.*

The lettering was not his father's. He had seen it written on all of his gifts and on the letters written to and from knights. It was courtesy of the Knight Commander. Finley wondered if that was what his life would be as knight commander. Just an errand boy for the King or if there was more.

He tore the wrapping open to find a wooden box carved with the Seelie Courts sigil. He ran his fingers over it. When he lifted the lid he found a dagger. Hand crafted the hilt formed a dragon with Celtic patterns and emeralds for eyes. He slid the blade out of its sheath. It was sharp, paper thin with iron. It was a work of beauty.

Finley concealed the blade back into its sheath. The package should have said Knight Commander. He took the box and threw it against the far wall. The noise it made carried through his chambers.

"Finley? What are you doing?" His mother stood in the doorway. Her velvet emerald gown fell to the floor in layers. The crown upon her head, golden, striking the light in such a way it appeared to glow.

Finley looked away. He wiped the tears in his eyes he hadn't realized were there. "I…" he began. He searched his mind for the right words. "The King's gift hurt me," he finished quietly. Finley fabricated his way through the truth. He couldn't admit to his mother any further details of his pain. Though it was a gift, a valuable one, it came with no love.

His mother entered the room, her dress swishing along the floor. She walked over to where the box had landed and picked it up. She glanced over at Finley before she approached him.

She lowered herself to meet his eye. She reached out and wiped his face. Despite being over four hundred years old, she never looked a day over forty. The same green eyes Finleym had, stared back at him. "Finley Treasach," she said. "There is much you have learned in your life and I could not be prouder. But there is also so much you don't understand yet."

"He doesn't love me," Finley replied. A few tears streamed down his cheek. "I know he couldn't wait for this day."

"Listen to me, Finley." She lifted his chin so he wouldn't drop his gaze to the floor. "Everyone's heart is as fragile as glass. Some of us cannot help but lock theirs inside an iron box for no one to see. Do you know who taught me this?" Finley shook his head. "My mother. And do you know who taught her?" she asked. "Her mother. Finley, we are creatures of understanding. Though it does not condone one's actions. We must believe in the best in everyone. He does love you, he just does not know how to show it."

"I don't want to leave," Finley admitted. "This is my home."

A smile curled her lip. "You are my brave little knight," she told him. Her smile was delicate, strong enough to make the angriest man smile back. "And you will always be in our hearts. Always. But there is someone out there who needs you. We cannot be selfish and keep you to ourselves. You need to provide your beautiful soul to another Court. Teach them all that you know, guide them down the right path, and protect the vulnerable."

Doyle twirled a wrench in one hand, his back turned away from Finley. "One of the guards informed me that you were chatting amongst your fellow inmates." He wore the same rubber apron he had on when Finley first woke up in the prison. One spattered in blood.

The stench and gloom Finley had gotten used to, however the room alone sent his nerves on edge. A headache began to form with just his presence in the space. Though he hadn't been hit or poked or stabbed with anything yet.

The restraints that forced his arms and legs to the table beneath him carved chain link patterns into his flesh, burning iron to his bones. But the strap that ran over his temple, holding his head still was something he had never experienced before.

"I don't have to lock you up, do I?" Doyle's voice rang with delight.

"Well," Finley sighed. "There is that whole Freedom of Speech thing the Americans are always on about. Unless..." he paused. "We're somewhere else?"

A coy smile spread across Doyle's face as he turned. He rested one hand on the table beside Finley's head. Doyle leaned down, closer to Finley. The purple in his eyes, smokey and swirling with chaos.

"Enlighten me, Light fae," he said almost like a purr. He ran the wrench through Finley's brown locks. "What were you discussing?"

Finley caught the glint of the wrench against the fluorescent light, remnants of blood, fresh and dripping.

"The usual things prisoners talk about over a pathetic meal." Finley couldn't lie. Neither could Doyle or any faerie for that matter. Still, spending so much time in the human world, Finley had forgotten how difficult it was to bend the truth ever so slightly. "Who did we eat? Your tailor or perhaps your footmen?"

Amusement sparkled in Doyle's eyes as he swiftly smashed the wrench against Finley's skull. The sound dropped out of his ears leaving a piercing ringing in his head. The new gash split Finley's forehead open, dark red poured down the side of his face. "You're lucky I'm willing to throw you the scraps I do." Doyle turned away from him quickly, tossing the wrench with a clatter. "Some might call that merciful."

"Other's," Finley breathed heavily through the pain, "might see it as a precaution. So inmates don't turn on one another. So they don't turn on *you*."

"You really don't want me as an enemy," he warned. He placed one hand behind his back while the other lifted a jar.

"So this is friendship then?" Finley asked.

Doyle sucked in a breath, "If you don't answer my questions directly, I will have no choice but to bring in the other two inmates you were talking to. Not to mention...Nicolai."

Finley's jaw clenched. His heart pumped faster. Without realizing it, he found himself trying to pull free from his chains only to make the cuts deeper.

"I've been told you've grown quite fond of the boy." Doyle took a handful of the substance from the jar and turned around in the blink of an eye. He brought the small minerals to Finley's open wounds and sprinkled them.

Sizzling pain rippled against his flesh as salt pierced his gashes. Salt mixed with the iron seared and bubbled so harshly Finley began to see dots in his vision. The thought of Nicolai or anyone for that matter receiving the same agony cut him deeper than the iron chains. "We were discussing the crow," Finley seethed.

Doyle furrowed his brow, unsure if Finley was telling the truth. "You know about that?" he asked curiously. "Hmm." Doyle took a step back, out of the light. "I won't lie," he began.

"You can't lie," Finley corrected.

"Perhaps not," he exhaled. "But we know how to bend the truth, don't we?" Without seeing him, Finley knew a wicked smile spread across his face. "I'm surprised it took you this long."

Finley didn't say anything. His chest rose and fell in deep heaves as the bubbling of his skin died down.

"I like you." Doyle spun on his heel, placing the jar back on his table of unfortunate tools. "You're smart, quick witted."

"Do you tell that to all the inmates? Or am I your special friend?"

Doyle wiggled his index finger at him. "You've been here, what? Three months now? Do you ever wonder why your tongue hasn't been cut out?"

"I like to believe it's my incredible physique that turns

you on."

"Is it easier for you to hide behind your humor? It must be difficult knowing all the pain you caused those around you. Especially *that* young girl. Now, remind me, what was her name again?" Finley's teeth gritted together. "That's what I thought."

"What about the man in solitary?" Finley asked. "I hear he's been there for quite some time? Why have you kept him so long?"

Doyle cocked a half smile. "He's not mine to keep."

"So, if he's not yours," Finley said. "Whose is he?"

The edges of Doyle's eyes squinted. "Someone with mutual interests," Doyle said. "And when he arrives, I'm sure he'll like to meet you. He'll be very interested in your allegiance to the Dark fae."

"Allegiance?" he repeated. "To you?" Finley scoffed.

"Only time will tell," Doyle's hand danced over to the wrench again. "Unfortunately for you, you offended one of the guards. Now, under normal circumstances, I would send you to the crow. But," he raised the wrench back into his hand examining it as if it was a new toy. "Since we already have someone lined up for that position, I'll have to settle for this." Doyle gripped one hand tightly against Finley's jaw line. The hold that Doyle had forced Finley's mouth open and Finley realized why his head had been restrained. "Open wide."

CHAPTER IX

With night dusting the sky in stars, Kaden made her way back to Theordore's hole where she had left her two fugitives. Using the light on her phone, she followed the trails as best as she could remember. Every bit of wood was shrouded in darkness, not even the moon's light helped her. But the evening was peaceful, warm. Night enveloped her at every turn. Somewhere in the distance, she heard the faint giggle of children playing. It reminded her of Finley, the way the fae children reacted to seeing him again. Seeing how different he was, how much taller he stood in the Seelie Court.

Kaden stopped in her tracks with thick grass and weeds ankle deep. She glanced up through the canopy of trees, where the moon shimmered through. "Finley," she said in a faint whisper. "I don't know if you can hear me, but…I am going to find you." She half expected a reply, for him to just appear, but all she found were the giggles and night scape of crickets and cicadas.

With the duffel bag slung over her shoulder, she marched further into the wood. As slowly as her steps, the airy, bright melody of a flute reached her eardrum. The music grew louder the closer Kaden got to Theodore's home.

When she reached the clearing, she found Blaine atop a low tree branch, one leg dangling down. He bobbed and weaved his head along with the melody while Theodore jumped into the air to swat at his foot. "I said stop!" Theodore yelled. When he couldn't reach, Theodore grabbed a big stick. "Can you believe this?" his voice seethed. "I told you faeries were snobs! This is my home! Now, knock it off you faerie bastard!" Theodore smacked Blaine's foot with the stick. It did nothing.

"Blaine," Kaden warned. She aimed her phone's light in his direction. "Cut it out."

Blaine winced at the brightness, shielding his eyes from it.

"You're making too much noise. People will hear you."

"I will if you turn down that torch," Blaine said.

Kaden lowered the light back to the forest floor. "Where's Keeley?" She glanced around to find her nowhere.

"Here," she answered from the base of a tree trunk. Keeley leaned back, sharpening a branch into a spear head. "I was crafting a weapon to hit Blaine with," she admitted as she tested the spear's point with her index finger. "But it looks like you took care of his foolishness."

"You were going to stab him?" Kaden asked her.

She glanced up from her craftsmanship to Kaden. "He heals," she replied plainly with a shrug.

"Not emotionally!" Blaine shouted back.

Theodore stopped, out of breath. "Will you please remove these two from my presence?" He placed one hand on his forehead and shook his head.

"Keeley," Kaden said. The muscles in her spine stiffened. "Blaine, you two need to get a grip. If we're going to save Finley we need to work together."

Blaine furrowed his brow, "She started it," he whined.

Kaden's jaw clenched. She dropped the duffle bag at her feet and bent down, one knee against the cool ground. "Blaine," she said as she reached into her bag. Kaden tossed a grey beanie at him, "You get the hat." He then proceeded to examine it before pulling it over his head, covering his ears. "Keeley," she said. She stood up and pulled the silver necklace from her pocket. "Here's Finley's necklace."

Keeley took it, though it was made of silver, she acted as if it burned her like iron. "If Blaine is going to be helping us we will end up getting caught before we even get to Finley," she muttered under her breath.

"Excuse me!" Blaine yelled as he leaped down from the tree limp. "I am a proper knight of the Seelie Court."

Keeley shot him a quick glance, "You are a knight by default. Lack of warriors, if we're being honest. And you did break your oath when presented with your first challenge."

"That's it!" Kaden shouted. "If you two don't shut up and stop bickering I'm going to have Theodore send you back to the dungeon."

"It would be my pleasure," Theodore said with a nod.

The three of them stood in a circle, ignoring Theodore's comment. "Right now," Kaden began. "You are both out of your element, which makes me in charge." She looked over to both of them to see if they would challenge her words. "Both of you need to cover your ears. Blaine, make sure that hat stays on your head at all times. Keeley—" Kaden glanced down at the necklace, Finley's necklace falling between her breast bone. "Don't lose it."

The muscles in Keeley's jaw clenched, but she nodded.

"We need to take a cab and find Riley."

Keeley removed her bow from across her chest and handed it to Kaden. "How do you plan to find him?" she asked.

Kaden took the bow along with her satchel of arrows. "He was watching me," she told Keeley, "the other night. I don't know if he's keeping tabs on me or if he just…enjoys it."

"Where will we bring him once we have him? Surely not here."

"You bet your ass not here," Theodore chimed in.

Kaden looked down to Theodore, "No. We'll take him to Finley's apartment, he has more iron there." She pulled an iron frying pan out of her duffel. "We're going to hit him where it hurts."

"Um…I have a question," Blaine raised his pointer finger into the air. "What is a cab?"

Kaden leaned against a brick wall just across the street from her kick boxing classes. The last time she had been bait, circumstances were different. She didn't know what to expect. Then, it was about saving Megan. Trying and failing. The deep, hollow hole in her heart reminded her with each breath. Each inhale was a sharp pain tingling against her ribs. The feeling was similar to when she realized as a child her father was never coming home. Similar, and yet, different.

All she had was Megan. She had Quinn too once. But that broke the night she tried to convince her of fae. Even if she could show Quinn, even if she ended up believing, Quinn didn't trust her. Not the first time. Not when it mattered.

She brushed the thoughts away. Finley was going to be saved. He had to be.

The glow from the inside of the gym illuminated the street. She watched as Nancy was forced to partner up with the instructor and wondered if she was worried about her. Then, she saw Riley. He strutted down the sidewalk across from her with his hands in his pocket. Just the glimpse of him made her jaw clench. But she buried the anger that boiled her skin.

Kaden walked across the street.

"I see your running late," Riley grinned.

She threw up a little in her mouth.

She forced a smile across her face. "Yeah," she sighed. "Looks like they started without me." She reached the curb, hoping it would make her feel taller, more powerful than him. But Riley was still bigger.

He began to walk away. Kaden reached out quickly and grabbed his elbow. Riley glared down at her hand on him with a scrunched brow.

"Would you–" Kaden began to panic. He wasn't supposed to walk away. "Would you want to get...coffee?"

Riley squinted.

"I mean, I'm already really late so what's the point of going in?"

His coy lips curled upward. "I knew there was something between us," he purred.

Kaden bit her tongue, hard. "Why don't we cut through the alley?" she asked. "I know this great place."

Mischief swirled behind Riley's eyes. "The alley?" he repeated. "You know, bad things happen in alleys"

Kaden shrugged one shoulder. "Unless you're worried I will bite."

The edges of his eyes crinkled as his grin spread. "After you," he gestured toward the dark crevasse beside the building.

She smiled quickly, but as soon as she turned her back on him, it faded into a fine line.

There was no light in the alley, just the smell of days old garbage. The hairs on the back of Kaden's neck stood on end. She felt eyes on her and wanted nothing more than to whip around and cause him as much hurt as he caused her. But creatures like Riley don't hurt.

His finger tips graced her forearm. "Why don't we stop for a bit?"

Kaden cringed away from him, her attention on the large garbage bin a few feet away. "We don't have that far," she told him.

"Yes, but," he pulled her elbow back. Her skin crawled. Her muscles tensed under his touch. "We could get to know one another better first."

Riley took her and placed her back against the brick wall. He ran his thumb against her jaw line gently. Kaden fought the sensation not to squirm away or hit or punch the twisted look on his face. "We could have fun," he added. His breath was hot against her ear. Heat fueled her heart, spreading wild fire through her veins.

The moon above glowed silver-white against Keeley's hair. She was easy to spot as she approached Riley from behind. Her footsteps were non-existent. Her movements, graceful like a wolf hunting its prey.

Kaden relaxed as she watched Keeley raise the iron frying pan up and swiftly back down against the base of Riley's skull. The sound it made crackled, like a bowling ball hitting the floor with its dead weight.

Riley fell, still for a moment. He reached his hand behind his head only to find traces of his own blood. When he glanced up to the two of them, his face was red with anger. "You little—"

Keeley struck him again, knocking him out cold. His body fell limp against the asphalt. "Nice to make your acquaintance, Riley," Keeley said.

With Riley unconscious, Kaden was able to move and squirm her body free of him. "Come on," she said. She bent down over his body, "We have to get him into a cab before he wakes up."

The tip tap of footsteps echoed down the alley as

Blaine approached. "That…was…incredible!" He raised his arms above his head and spun around. "I adore this city!"

Keeley shot him a glare as she helped Kaden lift Riley's body off the ground. "You did nothing to execute this plan."

"Perhaps," Blaine admitted easily. "But I was here when it took place."

Keeley pressed her lips together in a fine line to prevent herself from saying anything she might regret. She tossed Riley's arm over her shoulder, "How does one explain a limp body to the vehicle's driver?" she asked.

Kaden took his other arm around her neck. His touch was no better alive than it was unconscious. "It's Seattle," Kaden said plainly. "If anyone asks, we'll just say he got drunk and passed out."

"This is just so riveting." Blaine smiled wildly. "I could just kiss you, Keeley!"

"Touch me and I will break you," she told him flatly.

"Blaine," Kaden said.

"Yes?" he answered.

"Remeber what we talked about," she reminded him. "No talking in the cab."

Blaine's face fell with utter disappointment, "How am I supposed to get to know the humans without words?"

CHAPTER X

Seattle, 1934

Finley sat in the garden eating an apple as he watched the sun dip below the horizon. The mid-afternoon glow was a beautiful sight after a long day of training under the Knight Commander. Training and fighting were among Finley's favorite things, but his solitude at the end of each day was more rewarding. The botany of the Seelie Court was different from the one he had at home. It was vast with greenery from all parts of the world. The forest beyond the village was like a rainforest. The village itself, much like the nature of North America, and the Court, a slice of home.

It was in the peaceful moments he found himself. Training all day only allowed for some much peace.

"Enjoying your apple?" A female voice pierced through Finley's quiet.

"Well, I'm eating it aren't I?" he answered. He sank his teeth into another bite. The juice dripped down from his chin as he turned to see who had interrupted his company.

Deep doe eyes stared back at him. With the glow from the sun, they looked gold. Her beige dress stood out among the shades of green. And her hair, her hair fell past her shoulders in auburn locks. "Oh, um...your royal Highness. I meant no disrespect. Please forgive my rudeness." His word fumbled out of his mouth along with bits of apple. He stood from the bench suddenly and bowed his head.

"That's quite alright," the young princess said.

Finley raised his head up, catching the delicate lightness of her smile.

"I imagine you came here to be alone. It seems we had a similar idea."

"Yes," he said quickly. "Your Highness. I will be on my way." Finley stood up straight, but bowed his head once more.

"What for?" she asked. Her brows furrowed.

"Do you not wish to be alone?" he asked her.

She followed the cobbled pathway to the bench and sat down. "As do you," she said. She glanced down to the stone bench and looked back up at him. "We can be alone together."

Finley hesitated before he took his seat once more. "Would you like some apple, Your Highness?" He held out his apple for her. His teeth marks cut a circle in the center to the core.

"No," she let out a gentle laugh. "However, your offer

is kindly noted."

Finley smiled weakly, returning the apple to his lap.

"You're to be the new Knight Commander? From Ireland?" she questioned.

"Yes, Your Highness. Although I am only an apprentice."

"You don't have to do that," she told him.

Finley glanced over at her. The way the sun kissed her skin made the freckles along her nose visible. "Do what, Your Highness?"

"Refer to me as 'Your Highness'," she said. "I have a name you know."

"Yes," he nodded. He looked away before he couldn't stop looking. "Of course."

"Well aren't you going to ask me what it is?" she wondered.

Finley tried not to grin. "And what is your name?" he asked her.

Her tenderness swept through her smile. "Linette."

"Forgive me," he said. "But it is proper to refer to the royal family with the appropriate title."

Linette raised an auburn brow, "It is also proper to do what your princess tells you to do." Her grin turned coy, making the dimples in her cheeks stand out.

Finley smiled back, "You are right," he agreed. "My apologies...Linette." Her name on his tongue was against every bit of royal protocol. Had his mother been present, she would have corrected his mistake instantly or insisted he treat her as a lady. If his father had heard him... "May I ask you a question?" he asked suddenly.

Linette turned away from the setting sun, "You may," she said.

He fidgeted with the apple in his hand, "Why do you wish to be alone?"

Her features dulled. The kind smile she once wore, faded. "Mother wishes to teach me everything, around every corner of every day."

Finley cocked his head. "Forgive me if I'm wrong," he began. "But is that not something you want to learn as heir to the crown?"

"I never asked to be Queen," she answered quickly.

"I never asked to be Knight Commander," he shrugged. "But here I am. I actually find I quite enjoy it. Perhaps you will learn to enjoy being Queen."

"I doubt that possibility," she said softly. "It may sound easy, but it's much more complicated. Having no siblings doesn't make it easier. An arranged betrothal isn't something I dream about."

Finley's gaze fell to his apple as the oxygen began to turn it brown. "I never quite thought about it I guess."

"About what?" Linette asked him.

"In the eyes of the bride," he admitted. Finley looked back up at her to find she was staring at him, listening. "My brother didn't seem to care much that he would marry someone he didn't really know."

A weak smile curled her lip. "And you are out here, why?"

Finley found himself looking past the garden to the pasture beyond. "The other knights told me my horse had to be trained before I could see her again," he told her. "I usually share an apple with her about this time."

"Lucky for you I have some authority with the knights," she said proudly.

"Oh, no," Finley shook his head. "That's very kind of you, but I don't want any attention drawn to myself."

"Alright," she nodded. Linette peered around at the light fading on the leaves. "I should probably go before Mother sends a whole garrison out to look for me," she said. Linette stood from the bench and so did Finley. "Until next time."

Her dress swooshed as she walked. Panic swirled against Finley's chest watching her get further and further away. "Finley," he blurted out.

She glanced over her shoulder. "What?"she asked.

"My name," he answered. "It's Finley."

Linette smiled one last time, "I know," she said before she disappeared.

The prisoners lined up in rows three stories down from where their cells were. What was referred to as 'recreational time' was an opportunity to sweep through the cells to ensure no one had dug a hole or managed to steal anything that could be used to escape.

The guards made their way from cell to cell, tossing over beds and buckets.

"Like a plastic fork could help us claw through these walls," William grumbled under his breath. William was one of the more unusual looking fae in the prison. Thick, black hair covered all of his body aside from part of his face. His nails were sharpened into perfect points, more like claws. But it was his nose that made him stand out the most.

Each level had their chance at standing around the main floor in chains. It was what Nicolai referred to as a good time, but for Finley it was a way for him to study the function of the prison.

"At least we get to stand in a different environment for a few minutes," Finley replied. He made sure to speak without moving his jaw much as both sides were painted with yellow, turning purple, bruises. He couldn't see himself, but Nicolai had told him his face looked as swollen as some of the other wounds he had on his body.

"What happened to you?" Hugo asked from beside William.

"Doyle decided he wanted to role-play as the tooth fairy." Finley's jaw locked at the thought but the soreness of his mouth caused him to stop.

"He pulled out two of his back molars," Nicolai whispered to them. "Finley was throwing up blood for a while." The boy patted Finley on the back gingerly.

"I suppose we ought to thank you then," Hugo said. Finley squinted over at him curiously. "For taking the beating," he added.

Finley looked away. It never crossed his mind to allow someone else to get tortured. The faerie side of him wished he hadn't said 'thank you', but he wasn't about to correct Hugo. He leaned forward slightly, "I doubt either of us will be alive much longer though."

"How long does he keep prisoners alive?" Finley asked. The metallic taste of blood filled his mouth.

"It depends," Hugo replied. "Most of the time, just until he gets whatever he wants out of us."

"Where does that leave you two?" he wondered.

Hugo shrugged. "Who knows." The clash of metal rippled from the balcony above as a guard chucked a bed frame out the cell door. Every prisoner looked up. "He still needs William to draw a map to the Buggane market," Hugo whispered.

Finley recalled his brother teaching him about the Buggane market. It was much like the black market of the fae world. Bugganes were difficult fae to track. Their nature had them awake at night in places of ruin which was why the market was well hidden.

"I thought that market was destroyed ages ago?" he asked him.

"So you're a Buggane?" Nicolai asked, hidden behind Finley from his fear of talking to other inmates.

"It's the fae market," William hissed at him. "It never closes for long."

"Why do they need to get to the market?" Finley asked him.

William grunted. "Why would I tell the likes of you?" he shot back.

"Obviously they want something from there. When we get out of here we need to—"

"*When? When?*" William spat on the floor by Finley's feet. "There's no getting out."

"Of course there is," he replied with certainty. "All I need is a plan."

"I'm afraid William is right," Hugo added. "The only

way out is in a coffin." Hugo looked down at Nicolai with sadness in his eyes.

Finley turned his head to see Nicolai's eyes beginning to water with tears. The boy clutched the shreds of Finley's clothing that still managed to survive. "Don't worry," Finley whispered down to him. "They're only old men." He gave Nicolai a quick wink. Finley tucked Nicolai further behind him as if it would protect him from their conversation. "What about the guy in solitary?" he asked them.

"What about him?" William grumbled.

"He tried to escape."

Hugo leaned out of line, "That's just a rumor," he told him. "Solitary only leads to the crow. There's no way of knowing if there even *is* someone there because no one ever comes back."

Finley sucked in his lips. "What is this crow you all seem to be terrified of? It sounds to me more like an empty threat and poorly named."

"It's short for scarecrow, jackass," William snapped. He shifted uncomfortably under the weight of the chains.

"What is it?" Finley pressed.

William's lip curled. "When a prisoner's time has come," he began.

"Or a prison misbehaves," Hugo added.

"They get sent to solitary. They stay there for a few days at most. Then they take them outside and string them up on a post for the vultures to pluck out their eyes and their livers. If they're lucky enough to bleed out first, it's really not so bad. But if they don't, the hounds shred away the meat from their bones until there's nothing left."

Hugo swallowed. "If you listen carefully enough," his words became a whisper. "You can hear their screams at night."

"I need to get to solitary," Finley said plainly.

"Are you mad?" William shouted. His voice carried throughout the open area, forcing everyone to silence before a guard appeared. He lowered his voice, "Are you mad, boy?"

With his head bowed, he eyed the guards positions. "If there is someone up there, I need to talk to him." Finley wondered why he was so important to keep. What he knew or was that he couldn't be placed with the rest of them.

Finley hadn't realized both Hugo and William's eyes were dead set on him. "What for?" William asked. "There's no way you'll be able to talk to him without getting yourself killed."

"We need to make an escape plan and he seems like a way to do it."

"Who said we would join you?" William snapped.

Finley shot him a glare, "You're dead either way, aren't you?" he said.

"Treasach!" A menacing voice shouted from across the room. Nicolai shrunk further behind him. Both Hugo and William lowered their heads.

The guard from the cafeteria that had nothing more to do with his life then cause pain approached him with a vile grin across his face.

"You're coming with us," he seethed. He was accompanied by a rather bulky fae who unchained Finley roughly from the link.

"What for?" he asked them, fearful they had caught wind of their conversation. "Is Doyle ready for another round of role-palying?"

The larger guard tugged Finley by his upper arm so aggressively he thought his arm might pull it out of his socket. "Let's go," he coughed.

The two lead him down halls he had never seen before with stairwells going up and down, corridors stretching far beyond the scope he had formed in his mind of the layout.

When they turned a corner, he was met with a brick wall. They shoved Finley out in front of them, Finley forced himself to resist the push as much as he could. "I know some of the other inmates are into this sort of scenario," Finley turned around slowly and gestured to the triangle they made. "Maybe you should get one of them."

The thicker of the two snarled at him.

"Some of us," the gruesome one began, "are getting tired of how much you get away with." He stepped closer. "The boss says we can't kill you..." he cocked his head slightly to the side. "But we can make you wish you were dead."

CHAPTER XI

Riley began to stir. The more aware he became, the more he struggled under the burn of the iron chains that Kaden used to tie him to the chair. His eyes shot open. Wildly, he glanced around the unfamiliar surroundings.

Finley's apartment was bright, furnished with leather and velvet, marble and stainless steele. As soon as Riley settled around his whereabouts, his attention fell to the other three occupants in the space.

Blaine sat on the kitchen island that separated the living room from the kitchen itself. Keeley blocked the exit, her back to the front door while Kaden simmered, anger under her skin, in front of him.

"Morning sunshine." Kaden flashed him a cocky grin before it fell from her face to a flat line.

Blaine leaned in closer, "Is sunshine an insult to

humans?" he wondered. Keeley stole a sharp glance his way, making Blaine recoil back further.

"You remember me," Riley said with curiosity. He studied her quietly for a moment, his eyes intrigued. "How?"

Kaden stood with her arms crossed over her chest using one leg to hold most of her weight. "Let's just say someone branded me with a favor." Her jaw clenched, the muscles tightening the features of her face. She wanted nothing more than to grab him by the locks of his hair and make him pay. But she remained still. "It brought back a lot of missing memories."

Riley half smiled, almost impressed. "Of course someone as naive as you would agree to a favor," he scoffed.

The ease in Riley's demeanor was unnerving. She inspected the points at which the chains linked without moving. "Worried your work won't hold me for long?" Riley asked her.

The edge of her right eye flinched at the sound of his voice. "How did Doyle pull it off?" she asked quickly.

Riley grinned the kind of grin that forced goosebumps to run up and down the spine. "It was a hallucination," he answered plainly. "You *murdered* an illusion of your own friend."

"I didn't murder anyone," she corrected sharply.

"Maybe," he said. "But you would have."

Kaden took a step closer to him. "The blood was real," she spat. "It didn't just vanish. Neither did the body in my arms. Not like the fake. Not like the Finley I saw on the balcony."

His wry smile twisted. "Doyle is the King of the Dark faeries," he told her. "Not in Seattle, not in Washington, but everywhere. He has enough power to erase your memory, do you really believe he can't conjure a terrifyingly realistic hallucination?"

Kaden's gaze held his. She looked for the lie in his eyes, the bent truth, but found none. The fire in her heart roared. She just wanted to throw something, hit something, make something bleed.

"Hit me," Riley said. He leaned against the chair slightly. "I don't bite."

Before Kaden could respond, Keeley pulled her away from him and took her position. "Faeries don't have that kind of strength anymore," she said. "Not even the King of the Unholy."

Riley didn't take his attention off Kaden. He watched her. Studied her. She was vulnerable and he knew it. It made Kaden's skin crawl with the heat of a thousand fire ants. "I guess you'll just have to ask him yourself then."

Kaden sucked in her breath.

Breathe. She told herself.

"Where is he?" she asked him.

Riley cocked his head slightly, "You'll have to be more specific."

Her lip curled. "Finley."

"Ah," he sank back into his seat almost as if he wanted to tip the front legs back. "The million dollar question."

"Answer her," Keeley demanded. Kaden watched as Keeley's grip on her sai swords tightened.

Riley caught the same gesture. The smile he had slipped off his face. "A prison," he replied. He swallowed hard.

Kaden looked at Keeley. If it were Quinn she was looking at, she would have known Kaden was wary of Riley. But it wasn't.

"Where?" Kaden pressed.

Riley looked between Keeley and Kaden, not paying much attention to Blaine, who Kaden almost forgot was present. "If I knew," he started. "I wouldn't be here in Seattle now, would I?"

Kaden moved closer, making sure not to get too close in case she wrapped her hands around his neck. "You're basically Doyle's second," she pointed out. "You must know something. Unless…" The devious part of Kaden hummed under her skin. "You're just his little bitch."

His face contorted in the same way it had the night Megan went missing. He was seething. A smile spread across her face.

"Doyle's second?" he scoffed. "Doyle has *hundreds* of us scattered all over the world. And if anyone's a bitch here, it's you, lass."

"So he's not in Seattle, then?" she said.

Riley's nostrils flared. His lip fell into a fine straight line.

Kaden began to pace behind Keeley, collecting her thoughts. The possibilities were endless if Finley wasn't in Seattle or North America for that matter. "Alright," Kaden sighed. She shared a glance with Keeley and nodded.

Without a word, Keeley drew her weapon swiftly,

resting the sharp end of the blade against Riley's neck. "The time for games is over," she told him.

Riley leaned back, as far away from the blade as he could, but to no avail. The veins in his neck formed a system of rivers as they waited, exposed to the light.

"Keeley, here will be happy to cut out the answers we need," Kaden said. The words sounded funny coming out of her mouth. Like the voice that spoke wasn't hers at all. They were unusual and threatening. They fueled the fire growing inside of her.

Riley squirmed under the pressure of the blade. "Perhaps," he began, his voice raising pitch slightly. "I know…a secret."

"What kind of secret?!" Blaine asked from the kitchen.

Riley's attention didn't veer off the deadly weapon at his throat. "One that *may* lead you to where you need to go."

Keeley pressed her blade against his neck, enough to draw blood. Riley seethed. "Go on," Keeley told him.

He glared at her sharply. "I am aware of a realm that Doyle has visited," he explained. "One that very few fae have been to, most don't believe it exists."

"What realm?" Keeley asked bitterly.

Riley clenched his teeth. "I didn't say I knew what realm it was, now, did I?" he snapped. Keeley punctured the tip of her blade into his throat enough for more crimson to run down his neck, a stream of blood. "Okay! Wait!" Riley squeezed his eyes shut. He struggled under the chains. The veins in his neck bulged making more blood seep out.

Keeley pulled back only a little. "There is a group of fae who have been to the realm and made it out alive," he offered.

"Who?" Blaine asked. Kaden shot him a quick glance before returning her attention back to Riley.

"All I have is a last name and a location of their last whereabouts," Riley huffed.

"Tell us," Keeley demanded.

Riley licked his lips.

"Now." Keeley moved the blade off his throat to the base of his earlobe. She pulled his ear away from his head and, slowly, delicately began to carve upwards.

Riley's scream reverberated off the walls for deaf ears to hear. "Canem," he answered quickly. Foam and saliva gathered at the corners of his mouth. "Their last name is Canem. Last location, Darrington."

Keeley paused. She glanced over her shoulder to Kaden.

Kaden furrowed her brow, "They're here in Washington?" she asked him. "If they know where the prison is, why hasn't Doyle killed them?"

"I told you what I know," he replied. His chest rose and fell with the heaves of his breath. "Just...don't kill me."

"How did you come to know this information?" Keeley asked as she turned back to him.

"Doyle wanted me to keep my ears open," he spat. "He wanted me to make sure no one found them."

Kaden drew closer. "Why would he want to protect them?" she asked him. She found it hard to believe Doyle had a bleeding heart or any heart for that matter.

"Like I told you," he began. "I don't know."

Keeley cocked her head to the side. "You mean for us to believe that Doyle wants to protect these people?" She lowered her blade slightly. Riley winced, worried she would run it across his neck. "People who know his secret?"

"Given that Doyle and I were the only ones to know about them," he said as he relaxed enough for his veins to return to normal. "You want more answers, ask them."

"Alright," Keeley said. "I'll finish him off." She had the sword under his neck again in seconds, but Kaden grabbed her elbow before she could harm him further.

"Wait!"

Keeley's stone cold eyes found Kaden's grip.

"I told you everything!" Riley argued.

"Yes," Keeley replied. "We are grateful. But we cannot guarantee you won't tell Doyle or anyone else for that matter." She looked up to Kaden. "He must be killed."

"No no no no—"

"Shut up," Kaden yelled at him. She looked back at Keeley, "Don't kill him." The words were bitter on her tongue like poison.

"What?" Keeley asked her. "He is a witness."

"I knew I liked you," Riley sighed.

Kaden shot him a dirty look. "We could use him," she said. "And you're right, we can't let him go. But he might come in handy later."

The muscles in Keeley's jaws tightened. "You cannot be serious?"

"I am very handy," Riley said. "As long as you keep me alive."

Kaden pulled Keeley's arm further away from Riley's neck. "We need to get to Darrington," she told her. "We can keep him locked in the trunk of the car if we have to."

"I think I'd rather just be killed then," he admitted.

"Does this mean I can talk if we get a car?" Blaine asked from behind them. Kaden wondered when he had hopped off the kitchen island and how he managed to be so quiet.

Keeley released her blade from its place reluctantly, "You know, as Doyle's second in command I am awed to see how quickly you have fallen from his allegiance. It makes me wonder why that is?"

"I could say the same for you and your Queen," he replied. "Could I not?" Riley cocked a sly smile. "Dark faeries are only loyal to themselves, even Doyle knows that."

"The last faerie to be held captive here seemed pretty loyal," Kaden told him. "She even got a knife through the hand before she talked."

Keeley stood from her spot, and stabbed her sword into the coffee table.

"Look what happened to her," he said pointedly. "Loyalty gets you nothing but death."

CHAPTER XII

Behind the wheel of a rusted 1996 car they had acquired from a parking garage not far from Finley's apartment, Kaden drove with a firm grip on the steering wheel. The thumping sound of Riley's head against the bed of the trunk had stopped a few miles prior while Blaine sat in the back seat trying to make the windows of the car steam with his breath so he could write his name. Keeley rode shotgun with her bare feet up on the dashboard like there was some other, better, place she should be.

The morning glow rose over the mountains. Dew frosted the tips of grass along the highway.

The drive from Seattle to Darrington was not a long one. But with Blaine bouncing around in the back seat after his first experience with coffee and Riley either trying to knock himself out or escape, Kaden wasn't sure, the ride seemed to last forever.

Kaden reached into the center console for her coffee. The taste of it was bitter, making her wish she had sampled it before they left the coffee shop. Keeley managed to balance the mug she had stolen on the dashboard beside her feet. Kaden didn't know if the 'Man Tears' cup was being magically protected from bumps and potholes or if Keeley just had that kind of luck.

Beside her, Keeley wore black riding pants much like the ones she was used to wearing that allowed for free movement. Her jacket of choice was a wine colored bomber that would have gone well with the band of red she wore across her eyes, but Kaden made her wipe it off.

Blaine had chosen a dark green t-shirt with a pair of jeans he almost refused to wear because of their bagginess. To Kaden's surprise, he managed to keep the beanie pulled over his ears.

Kaden wore her dark blue jacket, pants similar to Keeley's with a black t-shirt. In any other scenario, Kaden would have opposed stealing, but she wanted to save as much as her mother's money as possible. She did, however, leave a nice 'I.O.U' note for the cars' owner.

She took a quick glimpse of herself in the rearview mirror. The bags under her eyes were dark and purple. She looked away.

"Hey look!" Blaine shouted. He leaned forward in between Kaden and Keeley and pointed.

"Blaine," Kaden replied calmly. She glanced at him out of the corner of her eye. "You can't shout something like that in a driver's ear. We're going to get into a car accident."

"Oh," he said, the concept of car rules being foreign to him. "Sorry." He waited a second longer before reaching his arm out and pointing out the windshield. "Look at that sign." Billboards he found fascinating.

"I can't read it while I'm driving," Kaden told him.

As Kaden passed by, Blaine followed the sign. "'The President lied to us'," he read.

Kaden scoffed to herself. "Which one?"

Blaine pondered the billboard and put his elbows on the console. "What is a president?"

"It's the equivalent of our Queen in this country," Keeley answered. She leaned back into her seat and closed her eyes.

"Oh," he said to himself. "Hey look over there!" Blaine jumped to one of the back windows. Kaden was positive that if he knew the windows could open, he would hang out of one.

"How do you know so much about this world?" Kaden asked Keeley.

"That's no concern of yours," she replied, still with her eyes closed. Kaden shifted her attention off the road to Keeley. She seemed at ease, but not at all interested in her surroundings. It made Kaden notice how different Keeley was to Finley. He had charm while she always seemed neutral. She was more controlled in her mission when Finley wanted to order breakfast at diners. "How much longer until we're in Darrington?"

Kaden drew her gaze back to the road. "Not long."

She stared ahead to the asphalt and the white lines of

the road. Every inch seemed the same. The same trees, the same landscape, the same guardrail.

She sunk further into her seat. A sigh escaped her lungs, but her knuckles grew white under her grip of the steering wheel.

Her thoughts drifted to Megan. They ran wild like a stallion in a meadow.

If I do this, she thought, *then Megan will come back. They'll have to bring Megan back. I'll trade myself for Megan. It'll work. It has to work.*

The sharp squeaks of Blaine's pan pipe pierced her eardrum. She hated herself for not thinking to take it away from him.

"Darrington!" Blaine shouted suddenly, almost causing Kaden to swerve into the other lane. He pointed and wiggled his finger at the green sign. Kaden felt the muscles in between her shoulder blades tighten.

Keeley's eyes opened casually. "How do we plan on locating them?" she asked. She sat up, pulling her feet off the dash.

"It's a pretty small town," Kaden explained. She took the ramp for their exit. "I'll stop in a gas station and ask where I can find the Canem we're looking for."

"Why would they tell you where they are?" Keeley wondered.

Kaden shrugged. "Why wouldn't they?"

The lumber mill was not far from the main part of town. According to the gas station attendant, Kaden would be able to find Kane Canem there. "Excuse me," Kaden said. The small bell hanging off the door jingled when she opened and closed the door behind her.

A man with a clipboard in his hands stood behind the front desk, studying his orders. Kaden snuck a quick glance over her shoulder to the car where she left Keeley and Blaine to their own devices.

"How can I help you darlin'," he asked. He was a stout man, but with a build that told her he had worked at the lumber mill his whole life. The grey in his hair matched the grey in his beard she noted as he looked up from his clipboard.

"I'm looking for someone by the name of Kane Canem," she explained. Kaden took a few steps further inside, "I heard he would be here."

The man studied her for a brief moment. "You heard right," he said. "Is he expecting you?" He put down his clipboard and riffled through some papers on the desk.

"No," she admitted. "But it will only take a few minutes." The man didn't respond. Instead, he scratched his head as he searched for something on his desk. "I know it's not a good time since he's working but it's important," she added gingerly.

He looked up at her from behind the rim of his glasses. "He's out in the yard somewhere," he gestured toward the window that overviewed the piles of lumber and sheds of cut wood. "It'll just take a minute," he told her. He opened the back door, stepping one foot out the door before he leaned back inside. "What's your name darlin'?"

Kaden froze. She wondered if she should lie or not.

The man raised a grey eyebrow in her silence.

"Kaden Storm," she answered. It had been her name her whole life, but she wondered what her real name was. She swallowed, "I'll wait out front."

He nodded and headed out to the yard.

When she stepped back outside the morning sun reached high noon. Beads of sweat began to form against her skin as she headed around the side of the building. In the shadow of the building, she waited near a chain link fence that separated the yard from the parking lot. She scanned the few workers moving around beyond the fence, wondering which one was Kane Canem. She buried her hands in her back pockets and began to pace. Kaden thought about how she was going to bring up fae to a stranger. If he knew of fae or if he didn't. Or what or who he was. The last time she had a conversation with someone other than a fae themselves was with Quinn. And that ended badly.

Kaden bit down on her nail bed.

"So did you speak to him yet?" Blaine's voice whispered in Kaden's ear.

She jumped at the sound of his voice.

"No," she said. Kaden looked to both Keeley and Blaine who stood passively. "I thought I told you to wait in the car?"

"We *were*," Keeley replied harshly. "But someone saw a butterfly and decided to chase it. Then we couldn't get back in the mechanical horse you humans believe is better than a horse."

"You didn't have to follow me," Blaine argued. "It was

just so majestic, Kaden. I couldn't resist."

"If I didn't follow you," Keeley started, "you would have done something idiotic. Although, chasing a butterfly at your age is foolish enough."

Blaine clenched his fists at his side, "No I wouldn't have," he said. "It was a butterfly!"

"Percisly," she scoffed. "Humans don't care for nature, look!" Keeley walked closer to the fence and gestured with a nod of her head. "They cut down trees. I doubt they would chase butterflies."

"Stop speaking to me like I am a child! I am a guard of the——"

"Guys," Kaden broke in. "Shut up!" She glanced back over her shoulder to make sure no one was watching. "We are all here to save Finley and we can't do that if you keep arguing. So both of you keep your mouths shut or I will lock you back in the car with the windows closed."

Blaine appeared horrified by the idea of an airless trap, but Keeley just rolled her eyes.

Kaden let out a sigh and pinched the bridge of her nose. She gave Keeley and Blaine one last look before she turned back to the fence. A young man in dark blue jeans with loose threads and a navy t-shirt stained with patches of dirt headed toward them. "That's him," she urged, "so be quiet." His black hair was ruffled, glistening with sweat against the summer heat.

Kaden walked closer to the fence, leaving Keeley and Blaine in the shadow of the building.

He removed his working gloves from his hands as he stepped through the open part of the chain link that allowed trucks to come and go as they pleased.

"You're Kane?" she asked cautiously.

"Yeah," he said. "That's right." He eyed her with suspicion, but reached his hand out for her to shake.

She took it. The palms of them, rough with calluses. The strength in his grip crushed her hand slightly, but she tried not to show it.

"Sorry," she apologized. "I didn't mean to take you from your work. You don't know me," she glanced down at her feet. "Obviously. My name is Kaden Storm."

"Yeah," he said. Kane looked past Kaden's shoulder toward Keeley and Blaine. His lips were a fine line making him impossible for her to read. "My boss told me your name."

"Right," she said.

"Were you looking for some kind of construction help?" he asked her, though the muscles in his jaw tightened.

"What? No. I uh…" she fumbled over her words. Kaden rubbed her fingertips across her temple. "I came here for a *different* kind of help."

Kaden swallowed down the lump forming in her throat. She hoped she wouldn't have to explain *different* to him. Or *other* or *fae*.

She looked in his eyes for the answer. They were icy blue, though he wasn't much older than she was, his eyes made him look older.

"I don't think so," he said flatly. The features of his face tightened.

Kaden smiled faintly as if he was kidding. "What?"

she asked him. "But you don't even know what it's about."

"I don't..." Kane shot a harsh glance towards Keeley and Blaine, "associate with you people." The grip on his gloves tightened and he took a half step back. "So whatever help you need, I suggest you look somewhere else."

He turned away from her, but Kaden was quick to grab his upper arm. The grasp she had didn't seem to sway him at all, but he half-turned to face her. "I don't need to know," he said. "I know your kind."

"Your kind?" she repeated. "Aren't we all a part of the same world? You don't even know us." Kaden dropped her grip on his bicep.

Kane turned around fully, though his face suggested he didn't want to. He lowered his head so he was close enough to Kaden and gestured toward Keeley. "The necklace the snow queen is wearing?" Kaden glanced over to Keeley. She had her arms crossed over her chest and a frown on her face. "It's a Celtic talisman. And the boy, wearing a beanie in the middle of July? He's either a douche or you didn't have enough necklaces to go around."

Kaden's jaw locked. She turned to face him. "And what about me?" she asked him. "I don't have a necklace or a beanie. Do you know what that makes me?" Part of her wanted him to answer. But she knew he wouldn't have it. What he did have, was the location to where Finely was. And that was all she needed for the time being.

His eyes locked with hers. "It doesn't matter," he replied. "If you're helping faeries, you're just as dangerous." He waited a moment before turning away and walking back through the chain link fence.

She watched him slip his gloves back on his hands, running a hand through his hair before he did. She felt the fire again burning in her heart. The flames ran rampant in her veins.

Kaden turned sharply toward Keeley and Blaine. "Why didn't you guys say anything?" she asked them. Her irritation began to bubble at the surface.

Blaine furrowed his brow, "You told us to be quiet."

She sucked in a breath and slowly let it out before she hit Blaine over the head.

Keeley shrugged one shoulder, "I never thought this plan would work. Making friends may be your idea of how to get people to help you, but it's not mine."

"Alright," Kaden sighed. "What's your brilliant idea?"

"We wait for dusk and take him against his will," she said simply. "I'm sure he won't be a problem."

"We're not kidnapping him," Kaden told her. She snuck a glance over her shoulder, but Kane Canem was long gone behind the stack of trimmed lumber. "We need to reconvene. I'll convince him to help us."

"How?" Blaine asked. "He doesn't seem to care. The only thing he does is chop down trees and they did nothing wrong."

"That's not true," she corrected. She turned back to them. "He felt threatened by us," she said. "That means he has something to fear. Maybe someone in town will be willing to tell us where he lives, then we'll pay him another visit. Tonight."

"And if he doesn't want to help after a wholehearted conversation with you?" Keeley mocked.

Kaden pondered the question, "He won't have a choice."

CHAPTER XIII

Doyle strolled in through the double doors as if he were entering a grand ballroom and not the room he used for torment. "Well, well, well," he practically sang.

The new gashes and lashes and inflamed injuries on Finley's frail flesh appeared worse under the fluorescent light than they did in the darkness of his cell. The skin all along his spine was black and blue, yellows and greens. His left eye, still puffy and swollen. The exposed tears sporadically oozed some bodily liquid or another.

Finley tried and failed to hold his thinning stature away from the chair he found himself in once more. But the markings that ran up and down his spine kissed the solid steel regardless.

"Looks like someone had their fun with you," Doyle smiled. "Raw iron to the back, was it?"

"You know," Finley let out a sigh, but even that hurt. He watched as Doyle made his way into the light, "It's been months of you bringing me in here. And yet I still can't figure out why."

Doyle shrugged, "What can I say?" He grabbed a set of latex gloves off the table and slipped them over his delicate fingers. He snapped one of them for good measure, "I get bored."

"So you're bored, is that it?" Finley asked. "Because the first time you had me in here you said you were doing all this for Him. What exactly do you expect from Him?" He gently lowered his back against the chair and winced once his skin and the metal met fully.

"The Dark fae are interested in opening a particular door," Doyle said. He tilted his head slightly to the side as he approached Finley. "For decades we have been pushed around, driven to cowering in caves and other realms and for what? So the petty little humans can remain at the top of the food chain? So they may think we are merely a myth?"

"And your idea of living is joining someone who hates you so much that He refused to let you into hell?" A rush of something swirled inside Finley. Curiosity? Fear? He wasn't sure. He was raised never to speak of their dark past. "Even He doesn't think you're worth much."

Doyle raised a power drill into the light. He plucked two drill heads off the table. One spiral and one flat, both of which contained remnants of other fae. "What can you say about *your* kind?"

Finley's brow furrowed. "We have no desire to open any kind of door," he said. "The Light faeries don't run around slaughtering humans for pleasure, we embrace them."

"Ha!" Doyle's laugh echoed. "Embrace them? Is that what you call barricading your Courts up? Taking to your own realms like the cowards you are?" He decided to twist the spiral bit into the drill. Finley swallowed hard and hated himself for it. "*Your* kind," Doyle went on, "don't exactly save them either, do they? The ones who take lives freely know they are bad." He aimed the drill tip at Finley's temple. "But, the ones who can do something and ignore it? Why does that make you any better than me?" Doyle gave the drill a quick squeeze of power, its electrical sound bouncing off the walls.

Finley's jaw locked. "We don't have innocent blood on our hands."

"*Your* kind?" he asked with a chuckle. "Don't have blood on their hands? Who are you trying to fool? You may not have bloodstains under your finger nails or dream of ways to penetrate the skull, but you sure have your fair share of brutality." He grinned at Finley. "Believe it or not, Finley, I've always liked you." Doyle pulled a permanent marker out of thin air and drew an x on the back of Finley's right hand.

"That's comforting," Finley snorted. He watched the black ink stain his bruised skin.

"I wanted you," Doyle said. He practised aiming the drill against Finley's hand without powering it. "I wanted you to be King of Seattle."

"As foolish as I think you are," Finley spat. "We both know that could never happen." Each time Doyle drew the drill closer, his breath caught. The blood pumping through his veins ran faster to and from his heart. All Finley wanted to do was scream.

"But of course," Doyle said. "It could have." He hovered the drill just above his hand and gave it a gust of power. Even without it touching his skin Finley felt the energy it had. He felt the whirlwind it made in the open air. It sent a shiver down his beaten back. "You see," Doyle continued. "We noticed how much you and Linette loved each other. It was quite beautiful, really." He dipped the tip of the drill into some unmarked liquid substance.

"Would you like a tissue?" Finley asked through his gritted teeth.

"You are going to realize just how blind you really are. You think we can't get anything past you, but we did. Right. Under. Your. Nose."

Finley squirmed. "What are you talking about, you lunatic?" The combination of anticipation and irritation fluttered to the surface. Finley was tired. In pain. And expecting more.

Doyle flashed a smile. He placed the drill down on a small sliding table beside Finley. "Do you really think Linette's mother died of natural causes?"

Finley's muscles tightened. His brow furrowed and he stared at Doyle. "She was sick," he said flatly. "It happens." He remembered the moment he found Linette, distraught and crying in the garden after she found out her mother could not be healed, and how hopeless he felt to heal her pain.

"*Was* she sick?" he asked with a spark of humor and a wry smile to match.

"Is this your coy way of confessing to murder?" Finley shook his head, "Your kind couldn't get past my garrison even with the gates open."

"Trust me," Doyle said. "We have a network of turncoats. And with Linette devastated over her mother's passing we had hoped she would turn to you. Make you her King instead of that other moron we don't even know the name of."

"You're lying."

Doyle raised a brow. "Are you that desperate and naive?"

Finley shook his head, unwilling to believe Doyle. "She couldn't marry me, it's against the rules. You couldn't have turncoats without my knowledge. You could not have killed the Queen under my command."

A dark grin swept across his face. Purple mischief swirled behind his eyes. "Face the facts, darling," he said. His fingers traced the outline of the drill before he lifted it. "The Light faeries are more twisted than you were raised to believe."

Finley gritted his teeth. "If anyone's twisted here, it's the sadist who thinks Lucifer will have him."

Leila took Finley's hand gingerly. Chunks of his flesh fell to the floor with a plop. He could see the floor through the hole in his hand and wondered how long it would take to heal with the iron chains on.

She soaked her cloth in her wash bowl of lukewarm water even though it wouldn't prevent the wound from getting infected like the rest of his body. The blood diffused quickly in the water, spreading swirls of crimson against the clear liquid until it all became red.

Finley winced as she brought the cloth back to his skin. He looked over at her, at her focus on his injury. He searched his memory for the French he had learned. Though it was basic, he had to try. "You have a beautiful face."

His voice was frail and scratchy, dried from lack of water. But she smiled weakly to herself without looking up. "Your French is terrible," she replied.

A smile found its way to Finley's lips, "So she does speak."

Leila ripped fabric off the bottom of her skirt. She used it as gauze and wrapped it around his hand tightly. Finley winced from the pressure.

"You need to learn to control your tongue," she whispered to him. Leila didn't look at him. Finley wasn't sure if it was her fear or if he looked *that* awful.

"How do you know I'm not controlling my tongue?" he asked her back.

She didn't answer. Instead, she tied off the end of the wrap.

"I heard Doyle talk about you," she whispered. "He said you helped people." Leila started to analyze a severe gash that oozed some kind of puss. "You didn't have to, though."

"No," he admitted. "But it was very nice of me." Finley watched the doors. They remained still. He licked his dry lips, "Leila," he said. He leaned in closer to her, "Do you know where we are?"

She froze in her place. Her back straightened and she looked up at him for the first time. There was nothing but fear written in her eyes, "A dark realm."

"Which one?" he asked.

"...I...don't..." she stammered. Leila's hands began to tremble when she looked away quickly.

"Please, Leila," Finley begged. He reached out and took her hand. "We need to get out of here..."

"What?" she asked with anger rising in her tone. She pulled away from his touch sharply. "I—I can't be a part of that."

"Leila," he began softly. "I just need to know where we are so I can start to plan—"

"No!" she snapped. "Don't say anything else." Before Finley could speak again, she rushed, with her belongings, out the door.

CHAPTER XIV

Keeley slid into the window seat of the booth with Blaine right on her heels. She muttered something under her breath, but Kaden couldn't hear it. "Why is this place called a Burger Barn if there are no animals?" Blaine wondered as he scanned the menu the waitress set down in front of him. His eyes lit up as he looked at the images, instead of reading.

"Because they're all dead," Keeley answered flatly. Keeley's knowledge of the human world still intrigued Kaden. She wondered just how far it went. She brushed her curiosity aside, as she tried to read the words on the menu. All she could do was stare at the letters while questions wandered through the cracks of her focus. *Why would Doyle protect the Canem's? What were they? How many of them were there? Are they a threat?*

"Well?" Keeley's voice broke through Kaden's trance.

"Well what?" she asked her.

"Are you going to explain in more detail why there are no animals here or do I get handed that job as well?"

Kaden glanced up from her grease stained menu. She hadn't realized Blaine was staring at her earnestly. She released a sigh from her lungs, "Look," she said to Keeley. "I know it must be frustrating to have to take orders, especially from someone like me, but we all want the same thing." Kaden turned back to Blaine who discovered how bouncy the springs in the booth seat were. "It's just a name Blaine, it's not an actual barn." She lowered her menu back to the table, "Maybe you should stick to what you're used to."

"I don't want to!" he replied with disgust. "I want to experience new things, like Finley did!" He scanned the menu quickly, but stopped abruptly at the largest picture of a jumbo burger with a side of curly fries. "That," he pointed, "looks so...unhealthy. And I want this frosty brown drink with a stick."

"Which one?" Kaden asked him. Blaine pointed out the chocolate milkshake which to her, meant more sugar. "A chocolate milkshake with a burger and fries."

He beamed. "It sounds even better when you say it!"

The waitress walked over to their booth chomping on a stick of gum. "Do you know what you want yet?" She pulled a fuzzy pink pen from her apron with her notepad.

"Yes, fair maiden, I am going to have the..." Blaine paused and leaned across the table to Kaden. She repeated his order to him in his ear. "Right! The jumbo burger with curly fries and a milkshake."

"What kind of milkshake, hun?"

"Chocolate."

The waitress shifted her attention to Keeley, "For you?"

"I'll have a garden salad with grilled chicken and water," Keeley told her. She passed the menu back to her and Blaine followed suit.

When the waitress looked at Kaden, her stomach suddenly felt very empty and hollow but twisted and uneasy at the same time. "Just water for me."

"Okay," she said as she took the menus. "It'll be out in a jiffy."

"So," Keeley sighed. "What is the plan? How is this place going to help us capture Kane?"

"Number one," Kaden started. "Keep your voice down in public, someone might hear you."

"Then why did you talk to Kane about it at the lumber yard?" Keeley asked sharply.

"Because I asked him for help," she told her. "What you just mentioned is a felony. Plus, in a small town like this, everyone hears everything, which brings me to why we are here. The lumber yard is just down the road which means workers come here all the time for lunch."

Keeley leaned back against the booth. "How does that help us? Are we going to buy him lunch?"

"No," Kaden argued. "That means he probably talks to the waitress and owner all the time. One of them has to know where he lives and will point us in the right direction. It's just like when I asked the gas station attendant."

"What do you suppose he was?" Blaine asked. It was a burning question Kaden wanted answered herself.

"That's the only intelligent thing to come out of your mouth this whole time," Keeley said.

Kaden looked at Keeley, "What do you think?"

Keeley held her gaze for a moment. The corners of her eyes squinted so slightly, Kaden thought maybe they hadn't at all. "He's not a faerie, I can tell you that," she said. "I guess we'll just have to find out when we capture him."

Day fell to night, leaving the three parked in their stolen car at the end of a curvy driveway where Kane Canem lived. The house was set back, far enough it wasn't visible through the thickness of the national forest. The trees swallowed their land whole leaving nothing but shadow and moonlight. There was no way to predict how many Canem's there were. No way to get the lay of the land even when they drove by when the evening sun was still shining.

It was with great resistance that Kaden allowed Keeley to disappear into the darkness of the woods with her bow and arrow. But it was the best way for her to have backup.

She convinced Blaine to be in charge of Riley which he did not object to since he was falling from his sugar high.

Kaden worked her way up the driveway by foot which was mostly dirt with two ruts where car tires had travelled. She followed the pathway in the dark when a gnawing feeling pulled at her. She glanced behind her to the abyss of forest and wondered if it was Keeley perched in a tree someone she felt.

The path ahead led to answers, answers she needed. Deep down, Kaden told herself that if she saved Finley, she would save Megan too. It wasn't possible as far as she knew, it wasn't logical either, but it was what kept her feet from collapsing underneath her.

In the distance, the yellowish glow of lights appeared from inside the house. The front porch had dozens of dangling wind chimes that danced against the faint summer breeze. Nighttime buzzed all around. The house which looked more like a cabin stood motionless from both the inside and the outside.

Not too far away the bright burning of a bonfire crackled. Kaden counted two people seated in lawn chairs. As far as her sight allowed, neither one of them was Kane.

Kaden lightened her steps as she passed by an old Chevy Blazer that had seen better days. She paused in her tracks, watching the people near the fire converse. They didn't appear *different* or *other*. She wondered then if she was what they were.

Then, someone tugged her roughly by her upper arm. The grasp was strong enough to spin her around like a rag doll. It took Kaden's vision a moment to readjust to her surroundings only to land on Kane.

"What are you doing here?" he asked her. His temper was short, even under the slim waning of the moonlight she could see the anger in his eyes. "I told you to stay away from us."

"I just need a few minutes of your time and then I'm gone," she said. "You will never see me again, I promise."

He snuck a quick glance over her shoulder to the people enjoying the light of the bonfire, "Like I told you, I'm not helping you." Kane released his grip from her arm. He moved to side step her when she put her hand out against the car so he couldn't just walk away.

"And I told you, we needed your help."

Kane was taller than Kaden, like Finley, maybe slightly taller. His attention drifted from the people behind her to the woods and then the house. Kaden stood up on her tiptoes to catch his gaze, "You seem distracted, I'm trying to—"

"Clearly," he said. He looked down at her, the ice in his eyes cold. "You didn't understand that I was threatening you at the lumber yard." Kane took hold of her shoulders and moved her out of his way.

"I understood perfectly," she said. She spun around and followed behind his heels. "What you don't understand is that I'm very stubborn and when I want something badly, I'll do anything to get it."

Kane let out a sharp sigh. He turned around abruptly to face her, "Get in your car," he instructed as he pointed in the exact direction where she had parked, "and drive away."

Kaden didn't move.

Out of the corner of her eye, she caught sight of the two near the bonfire as they stood from the commotion.

"Not a chance," she told him.

"Kane!" An older voice called from the house's porch. Everyone in the near vicinity turned as the screen door slammed shut. An older woman, in her seventies, walked to the edge of the porch. "What's going on?"

Kane's jaw locked. "Nothing, Gigi," he reassured her and shifted a glare in Kaden's direction. "A hiker just lost her way, she was just leaving."

The woman wiped her hand with a kitchen towel. She stepped off the porch, careful not to fall and break a hip. As she walked toward the both of them, Kaden saw her cheek had a hint of flour on it.

She stopped suddenly. "Helena?" she asked.

Kaden looked over her shoulder, but there was no one else. "Excuse me?" she asked the woman.

Gigi smiled the kind of smile only a grandmother could have. She walked closer and placed a wrinkled hand on Kaden's shoulder. "You look just like her," she whispered. Her eyes studied Kaden's every feature.

Kaden caught the slight glint of tears forming at the bottom of her aged eyes. "Just like who?" she wondered.

"Your mother."

Chapter XV

"Gigi," Kane said. He stood in the threshold holding the screen door open. "You know this girl?" Gigi gripped Kaden by the elbow and escorted her inside. She seated her on the lumpy couch without resistance. Kaden fell into a daze as she sat amongst the low lighting. The breeze from outside drifted in, cooling her skin and the fire ants that threatened to crawl under her flesh. There was an ache in her chest she wanted to rub away, but she found herself unwilling to move.

"I was there when she was born," the old woman told Kane. "So were you. October 30, 1996." Kaden's brow furrowed. She had come for Finley, but she found herself itching to know more of what Gigi knew.

"How do you—" Kaden looked between Kane and the woman as she took a seat in a floral arm chair across from her. "Who are you people?"

Gigi flashed her a faint smile of sympathy. She pushed her curly grey hair from her face and eased herself further back into the chair. The warmth in her eyes swallowed Kaden whole. There was something unnerving about meeting someone who knew more about you then you did. "Gather her friends and offer them food," she told Kane.

Kane opened his mouth to object, but one glance from Gigi and he buried it.

"How–" Kaden looked back at Gigi. "How did you know I brought my friends?"

She smiled. "Do you like tea?"

Keeley sat beside Kaden, her bow in her hand and her satchel of arrows strapped to her back. Blaine made his way to the bonfire with the two other Canems she hadn't met. Inside, the house was filled with warm furnishings of various woods. Every blanket, pillow, and linen was made up of floral patterns. It smelled of cedar wood with a light twist of honey. The living room itself was honey colored with light from different lamps. When Gigi set the tray of tea down before Kaden, she understood where the honey came from.

"I knew your mother," she said again. Hearing it multiple times didn't help Kaden's mind to wrap around the thought. "Helena. She came to us," she poured the steaming tea into two teacups each patterned differently with flowers, "for help."

Kaden looked from the tea swirling in the cup to

Gigi's smile as she poured it to Kane who sat quietly in another arm chair. "Who are you?" she asked once more as Gigi lowered herself back into her chair.

"We're just a family living in Darrington," Kane answered with the ease of a robot.

"But…" Gigi glanced over at Kane whose gaze questioned her silently. "We come from a very long line of lupus relatives." Gigi brought her tea up to her lips, blowing slightly before she took a sip.

Kaden stared between the two. "Lupus?" she questioned. "Like wolves?" She waited for someone to object, but even Keeley remained perfectly still beside her. "Like… werewolves. That's a thing?"

"I came to understand werewolves were extinct recently," Keeley noted.

"Not all of us," Kane mumbled in his reply. He exchanged a sorrowful glance with Gigi.

"Why would Doyle want to keep a pack of wolves protected?" Keeley asked them.

"That's something you would have to ask him," Gigi said. She placed her tea delicately on the table beside her. "We don't know who he is."

"I don't understand," Kaden said, gesturing her hand in her confusion. "Why did my mother come to you? Where is she?"

"She came to us for protection," Gigi explained. "She was almost near her due date and needed a safe place to have you." She lifted a small plate of cookies off the coffee table and gestured for them to eat some. Kaden took one reluctantly while Keeley didn't bother moving.

"What would she need protection from?" Kaden asked her. She brought the cookie to her lips and nibbled on it, hoping it would ease the slight migraine beginning to form.

Gigi took her tea back in her hand and traced the rim with her finger. "Your father."

Kaden looked over to Keeley who had no reaction. "My birth father?" she asked. "Why?"

"He is a very powerful necromancer," Gigi told Kaden. "A Dark fae." Kaden's heart sank beneath her chest. Her palms became sweaty and she found herself looking at the floor. She knew she was of fae heritage, but she wasn't expecting to be of Dark fae heritage.

She sucked in a deep breath. "My parents were Dark fae?" Kaden nearly whispered the end of her sentence.

"No," Gigi answered flatly. Kaden's shoulders fell with relief. "Your mother was a Light wiccan," she continued. "From Connecticut."

"Is she there now?" Kaden asked abruptly. She could feel Keeley shift in her place as the conversation drifted to areas they were not meant to veer. Finley was their goal. But Kaden couldn't wait to know about her heritage any longer.

"I wouldn't know that," Gigi shrugged. "I just know she asked me to send her journal to her sister there." Kaden fell silent. Questions appeared in her mind and disappeared just as quickly.

"Why would she have a child with a Dark fae?" Keeley asked suddenly. She reached out and grabbed a cookie off the tray. "Is she uneducated about what they are capable of?"

"Some of us think so," Kane muttered under his breath.

"Kane." Gigi shot him a warning.

"What did she do to me?" Kaden wondered. "Why did she switch me with another baby?"

"Like I said, she was trying to protect you."

"How would that protect me?" Kaden asked back. She bit down hard on her cookie. The caramel and coconut melted in her mouth and she found herself wanting to shove more in her face.

"She needed to keep you safe so she could stop your father from getting his hands on you. After you were born she did a blood spell, dark magic. She stripped you of your fae heritage as much as she could so he wouldn't be able to find you."

"What about the other child?" Irritation coursed through Kaden. She couldn't wrap her brain around the idea of putting another innocent child in danger. "How could she just switch two babies? Didn't she feel guilty at all?"

Gigi scrunched her face, "She was." She placed her tea down again, "I was there. It broke her heart."

Kaden swallowed. "If it broke her heart so much then why did she do it?" she asked. "If she was a powerful witch, couldn't she protect me herself?"

Gigi sat back in her chair. She held onto Kaden's gaze, "She only wanted what was best for you."

"And screw the other kid and their family?" Kaden added. "Does she realize how much damage she has done?"

The older woman cleared her throat before speaking,

"I understand your anger," she said. "But I can tell you she did the right thing. It may not seem like it—"

Kaden shook her head. "It doesn't matter," she said abruptly. "We didn't come here for this."

Both Gigi and Kane looked at her with confusion swirling in their eyes. "Then what did you come for?" she asked Kaden.

"We are trying to find the location of Doyle's prison," Keeley answered. "We heard you were the only ones who have ever made it out of there. Do you know where it is?"

"Yes," Kane answered. He had been silently observing the scene. A wave of embarrassment washed over Kaden as she realized how childish she had sounded. "It's in the Black Forest," he told them.

"The Black Forest?" Kaden repeated. "Germany?"

"Is there another Black Forest?" Kane asked.

Gigi warned him again with a glare. "There's a portal you must take to get there," Gigi tucked strands of grey hair behind her ear. "The wolves used it to come and go to get to our village."

"Great," Keeley said. "If you'll just draw us a map to the location, we'll be on our way."

The room fell still.

Blaine's laughter drifted in on the summer breeze.

The antique clock ticked away.

It was a moment longer before Gigi spoke again. "I don't think you realize where you're going." Gigi's eyes hardened like stone.

"It doesn't matter," Kaden said. "We have to rescue someone from the prison."

"That forest is a dark, vicious place," she warned them. "It's changed since the wolves lived there."

"I think we can handle it," Keeley replied.

"You need someone to guide you through it, someone who knows the territory."

"I have two faeries with me," Kaden assured Gigi. "I'm sure they'll know what to do." She held back the part of her that wasn't so sure, the part of her that wanted the entire Seelie Court at her side.

Gigi looked at her. "You have two faeries who have never been to the forest," she argued. "They don't know what creatures lurk there or how to navigate it."

Kaden shrugged, "We don't exactly have any other volunteers."

Gigi paused for a moment before she replied. "Kane will take you."

"What?" Kaden asked.

"What!?" Kane shot up in his seat, not expecting those words to come out of Gigi's mouth. "Gigi, you can't be serious?"

She smiled softly and picked up the tray of tea off the coffee table. "I can't take them," she told him. "I'm too old. You are the oldest of the pack. You remember those woods better than the others. It has to be you." She stepped past Kane and into the galley kitchen behind him.

Kane lifted himself out of the chair and followed behind her, "Why should we help them? They clearly don't want it. If I go back we risk exposure."

"Whether they want it or not they will get it," Gigi told him. She began to put the dishes in the sink, "Help me will you?"

"Gigi—"

"Kane Canem, do not argue with your grandmother," she tossed a towel at his chest and he caught it. "Get these dishes done."

"What about work? I can't just leave," he said through his clenched teeth.

"Don't worry about that," she told him. "I'll have one of the others tell your boss I'm not well."

"Gigi," he said nervously. "I haven't been there since—"

"I know." She stepped toward him and placed a hand against his face. "You are a werewolf," she reminded him. "You will remember the scents just like it was yesterday." She patted him once before she entered the living room again. "The land is Dark fae now, you have to be careful. Can one of your faeries get you to Germany?"

"Keeley?" Kaden asked.

Keeley pondered the question. "I can get us to Paris."

"We'll have to take a train the rest of the way," Kaden noted.

"For now," Gigi said. "You will spend the night here. Kane will show you to the cots above the barn once he's finished."

"I will?" he asked.

"Yes," she replied with her hands on her hips. "And you will offer them whatever they need."

Moonlight shone through the window above the barn

door. It illuminated the loft in a white light where four cots rested, two on either side. "You can stay here for the night," Kane told them.

Blaine darted past him and plopped his body on one of the cots.

Kane pointed to a trunk resting under the window, "There are extra blankets in there if you need them."

Keeley strolled across the room to the cot furthest from Blaine and examined it.

Kaden was about to claim her spot, when Kane grabbed her elbow. "Who is in your car?" he asked her.

"How did you—"

"I can hear his heartbeat," Kane answered before she could finish. She had almost forgotten about Riley completely. "Do I need to be worried about him?" he asked her.

"This is so cool!" Blaine rolled off his bed and jumped over to the one across from him. "I have to be honest, this is the most exciting thing ever."

"Calm yourself before you get hurt," Keeley said. She stretched out on her cot as she had done once before in her prison cell.

"No," Kaden told Kane. "He's tied up. He won't get out." He looked at her with uncertainty. She didn't blame him, she was uncertain about him too. "Should I be worried you just happen to have four cots set up in your loft?"

"No," he said and nothing else as he climbed down the ladder to the floor below.

Kaden leaned over the balcony, "You're not even going to explain it to me?"

He paused at the bottom of the ladder and glanced up. "Nope."

She watched him make his way out of the barn, sliding the door closed behind him. She wondered how much sleep she would get, if she got any.

"Alright, ladies," Blaine stood up on the bed with a pillow clenched in his hand. "Who wants to have a pillow fight?"

Without warning, Keeley chucked a pillow off her bed and smacked Blaine in the back so hard he went tumbling to the floor with a thud. He remained there motionless for a moment. "Can you not hit me so aggressively next time?" he said with his mouth muffled against the floor.

Kaden sat Indian style on the cot closest to the window. The moon was bright casting shadows on the forest floor below. She could see the car Riley was caged in. She could see the house the Canem's slept in. She could even see the driveway that led to the road.

Blaine snored across from her.

Beside her, Keeley rested with her hands behind her head peacefully.

"I'll stay up," Kaden whispered to Keeley. "Make sure they don't try anything."

Keeley opened her eyes, "Why would they? I can kill them easily."

Kaden swallowed her doubt. "You can't be too sure," she said. The truth lay buried in her chest, under all the pain and achiness. She didn't trust anyone anymore. They were vulnerable and desperate to save Finley. She was vulnerable.

"Why would Doyle keep them alive?" Kaden asked

mostly to herself.

"You can ask him yourself when we rip his face from his skull," Keeley shrugged.

"Why do you trust them?" she asked. "How do we know they're not working for Doyle?"

"They seem genuine. They offered us food and shelter, a guide to the forest."

"Exactly," Kaden pointed out. "Why?" She leaned forward on her cot, closer to Keeley waiting for her answer.

Keeley turned on her side and used her arm to hold up her head. "They helped your mother once," she said. "Why wouldn't they help you?"

The muscles in Kaden's jaw locked. She turned away from Keeley.

"So you're going to stay up to make sure they don't slaughter us in our sleep?" Keeley asked through a yawn.

"You're welcome," Kaden said over her shoulder.

"You cannot execute a recuse mission with no sleep," she argued to her back. "Sleep deprivation is a highly elaborate form of torture."

"I'll sleep," she lied. "At some point." Kaden let out a sigh. She didn't want to think about the nightmares she saw whenever she closed her eyes. Her fears blended with her memories. Images of Megan drenched in her own blood, images of herself dripping in Finley's. Then there were her new fears. Fears about the truth. Her truth. "What about everything Gigi said," she whispered into the night. "About my parents. Do you think it's true?"

"I suppose," Keeley said. "They don't exactly have a reason to lie."

Kaden picked at her nailbeds. "Maybe we should get someone to undo the spell," she thought out loud. "So I have my…abilities?"

"Have you fallen on your head?" Keeley snapped.

Kaden twisted her body to face her. "Why not?" she asked. "Wouldn't it give us a better chance of not dying while we rescue Finley?"

Keeley scowled. "Witches learn how to control their powers from birth. This would be the equivalent of handing an explosive to a child who doesn't know to throw it away," Keeley argued in the dark. "And if your father really is a necromancer, we have no way of knowing you won't turn to the Dark fae once you have them."

"What are you talking about?" she shot back. "I would never go dark side."

"You don't know that," she said flatly. "Power like that is strong. Once you get it back, you won't know what you want anymore. Your judgement will be clouded."

"I hate to break it to you Keeley, but I'm pretty down strong."

"Not with magic."

CHAPTER XVI

Pain radiated through Finley like a scorched wildfire. The vertebrae along his spine exposed to the mildew air seethed with each passing breath. Each step he took, each inhale felt as though all his gashes and wounds only expanded deeper, ripped further. He tried to keep pace with the grizzled looking creatures that escorted him back to Nicolai, his nerves inflamed with each step.

The desperate cries and snarls from each cell sent a pulse shooting through his head. The jingleing of the keys at the guards sides made his eardrum wince. There was so much and so little.

Finley glared at the ring of keys. He wanted nothing more than to rip them off so his ears may rest. He just needed silence. Just for one moment.

The keys jingled again, and again, striking his temple

each time. Then, a thought crossed his mind.

Solitary.

He *needed* to get to solitary, to get to the man being held there, and to get some quiet so he could think.

Finley's hands were bound with iron chains, but his feet were free. Each guard held him by the elbow loosely. He had one chance.

Finley held out his foot in front of one of the guards. The man, thing, fell on his horribly constructed face. Behind the cells prisoners roared with excitement, screamed with delight. Within a second, the other guard forced him, faced forward, against the nearest cell bars. Finley elbowed him in the gut until his grip on him went slack. But before he could get far, the guard on the floor gripped Finley by the collar and flung him backwards against the railing.

The metal bars, rusted with time, dug into his flesh. "Victor!" the other guard warned. The grasp he held on Finley's neck tightened, cutting off air and blood to his brain. "You know the orders," he reminded him. Victor, whose teeth and breath smelled of rotten death, gnarled his lips close to Finley's face. "We can't kill him."

Finley's vision blotted with spots, the prison falling into further darkness. He thought about Nicolai who waited for him to return. He thought about William and Hugo and Leila. His head throbbed. His lungs gasped. Then he fell to the floor.

His hands and knees hit the stone hard. The prisoners cheering dulled in and out. His chest filled and filled, struggling to get as much oxygen as he could in case it went away again. When he glanced up, he saw Victor seething down at him. "Take him to solitary," he growled. The other guard dragged him to his feet, his vision still impaired. "And when you're done," he said. "Bring his cellmate to one of the torture rooms."

A cold chill sent a shiver down Finley's spine. The hair on the back of his neck stood on end. He froze. The guard dragged his limp body away. When his fear faded he yelled back, "He didn't do anything!" Finley pulled as much as he could, the anger inside of him bursting out. The guard pulled an iron rod from his belt and whacked him in the gut. He was sent down so quickly it took him a moment to realize what happened.

Victor grinned from a few feet away. Finley watched his feet as they drew closer to him. He looked up. Victor gripped his head by his hair and tilted it back. "He will suffer the pain of a thousand men for your actions. And you get to hear his agony as he wakes in the night from horrible nightmares like me."

Finley was taken down a dark hallway he was unfamiliar with. The walls were made of stone and the only source of light shone in through a few holes at the top of the wall. The guard dragged him up a set of crooked stairs. They spiraled up a tower and arrived at a landing that carried the smell of a thousand dead bodies. The air was stiff, allowing only the minimum oxygen into the lungs. His guard pushed him forward and he fumbled.

There were four stone doors, perfectly square and perfectly fit to their hinges. Everything was solid.

The guard flung one of the cement doors open and threw him inside. Finley thought the air outside was thick, but inside the air was so heavy it hurt to breathe.

When he closed the door behind him, his cell fell into darkness. On his knees, he felt liquid, wet puddles he assumed was urine based on stench alone. There was a sense of tension hanging in the space. Unspoken remnants of past guests.

"Not exactly the friendliest bunch of people," a muffled voice said from another cell.

"You could say that," Finley replied. He blindly crawled toward the cell wall, using the palm of his hand to trace its length. Dug into the stone, he felt the markings of claws gouged out of the cement. They were desperate, like a wild animal. "You're the one who's been here since the beginning?"

"It's been a while," he replied. "I'm Silas."

"Finley," he answered. He sat up against the cell door, lowering himself carefully. "Rumor has it you tried to escape," he said. "Is it true?"

There was a stillness for a moment. An emptiness. For a moment, Finley wondered if he made up the other man in his mind, but then he spoke again. "Most of the prisoners they send up here are terrified about what's going to happen to them," he said out of the silence. "I've heard hundreds of stories. Confessions made by completely innocent beings, sometimes even Dark fae. You're the first one to ask about me."

"I have an advantage they don't," Finley said. "I know Doyle isn't going to kill me." He almost felt a sense of pride.

But death never scared him, he was a warrior and faced death on countless occasions. There were far worse things he feared more than death. "They're just punishing me," he added. "I don't plan on dying in the hell hole."

"How do you know they aren't going to kill you?" Silas asked. In the acoustics, the mysterious voice sounded so close, and so yet far away.

Finley sighed, "Doyle wants me alive to meet some Dark fae. And he thinks I'm pretty."

"Oh." He replied.

"Oh?" Finley questioned back. "You know who it is?"

"I have had the unfortunate pleasure of meeting him," Silas answered. "He's a necromancer, Paxton Wylie."

Finley turned the name over in his head, but nothing. "Never heard of him," he said.

"Not many have," Silas told him. "That's the way he likes to keep it."

Finley paused and thought back to the conversation he had with Doyle, how Silas had not been his prisoner to keep. "You're *his* prisoner."

"The one and only," he sighed.

"Does he come here often?" Finley wondered.

"No," he answered.

Finley shifted his position, but slipped in the puddle of urine.

"He keeps to the shadows."

"I guess you're lucky then," Finley scoffed as he shook off some of the pungent liquid. "At least he isn't as cruel as Doyle." Finley rubbed the missing hole in his hand, the empty space. Even under the fabric of Leila's dress, he felt the missing piece.

"Doyle may be cruel," he said. "But he didn't order the extinction of an entire species."

Finley furrowed his brow, "What are you talking about?"

"Before I was captured," Silas began. "I was helping my charge escape from him."

"Charge?" Finley asked. He had heard the term before. It hit his ear with some sense of knowledge that he couldn't quite grasp it.

"I was a familiar, suppose I still am." Finley remembered. They were protectors of witches. Sworn to their charge through life, through secrets, and death. "It's why I'm still locked up here," Silas continued, breaking Finley's thoughts. "Paxton's convinced I'll tell him her most sacred secret."

"So how did you get caught?" Finley wondered.

"We retreated here," he answered. "To the Black Forest."

Finley sat up straighter. It hurt. "We're in the Black Forest?"

"Yes," he replied. "But before it was a prison, it was where a large village of wolves lived. Somehow, Paxton tracked us here." Silas hesitated for a moment. "He brought Doyle's faeries with him and slaughtered anyone who refused to turn to his aid. Any wolf who didn't give up their freedom was killed. And those that did…"

"Became hellhounds," Finley finished. Wolves were Light fae, loyal protectors he had read about in his bestiary. They were almost as old as the faeries, lore stretching back centuries. He remembered flipping through the pages in the library at home. The illustrations painted the wolves in shades of blue-grey, black and whites, hues of brown. But those pages turned from werewolves to hell hounds, beasts. Hell hounds were born from sacrifice. Through fear and hate. Through giving up their freedom to turn Dark fae. With it, they lose the ability to shift from man, trapped forever as a monster. "But it was only one pack of wolves," Finley said plainly. "How could he possibly cause them to go extinct?"

"Paxton is vengeful," Silas told him. "He was so enraged by those who helped her...us, that he had Doyle order any Dark faerie to either kill or turn them."

"What happened to your charge?"

"She died."

Finley heard the hollowness in his voice, even if he tried to hide it. The sting of guilt spread through his chest. He thought about Kaden even though he fought not to. He was supposed to help her. Instead, he ended up hurting her.

"I'm sorry," he whispered.

"It was my responsibility to protect her and I failed," Silas's voice murmured back.

Finley had felt grief. He had a lifetime of losses. Grief, twisted emotions. It was miserable and guilt and sorrow and hate and love all rolled up in one journey. But familiars, familiars were bonded to their charges. Their hearts beat as one.

"I lost a friend too," Finley admitted. "Before I was taken." The truth was bitter on his tongue. His stomach coiled and surged. "She was trying to save her best friend and I–I told her I would help her. I was supposed to help her. Now I'm here."

"I know the feeling all too well."

"So," Finley cleared his throat and blinked back the rim of tears forming in his eyes. "This Paxton character, he's been working with Doyle?"

"Yes. That's why I've been locked up here instead of somewhere else."

"Do you know what Doyle's been trying to do?" Finley asked. He wondered if Silas had more information. He hoped he did.

"I don't hear much from here," Silas answered. "Other than the screams."

Finley swallowed the lump in his throat knowing he would hear Nicolai's. The fear in the boy's gaze flashed in Finley's mind as he closed his eyes and swallowed again. "Doyle and his men want to open the gates of hell," he scoffed. The plan was propitious. It was insane. It was impossible.

"What?" Silas asked quickly.

"I know," Finley replied. "I don't know where they got the idea."

"I can," Silas said flatly. "Paxton."

"A necromancer and a faerie working together?" Finley shook his head. "They're more likely to tear each other apart."

"Maybe not," Silas pondered. "Both Paxton and Doyle want similar things."

"Like?"

"Paxton wants revenge on the world. He's angry. He's

always been silently boiling."

"Sounds like a real catch," Finley replied.

"And the Dark faeries have always wanted to return to hell. At least, that's what their history has shown us."

Finley remained quiet. "They're working together to open the gate," he said to himself. He shook his head, "No," he said. "There's no way. No one can open that realm."

"Who knows," Silas said. "Now that they're working together they have more resources to use."

And then the screams started.

CHAPTER XVII

The hustle and bustle of the Parisian streets, the delicate aroma of buttery croissants, and alluring cadence of the French language turned into the quaint countryside as the train headed for Germany. The sights were straight out of a movie, the landscapes and noises, all foreign to Kaden's eyes. It was the first time she stepped foot out of the country.

Travelling with two faeries, a Dark fae, and one reclusive werewolf took the awe out of the dream and shoved it somewhere between overwhelming family reunion and her first tooth removal.

The few moments of solitude she was able to steal traced the lines and blurs that swept past her out the window. She used one hand to hold her head up as her eyes grew heavy. Kaden felt the weight of her choice not to sleep. And she blamed Kane for it.

He sat across from her with his leg bouncing up and down restlessly. She wondered what he had to be so nervous about. He could leave if he wanted. He could show them the way and turn right back. She was the one with the razor thin chance of returning. "Anxious?" she asked.

The moment the words escaped her lips, his leg stopped. His cool blue eyes found hers, but he didn't say anything.

Kaden rolled her eyes.

With Keeley and Blaine off in different parts of the train, the private box car was quiet. Despite Kaden's objection to bringing Riley along, everything had gone smoothly. His hands had been chained together, bound in front of him with iron. Keeley kept him tight-lipped with her magic and just for the fun of it, she duct taped his mouth when no one could see.

"So is this how we're going to work together?" she asked him. "You ignore me and I try to pretend to trust you?"

"Your existence is the reason my family is dead," he told her coldly. "So, no, I don't like you."

Kaden leaned forward, "I'm sorry about what happened to your family," she said. She made sure to catch the waves of blue swirling in his eyes. "Really, I am. But I can't do anything about the past. Do you honestly think if I could, I would let that happen?"

"Gigi asked me to help you through the forest," he said. "But don't expect me to save you when things get bad."

"I wouldn't expect anything from you," she shot back.

Kane's mouth formed a fine line.

Riley, with his mouth sealed in tape, began to chuckle from beside Kaden. She shot him a sideways glare. "It's not going to be funny when we find you useless." Riley swallowed his last laugh.

Kane reached down to the backpack he stashed between his legs and pulled out a map.

When he unfolded it, Kaden saw hand drawn paths and symbols marked on the giant green blob that was the Black Forest.

The car door slid open, "I just spoke to the conductor," Keeley announced with Blaine hot on her heels. "It shouldn't be much longer until we are there." She took the seat beside Riley, sandwiching him between her and Kaden.

"Good," Kaden muttered. "I can't take much more of this train ride."

"Look what we got from the dining car!" Blaine plopped down beside Kane. He joyfully raised two bags of candy. "Sour worms! Do you want some Kaden?"

She shook her head. The gesture made Blaine shrug at her loss.

"Hey, Blaine," Kaden began.

"Yes, Kaden?" He gripped a handful of sour worms.

She scrunched her face slightly, hoping not to sound rude, "How old are you?"

"Eighteen."

Kaden rephrased her question, "How old in human years?"

He thought about it for a moment before answering. "One hundred and eighty years old." Blaine shoved the colorful array of candy into his mouth. "Hey guys," he said through chews, "look how many I can fit in my mouth."

"*You're* one hundred and eighty years old?" she repeated with disbelief.

"I know," Keeley sighed. "It's hard to believe, isn't it."

"So how do faeries age then?" She looked between Keeley and Blaine.

Keeley turned to her, "Ten human years is equivalent to one year for faeries. Time," she began, "for us is prolonged." For the first time since Kaden had broken Keeley out of her cell in the Seelie Court, there was no malice in her tone. No anger.

"Really?" she asked.

"Yes," Keeley answered. "Why would I make that up?"

"Why do you age so slowly?" she wondered. The further she dug herself deeper into the world of fae, the less she understood. The less she understood, the more she wanted to know.

"It's in our nature." Keeley answered quickly and directly unlike Finley who elaborated most of the time. She wondered if it had to do with his exposure to the human world or if it was just him.

"So where do you come from?" she asked her. "Faeries, I mean."

A few bits and pieces of Blaine's sour worms sprayed across the car as he sat up. "Can I tell her!?" He wiped his mouth of sugar. "Well," he began, "Once upon a time…"

"Enough," Keeley interrupted. "It's our ancestry, not a fairytale."

Blaine's smile turned to a frown.

Keeley turned to Kaden, "Faeries are descendants of the fallen."

Kaden waited for more. When it didn't come, she looked between the two, "The fallen?" she repeated. "Like dead people?"

"Celestial beings," Keeley corrected. Kaden raised her brow and waited for more. "Divine messengers," Keeley sighed.

Kaden furrowed her brow, she watched them with suspicion and shook her head slightly. "Wait," she said. "Are you talking about angels?" She glanced at Blaine and found it hard to believe he was a descendant of a righteous soldier of heaven. "Like heaven? Like there's a heaven?" She waited for Keeley to correct her but she didn't. Neither did Blaine. Then she started to laugh.

Keeley and Blaine exchange a quick glance. "Is there something funny we are unaware of?" Keeley asked her.

Her laughter slowed to a clumsy giggle. Kaden wiped the corners of her eyes free of tears. "You can't be serious. That's the most ridiculous thing I have ever heard...ever."

"Where did you think we came from?" Blaine asked her.

"I don't know..." she shrugged. Then she thought about the question, "A single raindrop from a petal of a four leaf clover."

"I have never been more offended," Keeley snapped. "I suppose I could say a human fell out of the ass of a donkey."

Blaine laughed hysterically. "That's a good one! It's like an ass came out of an ass of an ass. Oh my! Don't tell my mother I said that."

"So…you're not joking?" Kaden asked her. "I thought faeries were Celtic, not Christian."

"We're not much of either," Keeley explained. She put her right foot up on the bench across from her. "Angels are a sort of neutral entity. There aren't any set rules like humans believe. All there is, is the word of God."

"Did *you* know all this?" Kaden turned to Kane who was deeply studying his map.

He didn't look up when he responded. "I stay out of other fae business…especially faeries."

"There was a time when angels walked freely on Earth," Keeley added. "That's when you could say the doorway between worlds was open. The faerie ancestors were called Watchers, they were left with the task of guarding humanity. After a while, the Watchers became lustful, admiring humans and wished to take them as wives. When God heard of this, He refused them of their wish. Then they rebelled. When they lost the Great battle, their leader, Satanael, was cast out of Heaven. The rest were bound to Earth as punishment. Some wanted to join Satanael in damnation, they are the ancestors of Dark faeries. But Santanael wouldn't have them believing they weren't strong enough. So he left them on Earth."

"And the other rebels?" Kaden asked her. "The ones that didn't want to go to damnation?"

"They became Light. They procreated with humans,

forming hybrids you call faeries. Over time our abilities dwindled. Most faeries don't have wings anymore."

Kaden snuck a glance down at the Celtic cross necklace around Keeley's neck. "So then why all the Celtic designs? And the warrior's cross?"

"Many faeries took to the Celtic heritage," Keeley shrugged. "Somehow we got consumed by it. We wear the cross to mock Him for rejecting us."

"I could have made the story more interesting," Blaine argued. He leaned down to the floor and picked up bits and pieces of candy he had dropped.

"What about witches and …werewolves?" Kaden snuck a quick glance at Kane. "Where do they come in?"

"Those are different creatures," Keeley snuffed. "I only care for my own. You'll have to ask the dog himself."

She reluctantly turned to Kane, "Do you know then?" she asked him. "About witches and wolves?"

Kane crumpled the map when he glanced up, "That's not for me to say."

"I'm just trying to understand," Kaden said. Her lips formed a fine line as she sat back against the cushion of the bench. She crossed her arms over her chest, "Knowledge is power, after all."

The journey was long. Every time Kaden tried to close her eyes Blaine would speak. Every time she leaned her head against the cool glass, Riley would shift. Every time she tried to talk to Kane, he would stare.

When they finally reached the Black Forest region,

Kaden was surprised by how closely it resembled Olympic Park. The forest was dense, the mountains towering, the fog thick and hovering in between. There was a stillness among the mountains.

The town they found themselves in was made up of white buildings lined with dark wood. Strips of businesses with little wooden signs above the door. The streets were cobbled and crooked at times. A river carried water from the mountain down in a steady stream with tiny bridges and lush green grass all the while the pine needles of the forest were painted dark.

It reminded Kaden of Hansel and Gretel.

Kane led them through the town and out into the vast valley. The village grew smaller and smaller the further they got. They neared the forest itself with its full summer bloom, aside from one tree that rested just before the edge of the forest.

The bark was dead, greying in color and starving for life. Kane stopped abruptly at its base, "We're here." He lowered his backpack from his shoulder to the ground.

"Um…" Blaine placed his index finger on his chin and tapped. "I hate to be the one to break this to you, but, that's a tree."

Kane unzipped his bag, pulling a small axe from its depths. "That's the portal."

"Oh," Blaine said. "Well that makes more sense."

Kaden examined the twisted veins of the bark. "How do we get in?" she asked him. She clutched onto the straps of her own backpack for security.

He pulled his bag back over his shoulder. "We have to

crawl through the nook," he said. Kane gestured to the over side of the tree.

Kaden ran her finger tips along the dried bark as she made her way around. At the base of the trunk was a large hole carved and dressed in darkness. It made the hairs on the back of her neck stand on end. A frigid air seemed to slither out from the darkness. As eerie and haunting as it was, there was also an allure, a yearning to venture inside its depths. Kaden bit the inside of her cheek. "After you," she said to Kane.

The muscles in Kane's jaws clenched, but he slid sideways through the tight fit and disappeared. Keeley didn't wait very long to follow behind. She didn't have to twist her body as much as Kane did to get through, but she tugged Riley by the elbow through with her. Blaine stood at the base and leaned down, placing his hands on his knees. "Hello! Here I come!" He stepped inside disappearing like the rest of them.

Kaden sucked in her breath, clutched the straps of her back pack in her hands and stepped through.

Inside it was a dark tunnel covered with roots from the tree. Dampness clung to the earth. Teardrops dripped from the root network. The further she crawled and climbed, the more the sunshine from the world faded. The sunny summer day vanished as she made her way over slickness. Brown earth made way for black mud which coated her palms and knees.

When she finally reached the end of the tunnel, she stood among a foggy haze. A cough escaped her lungs and she waved her hand in front of her face. Twisted dead trees filled the dark forest. Not a single sound echoed through the air. The only light came from the low hanging moon above draping every bit of the forest in a grey-white glow.

Black birds stood silently above them on branches, watching, waiting, as if they would swoop down at any second to claim their dinner. "You used to live here?"

"It wasn't like this," Kane answered. He scanned the surrounding area, the treeline, the sky above.

Kaden stepped away from the portal as awe and fear struck her. The trees contorted into unusual shapes. Haunted, like ghosts of the past. She glanced up to the sky but there was none to be found through the fog. Under her feet she found black mud. She bent down to examine it. Against her pale skin it appeared harsh, like the earth that once was, had been poisoned.

She reached out for a leaf that seemed to have fallen, from where she didn't know. Her finger tip was met with a prick and she retracted her hand quickly from a sharp thorn. "Ow," she whispered under her breath. She glanced down at her index finger to find a pearl of blood forming.

"Kaden!" Keeley shouted. The sound rippled through the silence. She turned quickly toward Keeley's voice when a swoosh of air passed Kaden's ear. Her hair brushed against her cheek.

The crack of wood splitting hit her eardrum and she froze. When she glanced back over her shoulder, she found Kane's axe stuck in the trunk of the tree behind her. Split down the center of its body was a centipede the size of her forearm, squirming in its last moments alive.

Kaden jumped backwards at its squeals. She fell on

her butt and used her heels to kick herself a safe distance away from the tree. "You almost hit me," she told Kane. The dead insect slowly stopped moving until only a flinch remained.

Blaine took Kaden by the elbow to help her up while Kane walked over to his axe and tugged it out of the tree trunk.

"You're welcome," he said.

Keeley let go of Riley and brushed past Kaden and Blaine. She bent down to the fallen creature and inspected it. "What kind of creature is this?" she asked. "I've never seen it before."

"I should have just stayed in the car," Riley muttered under his breath.

"A parasite," Kane told them. He wiped the green slime off the blade of his axe onto his jeans. "Everyone needs to be on guard at all times," he instructed. "The further we get into the woods, the worse things will get."

"Finally," Blaine sighed. He pulled his sai sword from his belt, "I get to see some action!" He started to fake sword fight with an invisible enemy.

"Blaine," Keeley warned. She touched her fingertips to the insect's blood. "I'm only going to say this once. You are a trained warrior. Now is the time to act like it."

Blaine stopped and pulled his feet back together where he stood.

"Keep your weapons out," Kane told them.

Kaden slipped the dagger Finley had gifted her out from her back.

Keeley stood, pulling an arrow out for her bow.

Riley lifted his chained hands up in the air, the sound clanking throughout the forest. "I could be of some use to you," he offered.

"Not a chance," Kaden snapped.

"What happens if I need to fight?" Riley asked with a pouty face. "I'll be defenseless."

Kaden took him by the elbow roughly as Kane started forward. "Kind of like all those innocent girls you tried to kill?" she said. She pushed him and jerked him forward. "Karma's a bitch."

"Oh…" Riley sang. "So when you say 'innocent girls', are you referring to your newly departed friend?" He chuckled.

She took him by the shoulder without a second thought and pressed his back up against a tree. The iron of her blade sizzled against his neck.

"She's not dead," she told him through gritted teeth.

Keeley grabbed Kaden's wrist.

Riley twisted a smile, "Keep telling yourself that, lass."

Kaden's nostrils flared. All she had to do was press a little harder. But Keeley pulled her away and pushed Riley to Blaine who took him without a word.

"We still might need him," Keeley offered. "You were right to keep him alive, but do not let anger cloud your judgment."

Kane waited impatiently for the rest of them to catch up. "We have to keep moving," he said.

None of them responded.

Kaden stood, trying to push her anger as far down as she could, but it boiled in her. It rose every time she caught a glimpse of Riley.

Kane turned back, tracing the few steps they had made until he was near them, "I don't have time to stop for conversations," he told her. He found the fire in her eyes and held her gaze, "We don't know what's out here with us. Stay focused or you'll get us all killed."

CHAPTER XVIII

Screams haunted the night. They carried through the iron bars, through the desiccated air, and into the confined stone of Finley's cell. The cries bounced off the walls. They rang in his eardrum. They scraped the insides of his head. He couldn't escape the fowl aroma, he couldn't escape the noise or the thoughts tricking his mind. His chest rose and fell in heaves as if bricks weighed him down and slowly, more kept being added.

Finley clenched his chest, beads of sweat soaking his tattered shirt, "How are you breathing?" he asked Silas through his struggle.

"Paxton had Doyle put a vent in my cell," Silas said so easily. "It's why the screams get loud up here."

He let his head fall back against the brick and closed his eyes. The screams made him flinch. His skin crawled, although he wasn't sure if it was his own mind or if there were roaches scurrying about. "Can you get out of it?"

"And go where?" Silas wondered. "It wouldn't do me any good. It's probably safer in here than it is out there."

At least out there, there is air, Finley thought.

"Anything's better than being here and tortured," he said. His throat was so dry, when he swallowed it made him cough instead. The movement sent an ache through his rib cage.

"How often do they torture you?" Silas asked.

Finley stifled his cough. "It depends," he replied. "Sometimes three, four times."

"A week?" he questioned with a hint of astonishment.

Finley scoffed. "A day," he corrected. "I was trained for this sort of thing."

"A fae warrior?" Silas's voice echoed in the cell block. "I never would have guessed a faerie would be in the cell across from me."

A soft amused breath left Finley, "What gave me away as a faerie?"

"You're the only ones who still believe in warriors and garrisons. At least, that's how it was before I ended up here," Silas explained. "Those torture 'skills' you're talking about? They only benefit you *if* that's what they were trying to do."

Finley opened his eyes to the darkness. A black sheet of space opened up before him. It was hard to tell if his eyes were even open. "Of course that's what they want to do, more pain, more fun, more blood."

"Torture is easy for them Finley," he told him.

"They're trying to break you."

He swallowed down the thought as a shriek erupted from outside. "Yeah," he snuffed. "I'd like to see them try."

The muffled sound of footsteps against stone came closer. Suddenly, his cell door swung open. The light made him wince. What was once dull and faded hurt against his corneas. Finley shielded them with his arm enough for him to spot the guard who had ordered him to solitary, the guard who beat him, the guard who pinned him in the cafeteria. "Treasach," his voice felt slimy and made Finley's throat crave an ounce of water. "Here I was hoping to find your body, looks like I lost my bet."

"Here I was hoping the first sight I would see again was anything other than your face," Finley replied. "We all get disappointed, don't we?"

Finley half expected an iron chain to strike him across the face. Instead, a grin of crooked teeth spread from ear to ear on his face. "Your cellmate's been waiting for you," he told him with a twist of humor.

A knot formed in Finley's stomach. Rage quietly rose from his feet to his heart, forcing him off the ground as quickly as he was able to. A few months prior it would have been enough to wrap his bare hands around the guard's neck, but the guard was quicker and struck him with a hot iron rod.

Finley fell to the ground, cowering at the hot metal bubbling raw flesh. He glared up at him, "If there is one scratch on him, I swear..." he threatened through gritted teeth.

The guard kneeled down to his eye level, "You'll

what?" he whispered. "Kill me?" He chuckled. The sour laughter rippling through his throat echoed down the corridor and all Finley could do was listen.

They tossed him back in his cell, trading the pitch black for the dim green hue of the cell he called home for the past few months. The cell was empty. Nicolai was not in the corner he favored. Finley stepped further inside, panic rushing through his withered veins.

"Nicolai?" His whisper fell among the emptiness. He searched around the space, blood pumping faster and faster with each vacant inch.

A stirring came from underneath the bed. Finley dropped down to all fours where a shrivelled up human form curled in on itself. "Nicolai," he said softly.

He whimpered in response.

Finley reached under the bed and the fragile boy flinched away. "It's okay," Finley told him. "It's just me."

Nicolai pulled himself closer. A sob escaped his lips. Finley helped him out gingerly.

In the light, Finley saw Nicolai's eye was swollen enough, he couldn't open it. He placed his hands on either side of the boy's face to examine his injuries. Blood traced a line down his face. His teeth were stained with the same crimson. Gashes and bruises. Parts of his skin burned, other parts broken. Nicolai heaved a heavy cough that led to him spitting up blood. "Everthing hurts," he whispered.

Finley swallowed hard.

Tears started to form at the edges of Nicoali's eyes,

peeking through the little bit they could.

Finley turned him carefully so he could cradle him in his arms as he cried. His heart sank further in his chest. His body felt numb with Nicolai's limp body against his own. "I'm–" The words caught in his throat. "I'm so sorry–I didn't think–I didn't–" his voice trembled.

"I told them," Nicolai cried. His sobs grew into heaves. "I–I told them. I told them everything."

Finley stared at Nicolai's face, twisted with guilt and agony, cursed with grief and broken bones. He ran his hand over Nicolai's hair soothingly. "It's okay, it's my fault. I shouldn't have dragged you into this mess."

"They made me—watch—" Nicolai sobbed. "William," he cried. "They–they–cut—and blood–"

"It's not your fault," Finley rocked him as his own mother had when tears fell and words fumbled.

"They–told me if I—they would kill me–me too."

"Listen to me," Finley held Nicolai's face steady. "This was not your fault," he repeated. "It was my fault. And I promise, I will not let anything happen to you again."

Nicolai's tears soaked Finley's shirt, "I'm so–sorry."

CHAPTER XIX

They dragged Riley through the forest by his chains.

Blaine spent most of the time entranced by the crooked brambles and the unnatural twist of the trees which left Keeley more times than not with Riley. Her gaze was like a hawk's, following the faintest sound, the shift in the wind. Kaden stuck close by while Kane silently traced a path that only he could see.

"Where are you leading us?" Keeley asked him pointedly.

"In the right direction," he responded with an even tone. Kaden noticed he was more rigid than before. The muscles in his back were tight, the grip on his axe made his knuckles white, and with each step, he acted as if it were his last.

Kaden held her blade so the iron was parallel to her

forearm. Carrying a weapon, rescuing a friend, skulking around in places that shouldn't exist reminded her of when she was with Finley. When there was still Megan. The pulse of her heartbeat throbbed in her ear with each step. The lingering feeling of someone watching kissed her skin in a way she didn't like. She snuck a glance over her shoulder, but only found emptiness.

"We could be of assistance if we knew what we were looking for," Keeley called to him, just loud enough for him to hear. She forced Riley forward by the elbow to get closer to the front.

Kane cocked his head slightly to the side, "Keep your voice down," he told her.

"If I knew where we were headed," Keeley argued. "I wouldn't have to raise my voice."

"We need to cross a river," he answered reluctantly. "It's not far, I can hear the water from here."

Kaden eyed the back of Kane's head suspiciously. Werewolves were new. Anything outside a faerie or a gnome was foreign, and even then she only knew so much. It made her wonder about her own heritage. What she was capable of. It clawed at the nap of her neck with intrigue and fear. "Is there a bridge to get us over this river?" she asked him.

He tilted his head in the direction of her voice over his shoulder. "There's a tree that fell across it, we can use that as our bridge."

Blaine darted past Kaden, his excitement palpable. "What happens if we slip and fall in?" he asked.

Kane shot him a look out of the corner of his eye. "Don't."

Blaine nodded his head a few times and slowed his pace again so he lingered with Keeley and Riley. "Right then," he told himself. "Don't slip. I can do that."

Keeley shoved Riley over an exposed tree root. "What happens once we get over this bridge?"

"We head east," he told her.

The slick terrain was no friend to Kaden. The lumpy roots of the trees' threatened her at each step. The dampness in the air clung to the bark and soaked the ground. "How do you know that's the way we need to go?" she asked as she made her way over a large rock.

Kane was silent for a moment. Kaden thought it may have been him waiting for everyone to advance over the large obstacle. When she looked at him for his answer, his expression twisted. "The scent is stronger in that direction."

Kaden raised a brow at him. She followed his gaze in the direction they had been walking and found nothing in the fog. "What scent?" she wondered.

He glanced at her, "Not a good one."

She nodded, though she didn't understand. Despite her instincts, she walked beside him as they all landed on the other side of the rock. "How old were you," she began, "when your people were attacked?" The moment the words made their way out of her mouth, she wondered if the question was too much to ask.

"Why is that relevant?" Kaden asked her back. He didn't take his attention off of the path ahead.

"Just asking," she shrugged.

"If I may," Riley butted in with a cough.

"No," Keeley snapped. She tugged him closer to her

side in one quick move. "You may not."

"Sorry to piss on your parade, lassy," Riley said. He slowed his pace, purposely forcing Keeley to push him harder. "The prisoner is in need of a refreshment and a wee break."

"Not a chance," Kaden replied without giving it a second thought.

"No," Kane agreed.

"Actually..." Blaine hesitated. "I could use a brief break."

Kaden turned around, walking backwards to face the others, "We can't stop," she urged. The muscles in her calves disagreed.

"We have been walking for hours," Keeley admitted. "Perhaps we should." Kaden exchanged a glance with Keeley. "Even warriors need a break."

Kaden sighed and came to a halt. She looked back at Kane, who continued forward. "Wait," she called after him.

He took a few more steps before he stopped and turned. "You can't be serious?" he asked.

Riley leaned up against a tree with one shoulder. Kaden and Keeley kneeled before Kaden's backpack, rummaging through its contents. "Just for a few minutes."

"If we stop—" he began.

"Even if we don't stop," Kaden cut him off. "Something could happen." She pulled out a few power bars and handed them to Keeley who passed them around. "At least this way we'll be rested for when it does."

"Fine," Kane replied. His mouth tightened into a fine line as he turned around and kept walking.

Kaden shot up to her feet, "Where are you going?" she asked after him.

"To see how much further it is to the river while you take your break," he said as he disappeared through the fog. Kaden shook her head as she passed out water bottles to Keeley and Blaine.

"What about me?" Riley asked harshly. Kaden glared at him and reluctantly handed him a bottle. "What?" he shrugged. "No protein bar?"

"You're lucky you're getting anything," Kaden told him.

Both Keeley and Kaden decided Riley could lean against the tree, although Kaden hoped another parasite might climb down and suck the life out of him. "Do you think he's really going to see how far away the river is?" Kaden asked Keeley.

Keeley ripped a piece of the protein bar with her teeth before answering, "He can probably hear you," she told her. She sank her teeth into another bite while Kaden stared at her. "Werewolves'," she said, "they have heightened senses."

"Oh," Kaden said. She wished she had known that before she had spoken and before she had cursed him under her breath on numerous occasions. "Well," she cleared her throat. "I don't trust him."

"You trusted Finley," Riley said from behind them. Kaden turned around sharply at the sound of his voice against her ear and flipped him the bird, a gesture that confused Keeley.

"I'm starting to think we should put duck tape over his mouth again," Kaden said.

"Go ahead," he huffed. "It won't change the past like you seem to think."

A slight smirk slid across Keeley's face, "Maybe we *should* just kill him."

Kaden clenched her jaw, "Not yet," she found herself saying despite her eagerness to throttle him. Her grip around her water bottle crunched the plastic tighter. "We'll know when the time is right."

"Or you could *not* kill me." He shrugged one shoulder and threw his empty bottle to the ground.

"I will punch you in the throat!" Kaden snapped. The sound her voice made echoed in ripples through the forest more than she had anticipated.

"You could," he admitted easily. "You could pretend I am you since *you* were the one who got your friend murdered." His chuckle was sly and snarky. It taunted her, twisted her insides, and boiled her blood.

She felt the rush of warmth reach her cheeks as she took quick steps toward Riley. She stood inches from his face, the same face that threatened her friend, the same face that taunted her memories. She wanted a reason, any reason to hurt him. Under her chest, her heart thumped with lava. "Megan," she said her name with sharpness, as if it were a weapon. "Isn't dead."

Riley's eyes smiled.

Her hands clutched to fists at her side.

He's a liar, she told herself. *He's a manipulator. He's a bastard and she's not dead.*

Keeley snuck into her peripheral vision, she pulled Kaden by the upper arm a few inches away from Riley.

"Kaden," she said softly. "She is dead."

She turned her head sharply, her gaze boring into Keeley, "No," she told her. "She's not."

Kaden's insides swirled with the possibility. Her heart sank into her stomach, swallowed into the depths of her. Her throat dried up at the thought, at the lie. A numbness crawled its way up her feet through her legs to her knees. She shook her head before it could consume her.

Without so much as a word, Keeley slid Kaden's backpack from her shoulders. "What are you doing?" Kaden was realized at the distraction.

"Taping his mouth shut," Keeley replied. "I don't know what will happen here if I use magic," she added. She pulled the silver duct tape out and extended it to a decent size. "He's causing more trouble than he's worth."

"Of course," Riley sighed. "Why solve a problem, when you can just ignore it?"

Keeley bit the end off with her teeth.

"What the hell are you doing?" Kane's husk voice appeared out of thin air. He moved quickly, running toward them over roots and rocks alike.

Keeley's brow furrowed at the question, "Taping his mouth shut."

He pushed past them, past Riley and the tree trunk he leaned against to Blaine not far behind them in a small clearing. Blaine knelt beside a handful of sticks and twigs pitched together, forming a triangle. Smoke drifted, slowly, mingling with the fog.

"Are you trying to get us killed?" Kane knocked the pile of kindling down, stamping out the fire with his boot.

A cloud of black smoke rose up, with each stomp. The smokiness dissipated around them, causing each of them to cough the heaviness out of their lungs.

"I was getting cold," Blaine mumbled to himself. His eyes widened in the pure kind of way a childs' does when they've done something wrong.

"Hey!" Kaden shouted through a heaving breath. She walked over to Kane, turning him by his upper arm until he was facing her. "Don't talk to him like that," she said.

His expression twisted with anger, "Don't talk to him like that?" he asked her. "He obviously needs it since he was stupid enough to do something like this." The smoke died down around them to a faint haze, merging with fog. The embers from the fire faded to nothing but ash. "Why weren't you two watching him?"

"I am not a child!" Blaine yelled. He stood up from the would be campfire with a cough.

"Maybe you should stop being such a dick and talk to us like we're living beings," Kaden scolded him. "How were we supposed to know it was a stupid idea if you never tell us anything!"

"Hey!" Blaine whined. Kaden shot him a look to keep his mouth shut.

Kane sucked in a breath to reply when several low howls pierced through their disagreement. No one moved. Kaden felt the fiery hot blood in her veins turn cold. They all looked in the same direction, the direction the howls lingered. Then there was silence.

"We need to run," Kane said. "Now."

He started off in a dash into the dead wood.

Everyone followed without a single word, darting past trees as the earth beneath their feet rumbled. Not one among them dared turn around to catch a glimpse of what was chasing them. The heavy pounding against the forest floor urged them forward.

The instinct to run was palpable. Kaden ran fast enough that a low hanging branch cut her cheek. They hurtled over a decayed tree that had fallen and blocked their path. They stumbled and slipped on the charcoal mud beneath their feet.

A ripping pain stretched across Kaden's chest, "What do we do!?" she yelled to Kane who still managed to lead the way.

"We have to get to the river!" he shouted back.

The thunderous pounding mixed with low snarls persuaded Kaden to sprint faster, she passed Riley with no remorse. She knew whatever was chasing them was not about to stop until there was blood. And Kaden, was not willing to be the one to offer it.

Keeley had managed to remove her bow from across her chest, "How many are there?" she asked.

"I don't know," Kane answered. He showed no sign of having difficulty running like the rest of them, mostly Kaden and Riley. He ran as if it were just an everyday jog which left Kaden feeling he might just out run them all and save himself.

"We can take them," Keeley said with the confidence of a warrior.

"You're just going to piss them off," Kane told her. "We need to get over the river." Just as Kane finished his sentence, the raging river appeared on the horizon. The water moved with ease, fast and furious. The white caps licked the air and the jagged rocks beside the river's bed.

Crossing it would have been a challenge without something dangerous on their heels, rushing over a slippery log seemed impossible.

When the log Kane had spoken of came into view, it was nothing like Kaden had expected. It was a skinny thing, made for one person at a time, if that. The water soaked its trunk. Holes from decay and infestation riddled it with fragile spots. And the river did not look kind.

As they closed in on the river and the impossible task of crossing it, Blaine fumbled over a tree root. He hit the ground hard, staggering to get back to his feet.

"We need to climb," Kane decided for them. Both Keeley and Kane ascended a large tree beside the river where branches hung halfway out.

Riley hurtled over Blaine's body for the tree while Kaden turned back to pull Blaine up by the collar of his shirt. She caught a glimpse of the four legged beasts headed their way and froze.

"Hurry up!" Keeley screamed to Kaden who was paralyzed in her spot. The warning in Keeley's tone snapped Kaden back to life. She pushed Blaine up, urging him without words to move.

Kaden jumped up to a lower hanging branch, climbing parallel to Blaine, but closer to the roaring body of water beside her.

The beasts that hunted them barely slowed down in time, not to collide with the tree. They were over-sized, sharp toothed wolves. They were emaciated, ribs and bones sticking out leaving nothing of their form to the imagination. Their size was that of a grizzle. Drool dripped off their canines. The fur on their backs were matted and patchy. The hunger in their eyes, deadly.

Blaine froze against the tree like a squirrel being chased by a dog. "Blaine," Kaden called out over the rush of the river. His eyes fell to nothing but the emptiness between him and the beasts below. "Blaine," she called again.

One of the mangy creature's eyes locked on him. It pounced for his lowest leg.

Kaden instinctively dropped lower to kick it in the face before teeth met flesh. But its jaw was open and looking for blood. The beast's rabid canines clenched around her ankle.

A scream erupted from her lungs. She clung on to her tree branch with everything she had while using her other foot to kick it in the eye. She took in a gasping breath as it sank its teeth deeper. Her vision blurred, tiny dots. Kaden was sure she would either pass out and fall or the beast would rip her ankle clean off.

The cries of pain woke Blaine enough for him to pull out a sling shot from his back belt. He balanced himself on his branch easily, the dexterity in his feet accustomed to trees. A rock from his belt satchel made its way to the sling. He aimed and released, sending the jagged edge into the creature's eye.

The rabid dog whimpered as the rock lodged into its eye socket. Its jaw unclenched the locked grip from around Kaden's ankle, sending her off balance.

Kaden released the tree branch and fell into the raging river.

"Kaden!" Blaine shouted after her. The beasts clawed at the trunk of the tree and jumped on their hind legs. Their teeth chomped at the air as Blaine climbed up higher.

"What do we do now?" Keeley asked. She looked to Kane who was wrapping the straps of his backpack around his chest.

"They're dogs," he said. "Give them something to play with." He gestured his head toward Riley before jumping into the river after Kaden.

Keeley turned quickly. She swung down, using the branch beside hers as a bar, and kicked Riley clean off his branch and onto the forest floor.

Riley's screams carried throughout the forest, over the raging river. Their claws dug into his chest and tore his inside out. They nipped and bit at one another, fighting and chewing, blood dripping off their muzzles.

"Now what?" Blaine asked Keeley. Fear swirled in his eyes. The beasts were distracted, but there was only one of Riley and four of them. Keeley looked over her shoulder to the river's raging waters.

"That is an excellent question," she admitted. Her hawk eyes scanned her surroundings, the faint gurgle of Riley's dying breath lingering in the air.

Two of the beasts started jumping at the base of the tree again when a rumbling sound broke through the forest. The noise caught the attention of the creatures below, enough for them to stop eating.

The four of them turned to the darkness of the forest

and growled in a low, threatening tone. A creature that stood on two legs much like a human but very, very tall, kicked one of the beasts as it lunged to attack. The pale brown thing appeared as though it were a gnome on steroids but it was some other creature she had never encountered before. It was muscular enough to lift a tree clean out of the ground as if it were nothing but a twig.

"What the bloody hell is that?!" Blaine shrieked.

Keeley blinked. "I have no idea." The human-like creature had given them the distraction they needed to climb out of the tree and cross the river. The beasts were either attacking the huge thing or had already run off. "Let's get out of here," she tapped Blaine on the shoulder to get him to move. "Go!" she shouted at his reluctance.

"What about Kaden?" he asked Keeley.

Keeley gazed down the river only to see the wishing white caps engulf enormous boulders. "Kane said we needed to head east," she told him. "We'll have to meet them there."

CHAPTER XX

Purple velvet was not something Finley had particularly found inviting until he lowered himself among the soft comfort of the arm chair. At first, he thought he was dreaming. Then, he wondered if in his dehydrated state he conjured a hallucination of Doyle's private chambers.

The hearth was large enough to fill the grand space with warmth. The wood fire crackled and popped. The flames licked the air from the chimney. A smokey aroma filled the space like the comfort of a fire on a cold evening. The warmth hugged Finley's bones, heating the chill in his veins that had cursed him for months. He swallowed a hint of guilt, thinking about Nicolai.

He glanced away from the fireplace to a window that stretched from floor to ceiling. The glass's pattern revealed a distorted Black Forest. The wilderness had no ending, no beginning. Decrepit trees, blanketed with gloom, stood twisted and crooked, like they had been petrified in place.

Finley sank further into the chair. He examined the blood and mud and shit caked under his nailbeds. He traced the angles of his bones, both crooked and straight. His chains cut to the bone, though, there wasn't much for them to cut through. The burn of the iron had stopped hurting as much as when they first tied him up. The pain dulled to nothing but a tooth ache. Rust lingered and embedded in his skin and through his blood stream. The weight of them, harder and harder to hold with each passing breath. He wondered if he would have the strength to wrap the chains around Doyle's neck, but he doubted it.

Finley turned, just enough to look into Doyle's bed chambers attached to the sitting room. Purple velvet draped the dark wood canopy. The pillows were silk and smooth, shades of lavender. If he closed his eyes, he knew he would be able to smell lavender, like the wildflowers in the fields back home. Like where Shadow found him.

Even the thought of fresh air drew Finley's anger near. Nicolai had never smelled fresh flowers or slept in lavish beds or sat among the warmth of a fire. Finley clenched his jaw as the time passed by. Time he could be soothing Nicolai's pain.

The chamber door opened and closed just as easily, without a sound or a touch of Doyle's hand, but with magic. The King of the Dark faeries did as expected. He strolled across the room, passing by Finley and took the lush seat on the opposite side of the long coffee table. As he did, the fire roared purple flames.

"Nicolai did nothing," Finley said through gritted teeth. The heat he felt ran through his body. It flushed his cheeks and warmed the tips of his pointed ears. When he was young he was taught to hide such feelings among an enemy, but all he could do was picture Nicolai's crippled body shivering under the bed.

Doyle took a cheese Danish off the table beside him as if he hadn't heard Finley.

"If you wanted someone to torture," Finley said. He tried to move toward him, to lurch from the chair and strangle the life out of him, but the chains that bound him pulled him back. "You should have chosen me," he seethed.

Doyle smiled. "Frankly, I've had enough of you." He bit into the delicacy and moaned at its sweetness. "You may think me to be one of your moronic Light fae," he began before sipping a cup of tea. "But I've been studying you."

"Well fortunately for you," Finley sat back slowly, letting the fire in him fade. "There's not much to study."

Doyle crossed one leg over the other before he sat forward, "I've thought about killing you," he admitted. "A lot, actually. I could hang you upside down and slit your throat and watch as the blood drains from your body."

Finley glared over at Doyle with a half smile, "Nice to know you think of me when I'm not around."

"That wouldn't do anything," Doyle shrugged. He returned Finley's weak smile as he sat back against the velvet. "Not for you," he added. "Would you like to know what I've learned from you?"

"I have a feeling you'll tell me anyway, so…" Finley held his fire at bay and Doyle knew it.

"You're not bothered by pain," he stated. "You embrace it. After all, you are a warrior. But you, you can't stand the pain of those around you. I cut Nicolai and *you* bleed." Doyle watched as a vein bulged in Finley's neck and chuckled darkly to himself. "You see," he gestured to Finley's natural reactions. "You know I'm right." A devious smile lit up Doyle's face. "Now," he said, clapping his hands together as if he were getting back to business. "I am aware of this ridiculous plan of yours to escape which, by the way, I wouldn't recommend trying. When I woke this morning, I sat in my bed asking myself, 'Self, how on earth should we punish young Treasach for his crimes?'' Then it came to me," he snapped his fingers as though an image had appeared in front of him, "like a vision."

Finley sat silently seething under his skin. His aches and pains were nothing compared to having to listen to Doyle.

Beside him, Doyle lifted a silk cloth that rested on the side table next to his arm chair. Underneath the elegant fabric were a pair of wings. They were delicate, tracing the same shape of a butterfly's with the transparency of a dragonfly. Light purple mixed with silver and hues of blue sparkled in the fire light. At their base, where the wings would have met flesh were remnants of blood and skin from whomever they had been peeled from.

Wings were rare, sacred things. Finley leaned forward in his chair, hiding the desire to reach out and touch them. They had faded from existence in time, the gene long since erased. "Is this supposed to make me sick to my stomach?" he asked him.

"Well, don't you want to know where these once lovely wings came from?" Doyle raised a brow. Finley didn't respond. Doyle's face turned to a pout. "A little birdie told me you chatted with Leila."

The blood in Finley ran cold. His stomach churned into a knot.

"I'm guessing you weren't aware she was a beautiful inhabitant of the Basque region, in the southern part of France. A Laminak to be exact. Those faeries are some of the very rare faeries who still manage to produce wings every so often. And so, I felt I needed some...insurance, that she wouldn't be able to get away. So this morning, I called her into my bed chambers. I took the knife I used to spread the butter across my toast...and I carved them out."

Finley shook with rage. He had half a mind to break the chair apart so he could jump across the room to Doyle, but two guards held him down by the shoulders before the thought carried any weight. "She didn't want any part of my plan, you piece of shit!"

"She screamed," Doyle laughed.

"Leila is as innocent as the others!" Finley screamed at Doyle's smug face.

"She begged me to stop as I dug them out of her back."

"I will kill you!"

Doyle rose from his chair casually, "When she asked why she was being punished," he said with a dark, daring smile. "I told her it was in the name of Finley Treasach."

Finley's chains tore into him as he fought against the guards. Blood oozed down his arms into the velvety material of Doyle's chair . "I will burn you alive!"

"This is exactly what I was hoping for," he said as he slowly clapped like he was watching a magnificent performance. "Now I'm getting somewhere."

"If you touch any one of them again, I swear—"

"To what?" Doyle asked with intrigue. "God?" he let out a laugh. "I hate to break it to you, darling, but he's just an egotistical prick."

"And your 'god' is so much better?" Finley hissed.

"At least he acknowledges my kind," Doyle pointed out. He stepped closer to Finley. "I have one last party favor for you before I'm done for now." He opened a rusted metal container with a hollow needle of blue swirling liquid inside.

Finley's face fell the moment Doyle raised the needle into the air. "Doyle," he said softly, "don't."

"Ah, yes. Faerie dust. A favorite hallucinogen to humans, but for you, for us?" he aimed the end of the needle at Finley's face. "For our kind. It is the worst trip you could possibly imagine."

"Don't do this." Finley fought against the restraints. "What more do you want from me?" he shouted.

"Oh, darling," he said as he held Finley's forearm so the underside was exposed to the light of the fire. "This is just the beginning."

CHAPTER XXI

Rushing water swept Kaden down the river faster than she could imagine. The raging pull of the water dragged her under as she followed the river's dips and turns. When her head breached the surface she gasped for air only to be sucked down again. She grasped onto anything and everything in her path, but the slickness of the rocks and branches and the force of the water just threw her back into the river's flow. She knew there would be an end to the river, an end to the overflow in what she pictured to be a waterfall the size of Niagara Falls. As she got tossed and swept away she feared she wouldn't be able to stop herself from tumbling down it.

Suddenly something grabbed her in a firm hold. It wrapped around her waist, holding her head above the water. For a moment she thought she had caught onto a loose branch, but when she turned her head to look, she found Kane.

He swam with the current instead of against it, falling down into dips and curves. Ahead of them, Kane looked to a large branch off to the side. Without saying anything Kaden nodded. Kane grabbed the slippery bark while Kaden tightened her arms around his waist. He pulled himself further and further out of the river with Kaden clinging onto him for dear life. He managed to get them out of the main flow of the water to a place where they were both able to stand on solid ground. Kaden pressed down on her bitten leg and winced. She dragged herself the rest of the way to the muddy shoreline where they both collapsed from exhaustion.

Kaden coughed out some lingering water before rolling onto her back. She sucked in deep, long gasps of air to fill her lungs. Silently, they laid against the cold ground looking up at the stark sky above.

With everything falling back into stillness, the searing sharp pain rippled up her leg. She used her elbows to hold herself up and looked down to see dark red blood staining the bottom of her pants. "Son of a bitch," she muttered as she reached for the wound.

"Don't touch it," Kane instructed from his spot. "It could get infected."

"I think that thing broke my ankle," she said as she fell back down. She fought the pain by squeezing her eyes shut and exhaled. When she opened her eyes she found the dull light from the sky was blocked out by a slimy green looking man, or at least what she thought was a man.

The sight caught her by surprise. She almost jumped out of her skin, scrambling to get up, but the man quickly held a spear tip to her throat.

"Well would you look at this?" the ravenous man snickered. Kaden snuck a glance to Kane who had an almost identical man holding a ragged knife against his throat. "We got ourselves live meat."

"How much further?" Blaine asked with his feet dragging in the mud.

Keeley refused to shift her attention off anything other than what was in her nearby surroundings. "I'm not sure," she told him. She lifted one foot up to climb over a massive tree that disrupted their path. Blaine, on the other hand, climbed under it.

"Well," he began with a sigh. "How long do you think?"

"I do not know Blaine," Keeley answered through a wave of irritation. She shot a glare at Blaine who seemed more concerned with the tree tops than what was in front of him, "I don't even know where we're going."

Blaine kicked up some dirt that hit the back of Keeley's heels, "So not that long, then?"

Keeley's nostrils flared and she could feel her patience running thin. "I told you," she began with her jaw locked. "I don't know." A snap from a tree branch echoed in the distance. Keeley froze in her tracks.

"My feet are getting tired," Blaine complained as he almost walked into Keeley's back.

"Shh…" Keeley snapped. She removed an arrow from its satchel and placed it inside her bow. She raised the weapon in the direction the branch snapped in and waited.

There was nothing but a low hanging fog and a small black squirrel that scurried away at the sight of them. She dropped her shoulders slightly and lowered her bow. "Keep your voice down." The thought that he had been given a position amongst the garrison of her warriors nagged at her. Blaine was a boy, a child. He hid behind her as a shield instead of standing back to back like Finley would have.

"Maybe we should stop," he suggested with a hop-skip in his step.

"That is not a wise decision considering what took place last time," she reminded him with a glare.

Blaine stretched his arms out and through a yawn said, "I didn't know that would happen."

"That doesn't matter," she said. "You should have–" Keeley caught her words in her throat. Her patience began to fray and crack like broken glass.

"Should have what?" he asked her.

Keeley drew in a deep breath, "Someone your age should know not to do something so foolish."

"I miss Riley," he said. Keeley shot him another quick look of disgust. "I mean, I don't miss him. I feel bad he had to get torn apart like that."

"He was a murderer," Keeley reminded him. "And he captured our fellow warrior."

Blaine shrugged his shoulders, "Maybe he just needed a hug."

"Hugs do not fix people," she said flatly.

"No," Blaine admitted. "But love does."

"Neither does love."

"According to my mother it does. You know I have eleven older siblings." Blaine's drowsiness seemed to fade the more he spoke.

"Stop talking," Keeley replied.

"It's true," he continued. "I'm the youngest, so I always get their clothes. That's why my clothes are always patched up. Each of my siblings had a different shade of green, but mine's the best."

"I do not care," Keeley told him as she almost slipped on a patch of tar like mud, but she held onto a nearby branch.

"I know you love me, deep, *deep* down."

"Keep telling yourself that," she said as she jumped over the rest of the mud patch.

Blaine mimicked her, but landed on some of the mud which caused him to slip down a pathway of slick earth. He tumbled down the hill into a small ditch not far from Keeley. When his body finally stopped tumbling, he noticed the ground was shifting underneath him.

"Blaine," Keeley's eyes widened. "Get up now!"

He glanced down at the mud he found himself in, wondering if it was some kind of quicksand. But when he looked closely, he realized it was a pile of wiggling critters he landed in. Slimy slug-like bugs attached themselves to him like leeches. He quickly jumped up and struggled to climb away while brushing bugs off his skin.

"Get them off!" he screeched. Keeley slid down and helped him swipe the critters off as quickly as she could.

"Get them off!"

"Alright," she told him. He squirmed away from the pile of leeches. "Calm down!" she said.

"Are they gone?" he asked. He spun around in a circle to examine his body. "Am I okay?"

"You're fine, Blaine," she reassured him.

"Pfft," he said as he settled back into his skin. "I told you this job was dangerous."

"Just keep walking," Keeley said and pushed him forward to keep moving.

CHAPTER XXII

Voices whispered, faint and haunting. Echoes of the past corrupted the inner sanctum of Finley's mind. Deciphering what was real and what was just a part of the hallucination blurred into a line Finley couldn't separate. The voices came and went. Sometimes, a whisper against his ear. Other times raging words scraping against his skull.

Finley watched as the ground beneath him crumbled with each step he took, allowing the fiery glow of hellfire to peek through the cracks of stone. The heat against his skin burned. Sweat dripped from his temple to the crevasses of his collar bone. He stumbled and fumbled along as something he couldn't see dragged him against his will to his cell.

He tried and failed to pull away, to squirm out of the toxins hold on him. The balcony was a cliff beside him, and he wanted to jump.

The things that forced him along the path turned, shifted from nothing to demon-like creatures, red skinned beings with horns and fire in their eyes. He wanted, needed to plunge himself down the three stories to get away, even if that meant breaking every bone in his body in the process. The hallucinations poisoned his mind. But to him, it was real.

As soon as the demons returned him to his cell, Finley flung himself onto the bed, shivering in the corner. His mind painted the bed as a boulder in a land of hellfire and lava. Across from him, stood his father. The expression on his face carried no emotion, a vacant thing that scared Finley as a child.

But it was only Nicolai huddled in his corner, still recovering from his injuries.

"It was only a matter of time before you ended up here," his father scoffed.

"At least I've lasted this long," Finley replied. His body trembled with fear and faerie dust.

Nicolai shifted his attention to Finley wondering why he stood on the bed, shaking violently. "You've lasted longer than many of my other cellmates," he admitted. He tried to sit up from his spot, but his body rejected the movement.

"You think you've lasted this long because you are strong?" His father lifted his chin. "You've lasted this long because you are weak."

Finley tried to step closer to him. He gazed down at the lava pit that surrounded him. "I am a warrior," he replied through a locked jaw. Between them the ground shifted and bubbled, swirls of liquified orange and yellow magma. The distance that separated them killed him. Every bone in his body, every fiber of his being felt ravenous with resentment.

"I know," Nicolai said. "You're m—my hero."

"You are a coward!" Spit flung into the lava making it sizzle. "They want to turn you into one of them," he hissed. "That's how weak you are."

The muscles in Finley tightened. He felt his jaw pop from the tension. "I. Am. Not. Weak."

"Finley," Nicolai whispered. "Are you feeling alright?" He shifted in his spot, wincing at the pain and reached out for Finley.

"You are weak," Finley's father mocked. "Too weak to save Kaden. Too weak to save anyone."

"Stop it," Finley snapped. He shook his head, desperately trying to make him go away.

"Finley," Nicolai pleaded. "Calm down. It's going to be alright. You told me that, remember?"

"You are useless. That girl was better off on her own."

"I said stop!" Finley lurched forward into flame, into lava for his father.

Nicolai cowarded backward. "You're scaring me."

Lava swarmed and pooled around Finley's ankles, wrapping him in third degree burns, more even the longer he stood among it. The heat melted his skin, his bones. The suffering crawled up his leg, the fire in his blood greeting the molten lava.

"She would have lived if it weren't for *you.*"

Finley shook, "You are the weak one!" He pointed at his father, at his warden, wishing his magic into the space. His magic could silence the unpleasant noise his father's voice made in his head, in his heart, but no magic came.

"They *all* would have been fine."

"Just shut up!" Finley clenched the roots of his hair through his fingers.

"When will you learn your arrogance will kill them all."

"I said shut up!" Finley wrapped his hands tightly around his father's throat. He felt the pulse beating faster and faster the tighter he held, the harder he grasped.

"Fin—I can't—breathe." But Nicolai's words sounded like nothing but the vile laughter of his father.

CHAPTER XXIII

With their hands bound, Kaden and Kane were escorted through the forest by the pale green creatures with large pointed ears and crooked noses. The two had hunched backs and scurried between the trees quickly, making sharp turns and brushing past brambles with ease. Kaden limped along as fast as she could keep up with her bitten ankle. Each step she wanted to cry out in pain, but she bit the inside of her cheek until she tasted blood.

Their camp wasn't far from the river. Just like their horrid appearance, it was patchy and mangy and smelled of rot. A small fire burned in the center that made Kaden wonder why the creatures that attacked them didn't come after whatever it was that held them captive.

A makeshift shelter made up of various bones and sticks stood alongside the camp fire. Fur hung off a low tree branch in a shape of what Kaden thought might be clothing. The dim light of the fire revealed two more of their kind. One was seated next to the fire plucking at a dead crow's feather while the other, which had a more feminine quality, tore a sharp object through the carcass of one of the beasts that had attacked them before. The beast's guts and intestine poured out as she drew the blade further down its stomach.

Kaden's head felt light and heavy as she watched the green being pull the heart out of the carcass. If it hadn't been for her captor, tossing her to the ground, she knew she would have made her way there regardless. "What's this?" the one seated by the fire asked.

"Found them by the river," the one who had dragged Kaden along answered in a nasal tone. "Better than fishies."

Kane was shoved so he was standing beside Kaden. He glared at his captor who expected him to seat himself onto the ground beside her. Both creatures cocked their heads to the side, "Make a nice meal we figured." Slime caked their teeth and sent an unpleasant smell in their direction.

"What you got there?" the female asked the two men. She pointed, with her blood stained knife, to Kaden and Kane's bags.

Kaden wiggled her toes slightly, then her foot, then her ankle. Each movement shot a warning through her that she would not be able to run.

"Carrying some goods," Kane's captor said. "Don't suppose they came from the hole."

"Where'd they come from, then?" she wondered as

she began to collect the guts into a bowl made from a pelvic skeleton.

"How should I know?" he asked her back. "Hey, you," he said to Kaden, "girlie. Where'd you come from?" He leaned his face towards hers, forcing her to push herself up against the tree trunk. His crooked nose touched her nose and she could smell death on his breath.

Kaden did the first thing she would think of. She spat in his face, causing him to pull away from her. He wiped the spit away and snarled. "Why you little—" He lifted his hand to strike her and she flinched.

"Regal," the one from the fire shouted. "Come. Let's see what they carry."

Regal ripped the bags off their shoulders and wobbled back to the fireside with the others. The way in which he moved reminded Kaden of Theodore. She wondered if he could reach them in the Black Forest.

She leaned back against the trunk, the uneven pattern of the bark, scratching at her skin. The warmth of the fire was a welcome treat after the plunge into the river. Her clothes were still soaked, shoes filled with water, even her ear had remnants of water in them.

They sat back and watched as the group poured out the contents of Kaden's bag first. She twisted her wrists but the rope that bound them was too tight for her to move. "What are they?" she whispered to Kane.

"Scavengers," he replied quietly. Kane brought his hands to his boot while the group was busy.

Kaden furrowed her brow, "Scavengers?"

"Ghouls," he told her.

She watched as they played with a flashlight she had packed. They flipped it every which way and it was only until one accidentally clicked it on that they 'awed' in unison. "And they're going to eat us?" she asked him.

"Probably," he said. Kaden looked over at him as he fiddled with his boot. When she looked back at the ghouls, one of them held up Finley's bestiary which was un-doubt ably destroyed from the damage of the river. Another seemed interested in the gold dagger.

"What are we going to do?" Kaden asked Kane.

"So which one do we eat first?" the female asked as she turned toward them, dagger in hand. Kane stopped moving. Kaden swallowed hard. The ghoul twirled the blade in her hand and then pointed it inches from Kane's face.

"The hurt one," one of the others called out from the fire. He appeared to be the leader, wearing the most fur of them all.

"Why not the handsome one?" she asked with a toothless smile.

"He has more meat in his bones," the ghoul told her. "We should save him."

Two of the ghouls wandered over, grabbing Kaden up by the elbows and onto her feet. They forced her to stand, which brought a numbing pain to her ankle, "Get off of me!" She tried to pull away from them but every move made her ankle worse and unbearable. The ghouls were forced to hold her upright as they struggled to carry her over to the burning fire. "Kane," she said. "Do something!"

"I like this one," the female smiled in Kane's face. "Maybe we could keep him." The female ghoul ruffled

Kane's dark locks as if he were her new pet. Kane jerked away from her touch. She grabbed him roughly by the hair and pulled his head back. "Would you like to stay with me?" she asked him.

Kane quickly and unexpectedly stabbed the ghoul through the bottom of her mouth into her skull.

"Fiona!" the leader yelled as she fell on her side to her death. Kane had his knife from his boot grasped firmly in his hand. He darted for the ghouls who were about to throw Kaden into the fire.

The ghouls dropped her inches from the flame. The heat kissed her skin, the flame bursting with shades of orange in her eye.

The hunched creatures pulled ragged blades from their furs when something big knocked down trees in the forest around them. Trees collapsed in the distance until a mud-like creature stormed into the camp. The ghouls shifted their focus off Kane, off Kaden, off Fiona's dead body. "Use the fire, you fools!"

Kaden rolled away from the fire as the ghouls grabbed branches to burn to force the creature away. The flame only seemed to make the being angrier, as it let out a roar.

Kane ran to Kaden and cut her rope. He grabbed his bag off the ground while the three ghouls defended their home by throwing skulls and pointed bones, but the creature lifted a log and tossed it at their shelter making it shatter to nothing but a pile of debris.

Kaden watched on in shock until Kane lifted her by the elbow off the ground. When reality found its way back to her, she made sure to grab the bestiary and dagger before limping away with Kane.

The creature roared again, the sound wave making the ground tremble. Kaden looked at Kane in the tree line and he looked back at her. Without a word, Kane lifted Kaden off her feet and ran as fast as he could into the forest.

Kaden watched over Kane's shoulder as they disappeared into the horrors of the forest with the ghouls and the creature behind them.

CHAPTER XXIV

"Paxton," Doyle said with his back to the door. He slipped a book back into its place on the shelf in front of him and turned. The sitting room lingered with the remnants of his prisoner's presence, a dull mix of anxiety and fear tingled his nostrils.

Paxton was nearly as tall as Doyle from height or simply the way he carried himself, Doyle did not know. His face was clean shaven, his dark brown hair perfectly parted with a black suit and tie that made him more suited for a board meeting than Doyle's humble abode.

"Always a surprise to see you." Doyle faked a smile. He took his seat behind his desk, covered in an array of tools he used for torture. Doyle gestured for Paxton to take the seat across from his desk. Paxton declined.

Doyle eyed Paxton as he rounded the desk towards

the floor to ceiling window behind him. "Has he said anything lately?" the man wondered. His expression was stone, always stone. Even his eyes were dead which made it harder for Doyle to assess what kind of mood he was harboring.

"He has not breathed a word of importance," Doyle replied. He leaned back in his chair so it stood on two legs.

"But he has spoken?" Paxton asked harshly.

Doyle dropped his chair back to all fours with a thud. "Of course," he said. "He's not mute." He lifted a wrench off his desk as if it were a dinner fork. He flipped it in between his fingers as Paxton turned away from the window and the doom and gloom that waited outside.

"Did I not specifically tell you to report every word he utters back to me?"

"You did," Doyle shrugged. "But I believe you're mistaking me for your own personal slave." He pointed the end of the wrench at Paxton who appeared unamused. "Did I ever actually agree to tell you his *every* word?" A smile spread across Doyle's face as he looked up at Paxton.

Paxton turned away from him. "The only reason you are still breathing," he said as he gazed out the window, "is because I am allowing it. And when I ask you to do something," he paused. "You do it."

Doyle propped his feet up on his desk. "How about you?" he asked. "Have you figured out why we are still mingling with the likes of humans? You siad—"

"I said I was working on it," he snapped. "If it weren't for me you would be two steps behind instead of one step ahead."

Doyle's jaw clenched. "The others are getting restless," he told him.

"All in due time," Paxton said softly.

"You said murdering those girls would work," Doyle began. "You said their innocence was the key." He tossed the wrench onto his desk. The loud clank filled Paxton's silence. "Now the others fear the Light fae may intervene."

Paxton turned to Doyle, slowly. "They have not intervened in years. What makes you think they will start now?" The leather sole of Paxton's shoes clicked as he stalked towards the bookcase. He scanned the shelves and removed one from its place, "The girls were a miscalculation on my part."

"A miscalculation?" Doyle repeated. His brow furrowed as Paxton began to leisurely flip through his book. "There were hundreds of them. How many more do we need before we prove ourselves to be as vile as He requires?"

Paxton looked up from the book in his hands, "The spell we must perform calls for great sacrifice." The book slapped shut in Paxton's hands. He placed it back among the others and walked in front of Doyle's desk, "I need more time to figure out what it requires."

Doyle's lips curled into a tight smile and fell again. He resisted the urge squirming inside of him to turn Paxton into the snake he was. Doyle sighed, "I am not closer to turning Treasach."

"I told you before," Paxton said, "we don't need him."

"You may not need him, but I do."

Paxton glared at Doyle, "For what?" he scoffed.

"More of your tricks and nonsense? This is exactly why your kind was not worthy enough."

"Not for nonsense," Doyler snapped. "For power." He sucked in a deep filling of fear that hung in the air. "With a loyal Light faerie on my side, I could turn others. Outweigh the good over to the evil."

"Just because one Light fae turns to you," Paxton started, "does not mean you will win."

"It's exactly what I need to win," Doyle told him.

"You are thinking of this as a child would," Paxton lowered himself into the chair across from him. "You must not worry about our war front on Earth but look beyond it."

"I am many things," Doyle said bitterly. "But a child is not one of them." He watched Paxton as blood boiled under his skin. Paxton didn't appear at all fazed. "Has it not occurred to you that with more fae power we could open those gates much more easily?" Doyle dropped his feet from his desk and sat upright. "We would have endless resources instead of a handful of Dark fae working in secrecy."

"We work in secrecy because no one can be trusted." Paxton answered sharply. He stared at Doyle, daring him to question his plans' efficiency. "It's safer to keep the others in the dark. The more fae that know, the more likely the Light fae will find out. The greater the chance we lose completely. So when I say we keep it quiet, we keep it quiet."

"Do not take me for a fool, Paxton," Doyle replied flatly. "I am older than you are–"

"Older," Paxton agreed. "But not wiser."

CHAPTER XXV

The forest stilled again as Kane carried Kaden away from the violent attack on the ghouls. His chest rose and fell, but not in the way someone who had been running since the moment they arrived would. Their clothes were still soaked, leaving little distance between her skin and his. Kaden squirmed at the thought, but realized she was warmer than she had been sitting near the fire.

"Cold?" Kane asked.

She looked away from the forest to him. The stubble on his cheek and along his jaw was longer than when she first met him. "No."

Kaden shifted her attention quickly back to the forest around them. She scanned for parasites, beasts, ghouls or muddy giants, all of which were things she didn't prepare herself for. More creatures lurked in the forest than she had ever experienced before. She started to understand why Gigi insisted on Kane guiding them through the forest. And she was thankful.

Kane slowed his pace from a speed walk down to a more casual one once he felt they were far enough away from danger. When his steps eased to something more hesitant, Kaden turned to see what lay ahead.

She found burnt remnants of a cabin, half engulfed by dead tree roots. The house was as black as charcoal, darker than the trees surrounding it. Beams dangled randomly, torched by fire, what was once a roof nothing more than charred lumber.

Kane stopped abruptly. He placed Kaden down on the porch half swallowed by soot before he slung his backpack off his shoulder. Kaden glanced around the decayed insides of the house to the ash pile of someone's life only to find a cluster of off white human remains. The empty eye sockets of the skull bore into her and she swallowed.

"What the hell was that back there?" she asked as she turned away from the skeleton.

Kane rummaged through his bag, "I don't know," he said. "I would say check your book there," he gestured to the sloppy remains of Finley's bestiary. Kaden opened the saturated book. Ink ran on the pages, blurring images with text. Gingerly, she turned another page and it ripped in two. "Looks like you'll need a new one."

Kaden closed her eyes and let out a sigh before she opened them again. "This was centuries old. I can't get a new one."

"Maybe you should start one." Kane pulled different items from his bag while Kaden sat helplessly on the dead wood.

"At least you still have your bag," she shrugged. At the very least she was able to save Finley's belongings. She didn't mind so much her food and water and bandages were gone. She just couldn't lose more of Finley than she already had. Kaden cleared her throat. "What were those dogs by the river?"

Kane froze for a brief moment before he continued searching his bag. "Hellhounds," he answered flatly.

"Oh."

She watched him quietly for a moment. Then she turned away from him and lifted her torn up ankle onto the porch. When she faced away, she caught sight of another cabin buried and burned in the trees. It was smaller, but its roof was caved in, windows shattered out.

Then she spotted another home and another and another. All houses swallowed by fire, fallen to nothing but ash. "Shit," she muttered under her breath.

"Don't touch it," Kane said. He hadn't looked up to see where her eyes had drifted.

Kaden glanced back down to her ankle to examine the bite. The hellhound's teeth had clamped down around her entire ankle. The markings were deep enough she caught a glimpse of her own bone. She nearly threw up in her mouth at the sight of her mangled leg. "I think it's broken." She sucked in a deep cleansing breath but her vision still wobbled. "How am I supposed to get to the prison now?"

"It's not broken," he said. He found a stick on the

ground and broke it in two. Kane gestured for her to give him her ankle and she winced. He removed her boot slowly, but even slowly felt sharp and agonizing. "You might need stitches at some point though."

"Ow." She squeezed her eyes shut and tried not to look. "Careful, careful."

"Don't be dramatic," he said. "*This* is going to hurt." He reached for a canteen from his pile of supplies.

"It already hurts," she argued. "How much more pain—"

He poured the liquid over her open wound, cutting her words off to a muffled curse.

It burned and bubbled through her ankle. As a reflex she pulled her leg out of his grasp. "Damn it!" she cried out. The piercing ache sent lighting up her leg. The trees around her began to wobble enough for her to lie back on the porch. She could smell the old wood. The sharp burn. Then something hit her nose that was remarkably familiar. "Did you just pour vodka on my ankle?" The question fumbled out of her mouth, feeling like cotton filled her mouth.

"You're welcome," he replied. She felt him wrap gauze around her ankle firmly enough for it to hold both sticks he had on either side.

"Why the hell did you bring vodka in your bag?" she asked him. She opened her eyes to find the dark branches of the trees trace a crooked pattern against the sky. "You know what? I don't even want to know, but if the rest of your supplies are as stupid as that, we're screwed."

"Believe it or not, I came prepared," he told her. He wrapped another layer of gauze over the splints, "What's in my survival bag is my business."

"But...*vodka*? Really?" Kaden asked.

Kane finished wrapping up her leg in silence.

"Do you think the others will meet us there?" she wondered suddenly.

"If they can manage," he answered honestly. Kaden buried the worry that cursed her chest and rippled through her nerves. If Keeley and Blaine had as much luck as they had, they may never make it out of the forest. "We can stay here for a few minutes for you to get your balance."

"My balance is fine," Kaden lied.

He scoffed. "Sure. That thing could still be following us, so we shouldn't linger."

Kaden sat up, using her elbows to hold her weight. "At least it distracted the ghouls," she reminded him. "And I did not get eaten."

"You were never going to get eaten," Kane told her. He started putting his things back in his bag.

"You mean you weren't just going to sit there and then run off?" she asked him. Kaden raised a brow at him.

He glanced up at her, "I had a plan. I always have a plan."

She squinted an eye at him, "How did you get so...so survivalist?" she wondered.

Kane swallowed before turning his back so he could lean up against the porch. She forced herself to sit up fully, looking down at him until he answered.

"Look around you," he said. His gaze swept across what was left of the village. "This was my home. This is where I lived with my parents," he paused. "This is where my people died…for you." Kane looked over at her.

Suddenly Kaden could see a vast ocean in the depths of his eyes. Then he looked away.

"And," he continued. "If I'm not careful, you'll end up getting me killed along with them."

Kaden's gaze fell to the forest floor, to her torn up ankle and the gauze protecting it from harm. "It wasn't my fault," she said softly. She imagined living in a small village in the forest. What the spruces and pines had smelled like on a warm summer day. What it sounded like. How safe it must have felt. "I'm sorry about your people." She watched her toes wiggle with less pain. "I've lost my family, too."

Megan.

Reality bubbled to the surface. As much as she wanted to bury it deep inside her, she knew it was real.

"I have no one left to go home to," she told him. "Finley is the only one. He's the reason I'm out here. With you."

"You don't even know if he's alive," Kane replied. He glanced over at her, "You're going off of something a Dark faerie told you. Someone who was ordered to protect what was left of my pack. How do you know this wasn't planned?"

Kaden had the same fears coiled up inside her. But a spark outweighed it all. "It doesn't matter," she told him. "Either way there are Dark fae holding people, beings, captive. I am not about to let more people get hurt."

"Why are you so concerned about fae you don't even know?" he asked her while fiddling with a nearby twig.

"Because I lost my friend to it." The words were

poison in her mouth. Her heart felt hollow enough to shatter. A wave of emptiness washed over her. "My best friend. And if I can prevent someone, anyone, from feeling the pain that I feel...I'm going to do it."

Kane fell silent.

Kaden fell silent.

The forest that engulfed them fell silent.

An ease filled her. It lessened the tension in her muscles. For the first time, Kaden felt a tiny window of hope appear since she remembered everything that happened.

"What was your friend's name?" Kane asked her suddenly.

The name rang in her ear. It swelled her heart. She could read it clear as day. But saying it, stung. "Megan."

"The Dark fae got her?"

Kaden's shoulder dropped. "It was Doyle and his people. They tore at her mind until there was nothing left to feel."

"Was there anything you could have done to stop it?" he asked her.

She furrowed her brow, "I don't know," she admitted.

"Was there?" he pressed. "Without getting yourself killed?"

"I guess...not. But I should—"

"No." His response was sharp and final. He turned to her before she could fill in some excuse. "If you keep telling yourself there was something you could have done, you will never move on."

Kaden wanted to shake her head. She wanted to find

some way to argue against him. She studied him and wondered who he had lost, what guilt he carried inside of him. "And you?" she asked him.

He turned away and placed his elbows on his knees. "My father," he said. He flicked away the last bit of twig he had dwindled down to nothing. "I thought I could help him fight this hellhound. The thing scratched my back, knocked me down before I even realized it. My father picked me up and told me to run. Instead, I distracted him and those things—they tore him apart in front of me." Kane let out a bitter sigh. "Gigi found me and we ran."

Kaden lifted a weak smile, "You should take your own advice," she told him. "You were a kid. It wasn't your job."

"Doesn't matter," he said. "He would have died anyway. There were too many of them and not enough of us."

"I will make sure that your people's death will not be in vain. We'll take down as many of them as we can."

Kane half turned to look up at her, "You seem stubborn enough to say something like that."

"Are you brave enough to follow me?" she asked him.

Grey clouds filled the sky, only adding to the eerie atmosphere outside the prison. The silence was heavy as Keeley and Blaine crept up behind a boulder which gave them an ideal visual of the broken building.

There was no movement, only the flapping of wings from crows circling a scarecrow just outside the structure. It was built of grey stone with black and dead vines crawling up the walls. There were no windows in sight aside from the top floor where a few stretched from floor to ceiling.

"Now what?" Blaine asked Keeley who was scanning the area.

"We need to check the perimeter," she told him. "We need to find the best entry point while we wait for Kane and Kaden's arrival."

"Good strategy, Silver Fox," he said.

Keeley shot him a glare and furrowed her brows, "Don't call me that."

"I just thought we should use code names."

"No," she replied flatly.

"Alright, your choice," Blaine stretched his arms over his head to crack his back. "Should I go to the left or the right?"

"We have to stick together," Keeley said. "I don't trust you by yourself. This way," she nodded. She crept to the left, hiding behind tree trunks and rocks that lay sporadically around the outside of the prison.

"Not much movement, is there?" he asked.

"No," she admitted. Her gaze followed the lines of the building, seeking faulty points and size. "No movement at all." The lack of security concerned her. There was no window into the building, no way to know what was on the inside. But then again she wondered who would be foolish enough to enter?

"Why do you suppose that is?" Blaine's face contorted to something uncomfortable as they hunched behind a ruined piece of what was probably part of the building.

Keeley pondered the question herself. "They have to

have another portal inside that they use to get in and out," she said.

"Really?" Blaine asked, shocked. "How would Doyle manage to create a portal?"

"It's the necromancer," she told him. "He must have created it or at least both of them worked together."

"Why would Doyle work with a necromancer?"

"I can't imagine it's anything good," Keeley said just as she was prepared to move behind a tree. Blaine fell over on his side before he was able to follow Keeley. She looked back sharply. "Now is not the time for games, Blaine."

"I know," he said. He lifted himself back up and glanced down at his body. "I just fell."

"What do you mean?" she asked as she waved for him to get to the next tree. He followed the gesture sluggishly.

Blaine made it to the tree and leaned against it, "I just fell," he told her again. He rubbed the lower part of his back and glanced up. "I don't know why. I couldn't control it."

Keeley rolled her eyes. Her patience for Blaine was thinner than she would have allowed for anyone else. But when Blaine glanced at her again, she saw fear. "Turn."

"What?" he asked her.

"Turn around," she commanded.

"Why?" he asked her.

"Do as you are told." When Blaine didn't turn around fast enough, she began to turn him. She started to raise his shirt up when Blaine tugged it back down from the front.

"I am not comfortable with this, Silver Fox." He held it down tightly before Keeley could move it anymore.

"Blaine," she said calmly. "I need to see if there is anything wrong with your back."

"Fine," he huffed. "But I don't like this."

Keeley lifted it up anyway. On his back, black lines traced in his veins like the roots of a tree. The closer to the spine, the darker the color. "Is there anything?" he asked in Keeley's silence.

"Do you remember when you fell into that pile?" she asked him as she lowered his shirt back down.

"Is there one on me?" Blaine began to spin rapidly in a circle, swatting at nothing.

"Blaine, stop it!" She grabbed him by the shoulders, steadying him. "You're going to draw attention to us."

"If there isn't one on me," he began, "then what is?"

"It will be okay," she offered in the calmest voice she could muster. Tenderness wasn't something she practiced and the little she had was not usually as kind as she wished.

"Oh no," Blaine said. His eyes widened. The fear spread faster than Keeley anticipated. "It's bad isn't it? That's what my mother always says when—"

"Listen to me," she told him. "I believe a parasite may have gotten...*into* you."

Blood rushed out of Blaine's face. The once cheerful boy was frozen in horror. "How? That's...that's disgusting."

"I can only tell you my opinion," she reminded him. "But," Keeley let out a sigh this time not of annoyance but of her own frustration and helplessness. "It probably went through your ear."

"Wait," he said. "We have to get it out. We don't know what it's doing, Silver Fox."

"Yes," she assured him. "And we will." Keeley hid the side of her, the small part that worried what kind of damage it was doing to him. And she hoped he wouldn't ask. "I don't know how to," she admitted. "Once we can, we will. Until then, you need to stay close to me."

"Oh," Blaine looked at the ground and twirled his foot in the mud. "Okay," he nodded.

"Look at me." Keeley held his head up by the chin. "We will fix this." But deep inside, she didn't know for sure.

CHAPTER XXVI

Nicolai's vision blurred with spots and dwindling light.

His feet scraped and wiggled against the cement floor, trying to pull free of Finley's grasp. The suffocating pressure drained his lungs of air. His head grew lighter, fuzzier. Finley's sharp ramblings were the only sound to hit his ears, even then, he couldn't understand any of it.

The pressure collapsing his throat vanished in one quick second. Air flooded to his lungs in a rush that made him cough and choke on it. Nicolai's chest heaved as he fell down against the cement.

"As much as we would like to see you strangle your friend to death," a wiry voice spoke out. When Nicolai was able, he looked up to find two guards filling the cell. "Your company is needed by request of Doyle."

Finley fought the guards, thrashing with spit foaming at the edges of his mouth. "Let me go!" His face flushed red, veins bulging out of his neck. Under their grasp, Finley's objections began to dwindle. The red horned demons they once were, faded into the green slim machines they had always been.

His gaze fell to the crumpled boy in the corner of the cell, the ground beneath his feet still ablaze. The faerie dust dried in his veins, transforming his father into nothing more than an apparition. The built up rage was still raw in his body when he pushed the guard away. "I saw Doyle not but five minutes ago, you ape!"

"Five minutes?" one guard repeated. "Five minutes?"

A wry smile spread across the other guard's face, "He doesn't even realize what he's been up to this whole time, does he?"

"I haven't done anything," Finley furrowed his brow. "It's the two of you who seem to be confused. Tell them Nicolai."

Nicolai coward further into his corner at the sound of his name.

Finley watched him grab instinctively at the fresh bruising around his neck, "Nicolai?" he asked.

He watched him swallow.

He watched as he wouldn't look Finley in the eye.

"You almost killed the boy," the guard snickered beside him. "We should have let him finish."

Nicolai raised his hands over his head.

Finley felt the adrenaline drain from his body. "What are you talking about?" he asked, though he didn't want the

"Fairy dust?" Paxton turned. "Why not Rowan?"

Doyle turned on his heel, "I do not wish to kill him. Just torment."

Finley drew his attention to Paxton as a rush delusion crept back to his mind. His body lingered with weightlessness again. For a moment, he saw Paxton as if he were half-man, half something else entirely. A man of conviction. "Is smoking allowed in the presence of the devil himself?" Finley asked. He held Paxton's gaze. There was a darkness surrounding him, a black cloud following in his shadow.

"I can assure you there is no devil here, only the demons of our pasts." Doyle hopped onto his desk to sit, turning his back on Finley to Paxton.

"What does he see?" Paxton asked with intrigue. He squinted at Finley, studying him as Finley drifted again into fever and mayhem.

"How am I to know?" Doyle shrugged, he glanced over his shoulder to Finley whose gaze wandered wildly. "Whatever it is, it will bring him closer to us."

"Sir." A guard stepped into the room behind Finley. Heat tickled the back of Finley's neck, he tried desperately to shake it off, to shake himself out of the fairy dust. "There is something you may find interesting."

"Were you not asked to leave?" Paxton questioned. He scolded the guard with a simple expression.

"That's alright, Paxton," Doyle said. He waved the guard further into the room. "Go on."

"Treasach was strangling the boy in his cell, on and off for hours." Finley felt hollow. He would never. "If we weren't there to get him, he would have killed him." The words rang in his ears. He would never.

It all felt so distant as though he were a thousand miles away. Even as he struggled, he sensed whatever Paxton and Doyle had going, would ruin the fae world one way or the other.

Doyle smiled. "You see?" He clapped his hands together as he hopped off the desk. Doyle spun on his heels toward Paxton, his coat dancing along behind him. "My plan is already working."

Paxton lifted his head to Doyle. "You consider a drugged Light fae murdering another, a plan?"

"If the plan is to turn him," Doyle paused, "then yes. He is but one of many, a very popular one if I may add. If he sees what he is truly capable of, he may wish to embrace it rather than run away from it."

Paxton rubbed his thumb and middle finger together as he pondered Doyle's thought process. "I have tried that plan before." He examined Finley from afar, "I can assure you, it doesn't work."

"Have you now?" Doyle asked suspiciously. "I've known you for some time now, and yet, I know not of this. Perhaps if you would share your knowledge we wouldn't meet at a crossroads."

Paxton glared at Doyle with uncertainty. "You are aware there are not many of my kind," he said.

"Of your kind?" Doyle asked through a laugh. "There are plenty of wiccans on this Earth."

"Not wiccans," Paxton corrected. "You incompetent maggot. Necromancers. Dark witches. I had the perfect plan to create more Dark witches. I was so close..." his thoughts trailed off as his mind wandered somewhere else.

"Helena?" Doyle recalled. He only had so much knowledge of the woman. Simply a name, a prisoner, and a call for vengeance. "You wanted my people to find her, to extinguish those wolves, and you told me to not ask questions. You said 'trust me. It's all to help the Dark fae.' And I did not question it."

"Helena was with child," he replied angrily. "If her family's blood merged with my family blood, it would have been catastrophic."

"Then why do you wish for me to stop?" Doyle asked him. "If you have this child and I manage to get Tre–"

"I do not have the child," he said sharply.

"But, the night we destroyed that village–" Doyle began.

"What I thought was a victory," Paxton said. The muscles in his jaw tightened, "Ended as a failure. Helena deceived me. I have since misplaced the child."

"All the more reason for us to turn Treasach." Doyle leaned against his desk with his knuckles holding him up. "We need more power."

"He is not power!" Paxton shouted. Doyle bit his tongue. "He is a chore," he added. "A project that will distract you from what needs to be done. We have all the power we need."

"We don't know that for sure," Doyle argued. "None of your plans have worked so far."

Paxton glared. "If we need more power, we will simply take it," Paxton told Doyle. He gestured his hand towards Finley, "This is a waste of time, Doyle."

Doyle clenched his jaw so tightly he could have broken his own teeth. He had been working at Finley for years, more closely the past months. Doyle glanced at Paxton. "What do you suggest I do?" he wondered.

"That choice is yours," Paxton answered. "Now is the time for your fun and games."

Doyle pondered briefly. But in reality he had known for months how he would end Finley Treasach. "Guards!" he called. The room flooded with a handful of contorted beings. "Escort Treasach to the main floor," he said. "And bring the boy."

Chapter XXVII

"Wake up!" Kaden's eyes burst open from their slumber.

She rested against one of the burnt beams that once held up the roof to the porch when her eyes fell upon a familiar face. A face she never thought she would see again.

"Megan?" Kaden asked with disbelief.

Megan sat leisurely beside her, her dark curls with the same bounce they had the night she disappeared. When she looked over at Kaden, she didn't seem concerned by the confusion ridden in Kaden's eyes.

"What are you doing here?" Kaden asked her suddenly. She swallowed down her first instinct which was to ask her how she was seeing her in flesh and bone and instead wrapped her arms around her.

"Why are we hugging?" Megan asked her. Kaden felt

the warmth in her body, the smell of her shampoo, the air in her lungs. She squished Megan in her embrace, but Megan didn't hug her back, and she didn't care.

"How?" Kaden pulled away from her, though she didn't want to. She held her by the shoulders at arms length, "How did you—" Words fumbled out of her mouth as she looked Megan up and down, not a scratch in sight. "You were—" Kaden took her wrists in her hands and turned them in every direction, but there was no sign of what cursed her nightmares.

"Are you feeling alright?" Megan asked with a raised brow. She pulled her wrists out of Kaden's grasp. "Well, of course you're not *alright*. You're still an idiot." Kaden smiled happily at the remark. "I'm not here to tell you what you already know. You can't save him."

Kaden furrowed her brow. "Can't save who?"

"Finley," Megan shrugged as if it were obvious.

Kaden cocked her head to the side. "What?" she asked her. "How do you even know who Finley is?"

"You can't be here, Kaden." Megan watched her, her expression falling serious with no humor in sight. "It's not safe for you."

Kaden squinted, "It's not safe in general, Megan," she replied. "But I would do the same for him as I would do for you."

"Kaden," Megan turned. She took her hands and held them tight. The weight of her grasp felt so real, so alive. "I'm telling you, you cannot be here."

"I'm already here," Kaden told her. "But how are *you* here?" she wondered.

"We need to leave," Megan urged. "We need to leave. We need to leave. We need to leave," she repeated over and over, her sentences falling out of her mouth like a message on repeat.

"We need to leave," Kane's deep voice broke through her dream. He shook Kaden lightly by the shoulder until her eyes flashed open. She half expected to find Megan sitting beside her. She searched around the surroundings, but she was nowhere to be found.

"I was asleep?" she asked Kane.

"Only for a few minutes," he answered. "The pain from your ankle wiped you out."

"Why did you let me sleep?" she wondered. There was a good reason she had kept herself from sleeping too much. It was dreams, nightmares, like the one she had that prevented her from wanting to fall asleep. The nightmares were worse.

Kaden lifted herself off the porch, testing the condition of her ankle. A lighting strike shot through her body, "We need to keep moving."

"I didn't let you sleep," Kane corrected. "You just did." He stuffed the rest of his medical supplies into his bag along with a lighter, some food, and a flare gun. "Why?" he asked her. "Did you have a nightmare?"

She shook her head, "Just...a bizarre dream."

"I guess we'll be strolling through the rest of the forest then," he noted. He studied her as she tried to walk normally, but limped and held onto the loose beams from the torn up house.

Kaden glanced down at her ankle. "Or," she began,

"you could carry me," she scoffed.

Kane zipped his bag shut and looked at her as if there was no chance of that happening. "We'll be fine," she told him. "And who knows, maybe that giant will come back and clear a path for us."

Keeley studied the building as if it were a maze she had to solve, but instead of getting out, she had to get in. She watched where the crows flew and the scarecrow stood. She judged how high the walls were and at what point there would be a second and third story.

Her eyes followed a dirt pathway that led to and from the post separated from the structure as it seemed to be the only point in which anyone came and went.

Out of the corner of her eye, Keeley checked on Blaine who rested up against the trunk of a tree, his eyelids opening and closing as if he were trying not to fall asleep. His head drooped progressively lower and lower as did his breathing.

Keeley whacked him on the arm to keep him alert, but it only seemed to give him a jolt of life for a few moments.

A twig snapped behind them. Keeley turned swiftly, her bow and arrow aimed. She discharged an arrow from her bow in the direction of the movement and began to reload another when she realized shooting it wasn't necessary. She had the next arrow aimed and lowered the point when she recognized the two people walking out of the brush. "I almost shot you," she said plainly.

Kane had the arrow in his hand inches from his face. He flipped the point and handed it back to her, "I can see that."

"How bad is it?" Blaine asked Kaden from the ground. He gestured to the gauze wrapped around her leg.

Kaden looked down and shrugged, "I'll live." She limped her way closer to Keeley to get a better view of the prison. The structure reminded Kaden of the warehouse the Dark fae had taken Magen to, only it was much larger and more ruined. "Some ghouls got us by the river," she explained. "But this giant thing attacked them before they could eat me. Lucky us."

Keeley shot Kaden a quick glance, "We saw a giant creature as well, right after Kane jumped into the river. It killed the beasts that chased us up the tree."

"Hellhounds," Kane corrected from beside them.

They stood in silence as a scream carried through the dead space between them and the prison. Kaden looked down to Blaine, "What's wrong Blaine?" she asked him. His head barely moved to look up at her as if it were ten times as heavy as it should be.

"What do you mean?" Keeley asked her back.

Kaden lowered herself so she was eye level with him. His eyes were glazed over with water, hardly able to focus. She took his head in her hands and held him steady. He gave her a weak smile. "His lips," she said. "They're turning dark blue."

Kane walked up behind her while Keeley kneeled to see the dark blue lines forming around Blaine's lips. The veins around his mouth matched the one that formed on his back. Cracked and spreading quickly.

"I guess I should mention I had a bit of an accident," he mumbled. The green of his irises thinned enough for his pupils to take up most of his eyes.

"What kind of accident?" Kane asked.

Keeley sucked in a breath and sighed as she stood. "Blaine fell into a pile of those....parasite things."

"He what?!" Kaden shouted. She covered her hand over her mouth as her voice carried through the Black Forest.

"When?" Kane asked Keeley calmly.

"A while ago," Keeley answered reluctantly.

Kaden drew her gaze away from Blaine to Keeley. Her expression was vacant, but her knuckles turned white from her grip on her bow. Kaden stood up and peeled Kane's backpack off his shoulder.

"How long is 'a while'?" Kane asked her.

"Niether now or when we first arrived," she replied evasively.

"What does that mean?" Kaden pressed. She took the canteen out of his bag and began loosening the top when she realized it wasn't water inside.

"Do you know what kind of parasite it was?" Kane asked Keeley.

Keeley tightened her jaw. "No," she answered. "They were creatures I've never seen before."

Kane ran his fingers through his hair and clenched onto a tuft of it, "It's not good." He straightened his posture and paused. "Where is it on him?"

Kaden froze in her place and slowly leaned away from

Blaine in case the parasite could easily relocate itself to another host.

"I'm not sure it's on him," she said. "As far as I can tell, it's *inside* him."

Kaden shot Keeley a curious glance, "How did it—never mind. Lift up your shirt Blaine."

Blaine's glazed expression squinted as he weakly glanced up, "What? I already showed Keeley."

"Just do it," Keeley snapped. Blaine pushed himself away from the trunk and lifted his shirt. The black veins tracery stretched from his lower back upwards. "It's worse than before," Keeley said. The blackness of his veins had only gotten blacker and had started to stretch further up his spine.

Kaden looked up at both Kane and Keeley with concern she couldn't hide. Neither of them seemed to have answers and wore the same helpless expression Kaden had. She looked back at Blaine who smiled again weakly, "How do you feel?" she asked him.

"Light," he said.

"He fell over before," Keeley admitted. "We need to be careful if he's still coming inside with us."

"Maybe he should stay out here," Kane suggested. He stepped away, closer to the prison to get a better look.

"I'm right here!" Blaine yelled at Kane. His voice startled Kaden. She had never heard Blaine angry. "I have done everything you have asked me! Blaine Colin will not wait outside!"

"Alright then," Kaden assured him. She patted him on the back as she helped lower his shirt. "Keeley," she turned.

"Have you scoped out the building?"

"There aren't any guards outside," she replied. "The only windows are the ones on the third floor, so we have to use a door."

Kaden looked to where Keeley was pointing to find a rusted door and the sliver of it that was cracked open. "We don't exactly know what's inside those doors," she said doubtfully. "We'll need a plan to get out, too."

"We'll split into pairs," Kane broke in. "Keeley and I will go first and take out as many of them as we can. You and Blaine will go after to look for a way out."

"How will that work?" Kaden asked him. "There are probably hundreds of guards in there and Blaine's injured." She glanced down again at her own injury. She didn't want what happened to Megan to happen to them.

"I was trained for this!" Blaine exclaimed. "The Dark fae will fear the wrath of Blaine."

"For now," Keeley said. "We must use all the help we can get. And do not forget the prisoners." She adjusted her sai swords. They were visible at her sides and she pulled one out to practice wielding it since it had been months since the weight was in her hand. "If I can get some of them loose we will be able to use them, too."

"What about Doyle?" Kaden asked.

"He'll probably leave the moment he knows we're here," she answered. Kaden wanted a different answer. She wanted him first. But she would go through as many guards as she had to to get him. "There's bound to be a portal in the building that you and Blaine must find."

"What if Kane shifts?" Blaine asked suddenly.

They all looked down at the boy with the limp body then to Kane.

"I can only shift on a full moon," he explained.

Kaden crossed her arms over her chest, "I don't think we should go in blind."

Kane scratched the stubble on his cheek and took a glance at the building. "We don't have a choice," he told her.

"How will we find each other?" Kaden asked.

"Once they find the portal and we get Finley," Keeley began. "We'll....."

"My pipe!" Blaine shouted. He tugged out his pipe from his belt and waved it in the air.

Keeley squinted her eyes at him. "What?"

"I can use my pipe to signal we found it," he smiled with a light chuckle that seemed like it hurt him. "Kane should be able to hear it."

"Blaine," Kaden said. "That's brilliant."

Kane removed his axe from his belt, "I guess we're going in."

CHAPTER XXVIII

Finley was brought to the center of the first floor to what the guards referred to as the prisoners' recreational sandbox. Each prisoner was escorted out of their cell and lined up to the edge of the balconies. Against the railings, three stories high, chained up fae waited with anticipation and agitation. The prisoners on the first floor formed a square around the perimeter as Doyle coolly strolled around with his hands behind his back.

The room was nothing but hushed grumbles from the vicious fae who ached for a fight. Nothing changed shape, the floors weren't lava and Finley saw no demons, only the cursed souls of the prison like him. It was Nicoali's screaming that caught his attention.

At first he couldn't find him among the mess of creatures. His fear bounced off every wall and cell in the building. It made Finley's heart race under his chest and his weak body crumble in on itself.

He watched as guards forced Nicolai's kicking and shrieking body forward. It was the first time Finley had seen the boy fight back. His face was stricken with fear and a trail of tears.

Something inside Finley trembled. He elbowed the guard to his left in the face, elbow meeting nose with a quick crack to run for Nicolai.

Nicolai pulled backwards away from his guards, away from him.

In an instant, someone grabbed Finley by his shoulder and he heard a pop as it fell out of joint. He bit down on his lip, swallowing blood from the pain. The curse sitting on his tongue boiled as the fae around him laughed at his expense.

As the two were brought to the center of the room, Nicolai was thrown at Doyle's feet like a scrap of meat. The boy glanced up hesitantly, "Nice to meet you boy," Doyle said through a smile to the fragile child.

"You—you're Doyle," his voice quivered. Nicolai's eyes fixated on the man dressed in a purple suit as if he were the devil himself. He swallowed knowing that meeting Doyle was not a welcome achievement.

"What do they call you?" he asked him as Nicolai sat up on his knees.

"Nic—Nicolai," he said.

"Interesting." Doyle kneeled down to face the boy himself.

"Do you know what that name means?" he asked Nicolai as if he were his mentor and not a murderer.

Nicolai shook his head in response.

"It means victory of the people. Do you know why you are here, Nicolai?"

He shook his head.

Finley struggled under the hold of his guards, his arm dangling at his side.

"You are here because I wanted you here. You're a faerie of hail, rain, and frost. Did you know that?"

"Yes," he whispered. "Fin—Finley told me." Nicoali's eyes fell to the floor.

"Did he?" Doyle asked as he turned to see Finley wrestle with three guards restraining him. He wanted to rip the skin from Doyle's face and Doyle knew it. Out of spite, Doyle flashed Finley a wry smile before turning his attention back to Nicolai. "Did he tell you why I've kept you here so long?" he asked the boy.

"No," he answered. Unease washed through him. He began to fiddle with the iron chains that nipped at his skin.

"You see, Nicolai," Doyle began gently. "I wanted you here so you could join me one day. You are strong, and very powerful. It's why I took you at such a young age. I wanted you to grow up here to become the best you could be. But now," he paused. Nicolai's innocent face looked up at him. "*Now* I truly know why I brought you here." Doyle rose to his feet and turned to Finley, "Feast your eyes upon young Treasach!" he shouted for the entire prison to hear. "He who aligns with the Light! He who has slaughtered hundreds of Dark! Our people!" His voice echoed as he spoke to his guards and the prisoners with Dark running through their blood. "He who is nothing more than a fallen warrior now, shall be sent to the scarecrow! To suffer as his kind has made our kind suffer over the years! But first," Doyle stopped. He turned on his heels to Nicolai. "We have one more surprise for Treasach, one last going away present as the poison in his veins runs dry and the beasts of hell feed upon his flesh."

Half the crowd cheered while the others stood in silence.

"Doyle!" Finley clenched his teeth. He thrashed against the guard's grip. A fourth and a fifth appeared out of nowhere. "Please," he pleaded. "Just take me to the crow."

The smile Doyle had across his face made the prisoner's spine quiver. He held out his hand and waited for a servant to place a serrated knife in it. "That's not half as fun as this."

Nicolai's gaze found Finley's. He toyed with his chains and bit his lower lip. "Let Finley go!" he yelled to Doyle. "He hasn't done anything bad!"

"Hasn't done anything bad?" Doyle asked the small child. He turned toward him, the knife hidden behind his back. He strolled toward Nicolai causing the guards to nearly jump out of their skin with anticipation. "Did you hear that boys?" he asked his fellow Dark fae. "Treasach hasn't done anything bad."

"Nicolai," Finley warned. "It's okay, I deserve this." Finley felt the filthy hands of guards grabbing at his body. "Doyle, just end my life. Please."

"What was that?" Joy rang in Doyle's voice. "Treasach wants *me* to end his life?" Doyle waved his hand at Finley and looked up at his guards. "The warrior wants me to end his life," he scoffed. "A request you shall receive."

"I'll join you!" Finley blurted out.

The words were true.

The room fell silent.

Doyle lifted his chin in the air. "That's something I have been waiting a long time to hear," he said. "But, I'm afraid you're too late. The offer no longer stands."

"It's what you want!" Finley yelled as the remaining hope he had crumbled inside his chest. "What you have always wanted! What's changed?"

"I believe the expression you may be familiar with is, 'someone showed me the *light*.'" Doyle walked to Nicolai and stood behind him.

"Paxton?" Finley asked. "You're nothing to him."

Doyle grabbed Nicolai so his arm was around his neck and the knife was to his throat. The glint of the knife shimmered against the light. "Always a sharp tongue."

"Finley!" Nicolai screamed. His cry echoed. Tears streamed down his soft, frail face. He held onto Doyle's arm and tried to pry it away.

"Nicolai," Finley swallowed. "You're going to be alright."

Doyle chuckled in the boy's ear, "Don't worry boy, you weren't completely useless."

He swiftly slid the rigid blade across Nicolai's neck.

"No!" Finley crumbled.

Blood seeped down Nicoali's neck. He coughed and choked, reaching up to wrap his hands around his neck to keep the blood inside.

"It's okay," Finley told him. He fell forward so hard against the guards and reached out to the boy, who was like a brother, that the guards couldn't stop him from kneeling. He fell on the cement floor inches from Nicolai as the light behind his eyes dwindled and fought to stay alive.

Doyle dropped Nicoali's limp body. He snapped his fingers together, relieving Nicolai of his chains.

A gust of icy wind brushed between them. White and blue follicles formed at Nicolai's lips, crystals that spread from the tips of his fingers and lingered in a circle around him. Tiny flakes of ice formed on his eyelashes. And in his dying breath he smiled. "Frost."

The frigid chill pulled the air from Finley's lung as the frost and ice melted away to nothing.

Cheers broke out among the Dark fae.

But it was all muffled in Finley's ears.

His stomach coiled and twisted. Guilt stabbed him and tore him apart. Sorrow strangled him around the neck.

He was just a boy.

"Anyone else who wishes to test me," Doyle shouted as she flashed the freshly painted knife to the others. "Will see a similar fate." Doyle stepped over Nicolai's body and leaned over to Finley. "If it brings you any comfort, we'll be feeding his meat scraps, along with yours, to the others tomorrow. Well, whatever's left of you anyway."

Finley stared at Nicolai as if he could get up any minute. He held his breath, waiting for him to get back up. But he didn't. Instead, the dark red liquid filled the dried, cracked skin that were his hands.

Someone began to pull Finley away. They dragged

him, limp and unable to move away from Nicolai. And Finley didn't fight it. He would have escorted himself to his own death.

CHAPTER XXIX

With the door cracked slightly, Keeley peered into the darkened hallway. A sliver of light from the moon shone in to reveal an abandoned corridor with moist walls. She hesitated before she stepped inside. With her back pressed up against the wall she made her way cautiously towards the first corner where the hallway intersected with another.

Keeley held her sai sword parallel to her forearm as she peered down the hall to the left, then the right. She caught a glimpse of two gruesome, almost deformed, Dark fae heading in her direction. A crooked grin spread across her face. She took one step back as adrenaline filled her veins.

As the two came to the edge of the hall where Keeley hid, she used the guard closer to her to lift herself high enough to wrap her thighs around the second one's neck.

While the muscles in her legs choked one, she used her sai sword to slit the other's throat before either of them could breathe a word.

The first guard collapsed with blood oozing from his throat while Keeley pulled herself around the second guard to do the same to him. As soon as the two were out cold, Keeley dragged their bodies by their feet into the hall which she entered from. She cracked the door open to signal for the rest of them to enter.

Kane came in with his axe at the ready and stepped over the two deceased bodies without comment. Kaden followed with her dagger in hand and Blaine at her side.

"Wow," Blaine whispered. "I knew Dark fae were ugly, but I didn't think they looked like this."

"Which way?" Kaden asked Keeley.

"The guards came from the right, so that's where Kane and I will go. You two take the left." Keeley flipped one of the dead bodies over on its side and patted him down. "Here," she said. She handed both Kane and Blaine extra blades, then proceeded to unhinge a large ring of keys off the other's belt.

Without another word, Kaden took Blaine to the left of the hallway, leaving Kane and Keeley to deal with whatever madness was taking place to the right.

Kane and Keeley made their way down the hall towards what looked like a large open floor plan. In the dim lighting, they could hardly make out what lay ahead. But the rustling of chains rippled through the hallway.

"How do you plan on unlocking those chains?" Kane asked her. They hovered in the darkness of the hall, watching as prisoners began to appear huddled together.

In the center of the room, a young boy's body lay limp while guards cheered and prisoners stood stiff with fear.

"I can change into a guard," Keeley told him. "They are too filled with their own ego to notice if I unlock the prisoners from behind."

"You have to change back once we start fighting otherwise I'll probably try to kill you," he said without looking at her.

In an instant, Keeley's fair-haired form with the leanness of a warrior shifted into a hideous green skinned Dark fae.

Kane caught a glimpse of her as she entered the room and recoiled from the smell. Inside, each level had prisoners and guards spread sporadically. She made her way behind the closest set of chains and grabbed them tightly in her hand. Her palms sizzled at their touch causing the fae to turn around sharply. "Keep quiet," she said into their ear before they could say anything.

The prisoner turned their head back to the scene in front of them as the chains fell to the floor. Keeley made her way down as quickly and as quietly as she could. It wasn't long before the other prisoners began to notice a guard unlinking their chains. The further she got, the more rambunctious they became.

One particular prisoner disobeyed her instruction to stay put until the time was right. He took a step out of line and she sharply pulled her blade to his neck. "If you wish to live," she spat into his ear, "do as you are told."

He swallowed against the blade, "I want them to

suffer," he hissed.

"So they shall," she told him. She pressed her blade tighter against his neck, daring him to disobey. They exchanged a glare before the prisoner nodded reluctantly. After Keeley roughly shoved him back into place, she continued down the row.

"Traitor!" someone grumbled. Keeley scanned the crowd to find a guard on the second level pointing her out. She glanced down at her work quickly, only a row of fae were free. "We have a traitor!" The guard shouted louder and caught the attention of the prisoners but only a handful of other guards.

Keeley narrowed her eyes at the shouting guard. She handed the keys to one of the newly released prisoners, "Unlock as many as you can."

He looked at her in shock, "What?"

"I am of the Light fae here to save you. Now go," she commanded. She swiftly pulled an arrow out from its satchel and aimed it at the guard who couldn't keep his mouth shut.

"Traitor! Look over—" The arrow shot through the air and landed in his chest, mid-sentence. His shouting hadn't caught the attention of his fellow Dark fae as much as he would have liked, but his body tipping over the balcony and landing with a thud in the center of the room did.

The joyous cheers of the fae silenced.

Keeley shifted back into herself and pulled out her sai swords. She stabbed the guard closest to her in the neck as Kane entered the room by chopping a guard's head clean off his shoulders. As the room came to comprehend what was taking place, the unlinked prisoners grew empowered and ran at various guards using iron chains and the magic they wielded at their mercy. The first level broke out in an uproar as guards fought loose prisoners. The battle had begun.

As a riot broke out behind them and the echoes of metal clanging against metal followed them down the corridor, Kaden and Blaine rushed in the opposite direction. The distant outbreak of battle faded behind them. "This way," Kaden instructed Blaine who had been limping along with Kaden.

She peeked through a set of double doors. The room was darker than the rest of the building, lit only with the flames burning underneath several stove tops. She pushed the kitchen door open reluctantly, scanning for any sign of life. The space was overwhelming with heat and bubbling liquid. Whatever was cooking spewed out of the pot and onto the stove tops. It almost looked like marinara sauce, but Kaden wasn't about to verify what she knew was *not* actually marinara.

They stealthy crept further into the room which Kaden first had thought was empty until they stumbled across a Dark fae sleeping in a chair next to a narrow staircase. Kaden held her arm out for Blaine to stop as soon as she saw the sleeping man, or what she assumed was a man.

With his eyes covered with a chef's hat, she couldn't

tell.

It was the fae's horse-like snore that reassured her he had been asleep for a while. She pointed to the staircase and nodded at Blaine.

Before she could take another step, Blaine grabbed Kaden by the arm. When she shot him a glance, he simply shook his head not with disapproval, but with fear. Kaden looked at the chef to make sure he hadn't moved. Then, she leaned closer to Blaine. "We have to go up."

"Maybe we should look down here first," he whispered back.

"No," she said sharply. "We should start at the top and work our way down."

The chef shifted his position in his deep slumber causing them to freeze.

"But there's a lot of fighting going on down here," Blaine pressed.

"Which is why we need to go upstairs," she told him. Kaden started towards the steps again, but Blaine pulled on her arm once more. She turned to him, what she found were eyes filled with dread. "What's wrong?" she asked him.

Blaine hesitated. His gaze dropped to his feet. "I–I'm not sure I can get up the stairs."

She furrowed her brow, "What do you mean?" she asked him. "You said you felt okay before?"

"I did," he said. "But...it hurts...to walk and steps are—" Blaine looked past Kaden, eyes wide. "Kaden!" he shouted. He withdrew his sword from its sheath.

She turned her head to find the Dark fae chef swinging a butcher's knife at her back. She ducked in time for him to miss and knock several boiling pots to the floor in the process. Blaine held his sword at arms length, "Halt you swine!"

The cook grinned at Blaine's failed threat. He charged for Blaine, but Kaden grabbed a frying pan off the floor and as she stood up, smacked him across the face with it. The hit dazed him, burning his face with a sizzle. He screamed and clawed at his skin. Kaden smacked him again, this time on the top of the head. His heavy body fell toward her, but she managed to step aside, tugging Blaine out of the way.

"Why would they use an iron frying pan?" she asked as she examined it in her hand.

Blaine glanced around cautiously, "Someone probably heard that." He tucked his sword back into its sheath.

"Yeah." Kaden dropped the frying pan next to the unconscious man. "I'll help you up the stairs, lean against me."

Blaine let his weight fall to Kaden as they made their way up the crooked stone stairs. The staircase was slick and curved up into a spiral making it harder for Kaden to see what was headed toward them.

"Kaden," Blaine said just before he dropped all his weight on her. She staggered back, almost tumbling back down until she caught herself.

She lowered Blaine down on a step for a moment, "Are you okay?" she asked him. The thundering sound of someone running down the stairs struck Kaden with fear. Blaine shifted, but couldn't move easily leaving them stuck in a narrow stairwell.

The only advantage she had was that she knew someone was coming, but they didn't know they were there until they turned the corner.

Kaden pulled out her dagger and waited for the fae to come around the bend. Adrenaline pulsed through her veins. She glanced down at Blaine who seemed paler than he had before.

Her jaw locked.

A guard appeared before her, darting down the bend. Kaden plunged her dagger into his gut and used the angle of the stairs to her advantage by flipping him over herself to send him tumbling down the stairs. The weight of him sent pain throughout her body as she strained her ankle. She swallowed a scream.

"I didn't mean to fall," Blaine whispered.

Kaden heaved in a breath. "If you hadn't," she said as she helped him back to his feet, "he would have killed us at the top of the stairs."

Kaden dragged herself and Blaine up the rest of the way to a closed dungeon-like door. She cracked it to see they had reached the second floor. The guards were struggling with the prisoners who remained chained. "There's a whole group of guards and prisoners," she whispered to Blaine.

"How many?" he asked her as he leaned up against the wall.

She looked at him in his weak condition, "Too many." Kaden slid Kane's bag off her shoulder. "I have an idea," she said.

She removed the flare gun and closed the bag back up,

slipping it back on her shoulders.

"What is it?" Blaine asked as he looked at the foreign object.

"It's a flare gun," she told him. "If I can hit the guards they'll catch on fire."

"Sounds good to me," he said weakly.

"What about the prisoners though?" she questioned herself. She knew the prisoners were helping them fight or at least were distracting the guards enough for them to complete their plan. She bit her lower lip.

"Maybe the heat can melt the chains," he suggested.

"I doubt it," she sighed. "But we don't have a choice." She swung the door open and shot the flare out of the gun. The bright orange-red glow startled everyone and most of the fae it hit flipped off the balcony. The brightness of the flare nearly blinded even Kaden, but it was the smokiness that suffocated the area and helped them escape without anyone taking notice. "Hurry!" She pulled Blaine to follow her as they searched for the next staircase.

CHAPTER XXX

They hauled Finley by his upper arms, his body and legs dragging against the stone behind him. The discomfort of his shoulder out of its socket made him want to vomit as they walked down a long corridor that ended with double doors. A faint light shone through the crack of the doors, moonlight. Finley realized he was taking his final breaths, his final steps even if they were just his feet dragging against stone. When the doors opened he would be free, free to fall prey to darkness.

"Do you hear that?" one of the guards asked abruptly. The creature came to a halt, turning half way down the hall where they had just been.

"It's just the chains of Treasach's restraints," his

comrade grumbled. He tugged Finley's arm, pulling him in two different directions.

In the distance, metal clashed with metal.

"No," he argued. He pulled Finley back. "It sounds like fighting."

"That's victory you hear," he brushed him off. "After all, look what we got." He tugged Finley forward with a huff when a scream echoed down the hall. The two guards both looked at the emptiness behind them as battle cries erupted.

"Something's wrong," one said.

"I told you," the other snapped. "They're rioting that's all, now let's get this filth out of here."

They tugged him forward, his body falling along like a rag doll when the soft echo of feet padded their way. They half turned again as the young girl ran down the hall, her head turned away to watch what was behind her. As she ran without looking, she collided with one of the guards. "Ahh!" she shouted as she jumped back and fell to the ground.

One of the guards lifted Leila to her feet, tossing her easily against the dewy wall. "Girl," he snarled in her face. "What's going on out there?"

Her fear stricken eyes locked onto the guards. She hesitated for a moment. He shook her roughly for an answer. "A riot," she responded through her trembling native French. "The prisoners..."

He grabbed a fist full of Leila's hair and forced her head back. She let out a whimper of pain as he clenched her messy braid in his hands like it was a rat's tail.

Finley glanced up at her as her feet wiggled in the air.

He wondered how long she would survive his touch. "Let her go," Finley snapped. His guard threw him up against the opposite wall. His spine scraped against the uneven stone.

"Not another word out of you," he warned, pressing a blade to his throat.

"Who started it?" the guard asked Leila. He forced his hideous face against her delicate cheek as she turned away from him and he sniffed.

"I don't know," she told him. He didn't like her answer. He pulled her hair back further exposing her neck as she let out a scream.

"I said," Finley kneed his guard between the legs causing him to hunch forward. "Let her go."

"Get a grip on him!" Leila's guard shouted.

The guard rose and plunged his blade into Finley's shoulder. The blade made its way through his flesh and bone out the other side. He stifled a scream, letting it settle in his throat as his chest heaved.

"Another word from your mouth," he threatened in a low voice. "And I'll cut out your tongue."

"Go ahead," Finley seethed. "I mean to die today anyway."

The guard's lip curled, "We should turn back," he said to his companion.

"Our job is to escort him to the crow," he snapped.

"It doesn't sound good," the other guards replied. He turned halfway as did the other guard. They exchanged angry glances as they argued. Leila glanced at Finley with tears forming at the edges of her eyes. He mouthed in her native tongue 'I'm sorry'. Finley closed his eyes tightly.

Nicolai was gone. Kaden was gone. Leila would be gone. Everyone he cared for.

"Doyle will have our heads if we do not complete our job," the guard snarled as he tossed Leila from his grasp to the ground.

"We won't have heads if the prisoners are loose."

"Paxton," Doyle said as he quickly waltzed through the doors of his chambers. "There is a riot with the prisoners. I recommend we leave while the guards take care of the problem." Doyle shuffled around tossing various important bottles and books into a bag.

Paxton calmly shifted in Doyle's seat as though a riot was no concern to him, "I can't leave without my prisoner."

"Your prisoner has not said anything useful nor do I believe he will." Doyle spun in several directions in search of anything he deemed worthy of his attention. His bag filled slowly. He moved so fast when he finally noticed Paxton had not moved an inch, he abruptly stopped in front of his desk. "We must go," he said, gesturing his hands for emphasis.

"Not without my prisoner," Paxton repeated. "If he does not give me information it doesn't matter. He will suffer for betraying me."

"It's your funeral," Doyle shrugged, although he thought Paxton's judgment was clouded with hatred. "But I'm taking my leave. You may use my guards as your own. Perhaps we shall meet again at your place of comfort?" Doyle didn't wait for a reply before he stepped into the giant hearth across the room like it was a normal thing to do. His figure blended with the flames as they burned purple and teleported him somewhere unknown.

"You," Paxton said sharply to a Dark fae hovering quietly in the corner. "Guard."

The grungy looking fae stepped forward, "Sir."

"How bad is it out there?" Paxton wondered as he gazed out the floor to ceiling window to the stillness of the forest. The screams and clatter of metal did not shake him.

The Dark fae hesitated before answering. "We have never had a riot like this one before," he answered. "Prisoners are loose."

Paxton took in a deep breath as he pondered his options. "I will stay here," he told the guard. "You will fetch me the man in solitary. He is *not* to be harmed," he warned the guard with sharp eyes. "Do you understand your task?"

"Yes, sir." The guard nodded respectfully as he turned to retrieve Paxton's most valuable resource.

CHAPTER XXXI

The battle progressed drastically, ever shifting as more prisoners became unchained, unhinged. As the wrath of those held captive grew overwhelming, the fight turned to Keeley and Kane's favor. The guards had more weapons, more numbers, but the prisoners carried the reason for the fight deep in their chests.

The two had executed the first of many kills, slaughtered their way through dozens of Dark fae. Their fellow fighters were fragile from months, years, of poor treatment. Keeley watched as several of them burned the fire for the fight, but fell just as quickly.

With a gesture of his wrist, Kane sent an arm clean off a guard's body with his axe. As he maimed Dark fae after Dark fae, more appeared from crevasses of the prison. "We can't kill them all!" he shouted to Keeley over the cries of the injured. Keeley forced her way closer to him, standing back to back. She shot arrows in any direction she could, her quiver laced with faerie magic so every arrow pulled replaced one lost.

Kane turned to his side as a Dark fae swung a black sword for his head. He used his axe to block the hit leaving the rest of him defenseless. Keeley maneuvered her way to use Kane's shoulder to aim her arrow at the guard. The clean shot hit him in the jugular and Kane kicked his dying body away.

Keeley watched as the second level of prisoners struggled, their chains still bound. She darted past fae for the stairway to the second landing as she shot arrows in front of her. The stairway was cramped with enemies both coming and going. One Dark fae clutched her by her silver locks from behind as another ran toward her with a blade. She lifted one of her sai swords from her side, reaching over her shoulder to stab the Dark fae behind her in the face. As warm liquid dripped down to her shoulder, staining her porcelain skin, she tugged the blade from his skull. Keeley kicked the guard charging her in between the legs, then swiftly slashed his cheek open with one swipe.

With each step she took, she used both her sai swords to stab the hearts of her enemies. She plunged her blade into ribs, lungs, and groins. Keeley flipped countless bodies over the railing of the second story to take other guards out onto the first floor below.

An unexpected rumbling shook the ground as if there

were an earthquake forming and Keeley thought the building was about to collapse underneath them. Bricks went plummeting out of the prison wall on the first floor. Dust clouded the scene below, but once it settled she saw the mud-like creature appear out of the debris. The creature, unharmed by the impact of breaking through the wall, lifted guard after guard off their feet and flung them around.

"Fantastic," Keeley said under her breath as she sent two fae to their death.

"It's helping us," a prisoner said as he used his chain to strangle a guard. Keeley shot him a quick glance and kicked the guard he was trying to kill in the face by lifting herself up with an exposed pipe.

She landed on her feet and shot an arrow to the first level where a guard was quickly making his way toward a distracted Kane. "What?" she asked as the arrow released.

"It's killing the Dark fae," the man said. "Not the Light." Keeley felt relief wash over her when a blaze of fire burst out of nowhere, spreading at a rapid pace.

She turned sharply to the man beside her, "Finley Treasach," she said. "Where is he?"

The man looked at her with a furrowed brow. "He was headed for the crow, first floor. *If* he's still alive." Without warning, a blade pierced through the man's chest from behind. It stuck straight out of his heart with blood dripping off its tip. Keeley grabbed a small blade from her boot and hurled it at the fae who stabbed him, hitting him directly in the heart.

She kneeled beside the prisoner as he gasped for air and his teeth reddened with blood. "You have been sacrificed for peace and now you shall receive it." Keeley pressed her lips to his forehead, gently laying him down on his back. This was what battle looked like. It was bloody and gruesome. She jumped over the balcony of the second floor onto the rubble the creature had made. "Kane," she said roughly when she landed. "Follow me."

"Kaden...I can't..." Blaine said as his legs gave way underneath him. "I can't." She carried him as best as she could, with her injured ankle. His weight along with her own made her want to scream in pain.

"Blaine," she said. "We can't stop here. More guards are coming." Kaden looked at him, his eyes closed and his mouth turned completely blue as if the parasite was sucking the life out of him.

The scuffling of guards echoed down the hall they found themselves in. With no choice, Kaden made a snap decision to drag Blaine into the nearest room. She opened a set of double doors, black with gold tracery. "Blaine," she whispered as she placed him on the floor against an armchair. She shook his shoulder lightly. "Keep your eyes open." Kaden lifted his head up, his skin was feverish and growing paler by the second.

"I guess as luck may have it, I made the right decision," a voice said suddenly. The sound sent a shiver down Kaden's spine. She turned sharply, startled to find the room was not empty.

Kaden aimed the flare gun at the unfamiliar man behind the desk with her finger on the trigger. "Don't even think about it," she warned him with an eerie tone. The man didn't flinch. His eyes never fell to the flare gun pointed at his head. He watched her curiously for a moment without so much as a word. "I have another flare in here and I won't hesitate to crisp you alive."

"We must keep moving!" One of the guards argued with saliva dripping from his teeth.

"No, we must go back!" The other shouted in reply. The two guards bickered, though their task had been simple enough.

Finley stood with his back against the wall, barely capable of holding himself up. His thoughts carried him down the hall and through the doors that lead to his death. He saw Nicolai each time he closed his eyes. Each blink hurt more than the last and he cursed his stubbornness. He watched as Leila quivered against the opposite wall. She was another victim of his too, torn apart but alive. He wondered if everything he knew was a lie, if everything he was taught led to a path of destruction.

Suddenly, one of the guards' gnarly voices quieted as an arrow lodged itself into his right eye socket. "Step away from them now!" Keeley's voice filled the space. Blood smeared against her skin and her eyes locked onto the one remaining guard.

When Finley saw her, he felt like he had drifted into a dream. Or a hallucination. Part of him wanted it to be the little fragments of fairy dust in his veins. Then Nicolai would be alive.

The guard with the arrow through his eye fell and as he did, the other guard took Leila off the floor, using her as a shield with a knife against her throat. "Drop the bow or I slit her right now."

Keeley held her position as someone Finley didn't recognize appeared behind her. The guard pressed harder against Leila's vocal guards and she whimpered. The muscles in Keeley's jaw tightened as she lowered her weapon.

The guard glanced behind his shoulder towards the doors. He slowly began to walk backwards, Leila as his hostage. She squeezed her eyes shut and whispered something under her breath.

Finley launched himself with the remaining energy he had left inside of him at the guard. He wrapped his chains around his neck and pulled. The knife fell to the floor with a clank as the guard reached up for the iron links. Leila ran out of his grasp and hid behind Keeley.

They watched as Finley strangled the guard. He choked and gargled on his own saliva. "You deserve worse," he whispered into his ear. The guard's legs collapsed underneath him. He stopped moving. He stopped fighting. He stopped breathing, but Finley clenched the chain around his neck for a moment longer. As soon as he was satisfied, Finley dropped his body and took the keys from his belt. He unchained the collar from around his neck. The iron peeled some skin off as he removed it, as much as it hurt, he was glad he could breathe again. "How did you find me?" he asked Keeley.

"Kaden," she said.

Finley's heart froze. "Kaden?" he asked her. "She's alive?"

"Yes," Keeley answered. "She's with Blaine now."

The dried and cracked skin that covered Finley's body began to heal with each layer of iron he peeled from his flesh. All his cuts and bruises erased as if they had never been there at all. He rubbed his wrists where the chains had restrained him and watched as his injuries sealed back up. Finley thought about how this would have felt for Nicolai. To be free. "She was dead," he said to himself.

"No." Keeley shook her head and took a step closer. "Doyle erased her memory."

Finley squeezed his eyes shut and glared up, "I'm going to kill him," he told her. He saw as the strange man Keeley had arrived with unchained the iron from Leila's wrists. "Who are you?" he asked sharply.

"Nobody," Kane replied. "Can we go before this place burns to the ground?"

Keeley turned with a nod, "Have you heard Blaine's pipe?" she wondered.

"Not yet," he sighed. "But we need to keep moving if we're going to make it through the portal."

"Wait," Finley said just as they were about to run.

"What?" Keeley asked.

"There' something I need to get first," Finley told them. He took the weapons off the guards' dead bodies.

"We don't have time, Finley," she said. She grabbed him by his arm and he pulled out of her grasp aggressively.

"I have to do this," he said. "Leila," he spoke in French. "Can you get them to the solitary block?" She stood for a moment frozen. "Leila?"

"Yes," she answered shyly. "But…why?"

"We need Silas," Finley told them.

"Who?" Kane asked.

"Trust me," Finley said. "We're going to need him." Keeley looked him in the eye and nodded. "Go," he urged. "Hurry!" He didn't waste another moment as he headed down the hall toward the riot, toward the fire and flame.

"How will he find the portal?" Keeley asked Kane.

"Doyle's chambers," Leila replied through broken English. She continued in French, "Finley's been there several times, he must know."

Kane glanced between the two as they exchanged words. Keeley tried to translate as fast as she could so he would understand. Frustration grew inside of him with everyone going in different directions. "Lead the way," he said with a sigh of irritation. Kane waved his arm for Leila to go in front of them toward the solitary wing before the fire could spread and ruin their chance of escaping unscathed.

Kaden kept the flare gun aimed at the man behind the desk. Her expression was stone and unyielding. He slid an admiring smile across his face, "You look just like her."

"I don't care about some stupid story about how you know my mother," she snapped. "Frankly, I've heard more than I can handle."

As he moved in front of the desk slowly, Kaden held the gun more firmly in her hand, following his every move.

She had threatened him with a death in flames, but she worried if she shot him, the room around them would engulf them all.

"What about your father?" he asked coyly.

Kaden furrowed her brow as he positioned himself so he leaned against the desk. He held his hands in front of him and studied her, Kaden groused, "You mean the psychopath who ordered the massacre of innocent people? I just want to shoot you for even asking."

His smile turned to a frown leaving his face unreadable, "You can shoot me, but then your friend will die."

"What?" she asked quickly. Kaden snuck a glance at Blaine. His chest barely rose and fell. The dark blue around his mouth turned black and threatening.

"I can save your friend," he offered.

She looked back at the man who was too serious to be kidding. "Or," she countered. "You could tell me how *I* can save my friend and I can still shoot you."

"That's clever," he laughed darkly. He turned away from her towards a bench-like table pressed up against the windows where various colored jars rested. "You're very clever. I know you won't though, because if you did want to shoot me, you would have done it. But..." he started to pour several liquids into own bowl. "You could save him yourself if you knew how."

"Okay, well, I don't know how, so are you going to help me or am I going to kill you?" She lifted the gun, aiming at the back of his head but he didn't turn around to face her.

"It's simple witchcraft," he replied. "You would know if you embraced your heritage."

"I grew up human, sorry to disappoint you." A pit began to form in Kaden's stomach. Her hand with the gun turned clammy and began to shake slightly. Her eyes narrowed on him. Her heart pounded against her rib cage. She didn't want to ask how he knew who she was because she was afraid of his answer, "Who are you?"

"I think," he said as he moved the bowl onto the desk, "deep down, you already know the answer to your own question."

CHAPTER XXXII

October 31, 1995

The sky was covered with a black blanket as trees brushed against one another from the passing breeze. Several campfires crackled against the wind sending sparks into the nightscape of wolves. A charge filled the air like electricity before a storm. "You should be resting," Gig told the new mother.

Helena had gotten hold of a small porch table and set it beside one of the burning fires, her ingredients spread out the way she liked. "We have to do this now," she told the old woman. "Before sunrise. Do you have everything?" Helena asked Silas. The man with long sandy hair settled the objects she requested onto the table.

"Right here," he replied.

A bulky man stepped out of the house. He was brawn enough to be mistaken for a lumberjack, and perhaps he was among many other things. He was the leader, the alpha of the pack Helena found herself hiding amongst. "What are you doing?" he asked her as he approached the table with peculiar objects. Although he had a rougher, meaner appearance, he seemed to be the most caring of the pack.

Helena didn't respond as she concentrated on her work at hand. "It's a protection spell," Silas explained, as he always seemed to speak for Helena. As her familiar, he was connected to Helena on a very unique level, one that allowed him to know exactly what she needed and when she needed it. "It will strip the baby of her fae heritage so she's safe."

"No one will be able to find her," Helena added. She properly formed everything she needed before creating the spell. She grabbed a handful of soil from the ground and added it to a separate bowl.

"What about Paxton?" the alpha asked. "If he's as strong as you claim he is—"

"The spell will drain my powers for a while," Helena snapped. She didn't mean her words to be so disrespectful to someone who had helped her in her time of need, but she had a plan and questions were not welcome. Especially when it came to protecting her daughter. "It's strong."

"Isn't strong magic what you're running from?" he asked her. He placed his hand on Gigi's shoulder and pulled her back as he moved closer to Helena.

"The purity of the Light is just as powerful as the malevolence of the Dark," Helena said. She looked him in the eye and held his gaze before she began to cast the spell.

"She needs to," Silas added. "It's the only way we can ensure the baby is hidden."

"Do you have the blood?" Helena asked Silas.

"Yes," he said, pulling a small vial of crimson out of his pocket.

"Who's blood is that?" the alpha asked.

"The baby's," Helena told him. She used the largest bowl and added the dirt to it, "Earth for birth." She poured fresh water from the nearby stream after, "Water for cleansing." Then, she added burning incense to the bowl, "Air for the breath of life." Helena took up a knife and cut across the palm of her hand, letting her blood drip into the bowl before adding the small vial of the baby's blood. "Spirit for everything and nothing." Lastly, she lit a match and tossed it into the bowl. The combination caused a small explosion in the bowl as the flames burned away all the elements with it, "Fire for purity."

The spell burned into the night, drifting far and wide mingling with magic when a woman came running up toward them. "How much time do we have before he gets here?" she asked them. Fear rippled through her eyes, her jaw set from the moment Silas and Helena first arrived seeking help.

"Not much," Silas answered. He took out a small handkerchief from his pocket and began to wrap it around Helena's cut hand. Helena didn't seem to notice. She stared vacantly as the flames that burned away her relationship with her daughter, that separated the bond.

"Our people are ready," the alpha told them along

with his mate.

"Dad!" A little boy yelled, running up behind the group so fast he couldn't stop in time and ran into his father's legs.

"Kane," his mother said, "you should go with Gigi." She gestured for Gigi to take the boy back into the house.

Gigi took his tiny hand in hers, "Come Kane, this way."

"I want to help," Kane pleaded as he tugged on his father's shirt.

His father bent down to talk to his son face to face, "You are helping me by protecting Gigi and the others." He glanced up to Gigi and smiled, "Remember?"

"But that's boring," Kane whined. His father ruffled his hair and Kane swatted his touch away.

"When you are a part of a pack," his father began, "sometimes you get stuck with the boring job, but that doesn't make it less important." He hugged his son tightly in his arms, "Now hurry." Kane gave his mother a kiss on the cheek before he walked with Gigi back to the house.

"It would be best if the children leave," Silas told them.

"They will," the alpha replied. "As soon as we have cleared the portal Gigi and the elders will take the children."

The flames of the spell died down, leaving nothing but ashes. "Is it finished?" Silas asked Helena.

She nodded first, "Yes." She began to move the bowls around again and both the alpha and his wife disappeared into the small village they had made for themselves. "She's safe."

"She's going to be protected and loved." Silas placed a comforting hand on Helena's shoulder but she didn't stop. He watched on as she pulled out new ingredients, "What are you doing?" he wondered.

"Just taking extra precaution," Helena told him.

"Helena," he said with hesitation. "You just did a very serious spell, your powers are drained. If you keep going you could—"

"It's not for me. It's for my daughter," she said. "If I can't watch her grow up...I can at least make sure she's safe." Helena took more soil from the ground and placed it into a bowl, she added more water creating a clay-like substance in her hands.

"What spell are you doing?" Silas asked her as she added more of her own blood.

"A blood spell," she answered. She flattened it out as much as she could and traced with her finger the Hebrew word, *Emet.* "If she bleeds on this soil a golem shall rise to destroy anything that means to harm her."

Silas watched Helena as she desperately worked to keep her daughter protected. "She's not going to be on this soil, Helena. She's not going to have her powers."

"We don't know that for sure," she argued. "Paxton is smart, he'll find her. He'll twist his methods into her mind, just like he did with me."

CHAPTER XXXIII

Kaden, with a lump in her throat, looked directly at Paxton and, with a sharpness in her tone said, "I don't intend on getting to know you." She rested Blaine's head against the armchair gently before she stood from the floor, lowering the flare gun. "So just heal my friend."

"I told you I would," he answered. "I always keep my promises, but..." Paxton began. Kaden held her breath. "I want something in exchange."

"Of course you do," she sniffed as she made her way slowly towards the desk where he started mixing an unknown concoction. "What would a father be if he didn't want something?"

Paxton froze mid-pour of a dark purple liquid, "I would have been a good father to you." He continued to grab mixtures and herbs from all over the room. Kaden eyed him wearily. She knew the room they stood in was Doyle chambers based on the lavish purple furnishings, but she wasn't sure faeries and witches used similar ingredients.

"Keep telling yourself that," she huffed as she shot him a sharp flatline smile even though he didn't look up from his spell work once.

"I had a nursery built for you," he said. "A lovely home built for your mother, for us to raise you in."

"She ran away from you," Kaden noted. "Hid me from you. I'm sure it wasn't because she didn't like the curtains you picked out."

"*She* ran away," he corrected. "*She* hid you. *She* took your powers. *She* stripped you of your heritage. She prevented you from knowing me, from knowing your true self. She painted me as the monster, but look where you are." He removed his concentration to Kaden for the first time since he started working on the potion to heal Blaine. He pointed to the closed doors of the chambers where the sound of hundreds of fae fought, "That is the sound of war. All her planning to prevent you from *that*, has led you right into the world she didn't want you a part of. Destiny brought you here, to me. If she hadn't taken your powers, you could have healed your friend by now." Kaden glanced over at Blaine as she watched the once happy-go-lucky boy struggle to breath. "And where is she?" Paxton asked her. "She's not the one here to help you, I am."

"You're insane," Kaden murmured. "You murdered—"

"I did what was necessary to find my child," he cut her off with a raised voice.

Kaden took a half step back, not anticipating a change in demeanor. She could tell by his tone and posture that he really did believe murdering was necessary.

Her eyes began to water. Her friend was dying on the floor, her other friends were lost in battle and she couldn't help but wonder if she did have her powers, could this all have been prevented. "So killing people," she said once Paxton broke his focus off Kaden. "Is a good thing?"

"Like the wolves are so innocent?" he argued. "When they shift on the night of the full moon, they have no control. If they get out into the human world and turn, there's no stopping them from tearing someone apart."

"They don't have control of their own bodies!" she found herself shouting. "You do!"

"Perhaps you're right," he sighed casually. As he paused he watched Kaden's emotions crumble before him, "I shouldn't have killed them. Perhaps Helena shouldn't have hidden behind them to defend her and what I thought to be you."

Kaden squinted her eyes at him as her mind went over his last words, "You have them," she said. "Don't you?"

"I have my surrogate daughter," Paxton admitted. "We live quite nicely together. Although, your mother's long gone by now. She left."

"I doubt she just left," Kaden snapped. If Helena had gone through all that trouble to protect her, Kaden knew her mother would not just give up. And if her mother was anything like herself, she wouldn't have left her surrogate daughter behind to play house with a psycho.

"Believe whatever you want."

"So what do you want?" she finally asked him. "To reunite as a family again? Or maybe you want a favor?"

"I don't want any of those things," he told her. "I want you to be you."

Kaden couldn't resist the laugh that escaped her throat, "How touching."

"She took your powers," he said. "I wish to return them to you."

"Why?" Kaden asked, "To use me?"

"So you can embrace this world without limitations. The world you were meant to be a part of."

"That's it?" she shrugged. "No strings?"

"Not unless you want there to be. With your powers, you can take on this world. You can do whatever you want, you can have whatever you need." Paxton had his mysterious potion mixed and ready. The dark liquid color lay resting in a bowl covered with various symbols Kaden had never seen before.

"What about the girl? Your 'surrogate' daughter." Kaden asked him as he graciously handed her the bowl. "What if I want to return her to her family?"

Paxton pondered the question as Kaden took the bowl from him. "You can save that for another day. Hurry," he gestured for Kaden to go to Blaine's aid, "he needs to drink it."

Kaden looked at it suspiciously but rushed to Blaine. He was quivering as cold sweat dripped down his face. She poured as much liquid into his mouth as she could, tilting his head back. But some of it spilled down the sides of his face. "Now what?" Kaden asked once the contents of the bowl were empty.

"He'll wake in time," Paxton told her.

"What's stopping me from shooting you now?" she asked as she turned back to look at him.

"Your curiosity," Paxton said flatly. He began something new, something that involved the skull of a human.

Kaden swallowed the lump she had in her throat as the screams from outside the doors seeped into her ears. "What do I have to do?"

Paxton gave her a half smile, "All I need from you," he began, "is your blood."

The thick black smoke from the burning building led Finley directly to the heart of the fighting. It was a place Finley had grown so used to seeing and fearing he would never leave. Smoke grew heavier in the air, blackening everything in a heated cloud. Finley covered his arm over his mouth and tried not to suck in the oxygenless air. Most of the fae were screaming to get out of the building as they struggled past him. But Finley was too driven by emotion to allow anyone to get in the way of what he was about to do. Anyone who tried quickly met their fate with the swipe of his blade.

Finley's foot caught on a large brick he hadn't seen causing him to fall forward. He was able to catch himself with the palms of his hands and looked to his right to see a gaping hole where cells used to be. The oxygen from outside the prison fueled the fire to spread at an unimaginable rate. Finley realized then that he had not felt fresh air, even if it was not-so fresh air in months. The sky was dark, polluting quickly with fumes. The trees were as dead as Finley felt inside, though he wouldn't allow anyone to know.

Despite the circumstance, it was a moment he had dreamed to share with Nicolai. He had wanted to see his face light up as he saw the magnificent coloring of the outside world, the smell of fresh air fill his lungs. For a brief moment, Finley wondered if perhaps this was his fate. If Doyle was right. If he should just lay among the fallen only to be consumed by flame. It would have been a better fate than what Nicolai had gotten.

A soft voice from Finley's past made its way into his mind, "*You are my brave little knight, Finley.*" His mother had told him the day of his departure, "*...but there are others who need you...you cannot be selfish.*" Finley thought about Kaden. How she had lost Megan to his world. How, though she must have been devastated and broken inside, she came to rescue him.

Finley lifted himself off the rubble and onto his feet. He walked barefoot on the sharp edges of the bricks to the center of the room which was covered with a mix of bodies and stone. He used all his strength to dig through the pile to the very bottom where a little boy lay motionless and broken.

Paxton placed the skull on top of Doyle's desk. The top of the skull had been cut off, allowing the skull to be hollowed out and used as a bowl. He dumped some dirt into the skull first, "Graveyard dirt," he said to himself.

Kaden shifted her focus from Paxton's spell to Blaine's still body then back to Paxton again. "I don't care what ingredients are involved in your spell," she told him.

"You need to start learning at some point. You've already missed so much." He took a vial of clear liquid off one of Doyle's shelves and added it to the graveyard dirt, "Tears of an innocent."

Innocent, she thought. What innocent person had suffered for her own gain? She swallowed hard.

Kaden looked away to Blaine's face for any signs of life, but there was still nothing changing. "This isn't working!" She shouted at Paxton. Kaden shot up from her spot beside Blaine and charged the desk, "You said he would heal."

Paxton glanced at her calmly as he opened a jar of pale yellow powder. "It takes time," he told her. With the lid of the jar open, Kaden smelled the strong stench of rotten eggs. "Th boys had the parasite in him for some time." Paxton took a small teaspoon of the powder and added it to the skull, "Magic does not mean miracle."

"What is that?" she asked harshly.

Paxton lifted his lips into a weak smile, "Sulfur. Now, I just need your hand."

"What for?"

"I told you," he said as he pulled out a small blade with a red jewel at the cross of the knife. "I need your blood for the spell." Kaden eyed the knife and took a step away. "Alright, I'll go first," Paxton said as he took the knife to his own palm. A fine red line appeared against his pale skin. Blood dripped into the bowl in a stream, mingling with everything else. Paxton wiped the blade on a small cloth from his pocket. He held the blade, handle first and waited for her to comply with her own hand.

Kaden took a deep breath before she took it, "If I get some blood disease from this, I'm sending you my medical bill." She mimicked him reluctantly. Kaden winced from the blade against her sensitive skin. Paxton held her hand over the bowl as her blood mixed with his. As soon as it was all combined, he gave her another cloth for her hand. "What now?" she asked.

"Now," he said. "We burn it." Paxton took a match and lit the mixture on fire. Kaden watched as the combination burned a bright blue flame. The sulfur bubbled together creating a red liquid that matched the color of their blood.

"I don't feel different," Kaden said.

"You will."

As the fire burned, Kaden made her way back to Blaine without turning her back on Paxton. The color in his face seemed to be coming back again, although he was pale to begin with. She felt his forehead with her hand and lifted his body so he was laying on her lap. When Kaden turned back to look at Paxton, the flame burning in the skull was beginning to die out and Paxton was gone. She scanned the room for any sign of his existence, but found none.

Kaden brushed Blaine's hair out of his face, "Come

on, Blaine. Wake up." Tears rolled out of the corner of her eyes, "How many more friends do I have to lose?"

The double doors to Doyle's chambers swung open. Kaden pulled out the flare gun and aimed to shoot. She half expected to find a Dark fae, but instead her eyes met Finley's. His body was frail, a skeleton with flesh.

He, too, was half expecting to find an enemy or Doyle himself behind the doors as he walked in, weapon ready.

Relief washed over Kaden. Finley was alive and breathing. He carried a body in his arms, a young boy while Kaden cradled Blaine in her arms. The room fell silent once they knew they were both safe. Kaden went to speak, but found nothing to say and everything to say. "I know," Finley said.

She flashed him a weak smile.

"Is he…" Finley began but his word died in his throat. He carried Nicolai's body inside and rested him beside Blaine.

"No," Kaden said quickly. "Or at least I don't think so, he's healing. What about your…" she asked, gesturing towards the boy. Finley looked down at the body but didn't answer. "I'm sorry."

"Me too," he mumbled.

As the two of them sat next to their friends, Kaden couldn't help as tears welled in her eyes. She wasn't crying, but she wanted to. She had lost so much and wasn't sure Blaine was healing. Seeing Finley again made that sliver of hope move through her, "I didn't think I'd ever see you again."

Finley looked at Kaden with a weak smile, "That

makes two of us."

"Have you seen Kane? Or Keeley?" she asked to avoid a total melt-down.

"Yeah," he answered. "I sent them to get someone from the solitary wing. They should be here soon." Finley reached over to examine Blaine. He titled his head to get a better look at the black veins that spread around his mouth, "How is Blaine healing?"

"It's complicated," Kaden murmured with a shrug. "Paxton was here—"

"Paxton?" Finley asked, confused. "You met him?"

"Yeah," she answered with surprise. "You know him?"

"We were acquainted recently," he told her. "What did he do?"

Kaden took in a deep breath, "It's a long story, and we don't exactly have time for it now. The building's burning down."

"Good," Keeley said as she burst through the doors, "You're all still alive." She made a b-line to Blaine once she saw his body limp in Kaden's arms. "What happened?"

"We need to get out of here," Kane interrupted as he entered the room with two others behind him.

Leila rushed past them to the fireplace, "Through the fire." She pointed to the hearth which was the only way Kane and Kaden understood what she was saying. "I've seen Doyle leave a dozen times."

"Helena?" A scruffy man stared at Kaden. His sandy blonde hair hung past his shoulders, his clothing torn and two sizes too big.

"Who are you?" Kaden asked.

"Silas," Finley said as he stood. "It's nice to put a face to a name."

"We don't have time for this," Kane argued. "Fire moves faster than you think."

"Kane's right," Kaden agreed. She tried to lift Blaine's body, but couldn't carry his dead weight any longer. Keeley helped, putting one of Blaine's arms behind her neck while Kaden did the same with the other. "We don't know where this leads."

"It doesn't matter," Finley said with Nicolai in his arms. "Just go!" Keeley and Kaden went through the portal first with Blaine dangling from them, followed by a very hesitant Leila. Then Finley carried Nicolai through with Silas and Kane shortly behind as the prison burned to the ground leaving nothing but ash.

EPILOGUE

Romania

The dew covered stone encaged an empty room with a single window too high for anyone to reach. The floor was stone, like the walls, and slippery from leaky pipes that hung above. A dark haired girl sat in the corner of the room, her fingers gliding across a small puddle. Her feet were bare, her knees were scraped from the roughness of the stone against her skin which was as pale as a ghost. She hummed a melody to herself as she always had. It was the only comfort she could provide herself with, alone in the dark room.

The dark wooden door with black iron tracery opened slowly as a maid entered to put a tray of food down for the girl, "Is Father back from his trip?" she asked the maid.

"Paxton returned the night before last," she answered

flatly. The woman waited patiently for the young girl to eat her meal. It had been her job for the past nineteen years. Every day she was instructed by her master to make sure the girl was fed and healthy.

"When can I see him?" she almost pleaded. The young girl crawled to her tray of food. She used her fingers to pick apart bits of finely cooked chicken, a baked potato, and some vegetables.

"He had not said," the maid told her.

"Has he said anything about me?" she spoke through her meal.

"Not a word." The girl ate slowly with the purpose of keeping the maid in her room for as long as possible. The maid was the only personal interaction she had gotten in the past month, and she wasn't about to rush it.

"Can you ask him?" she asked softly. "I just wish to see him."

"I will inform him of your request," the maid told her with her chin held high. "I cannot promise you will get it."

"I must see him," she said as she slid across the stone floor. "It has been over a month since we last spoke."

"He is aware and busy."

"Please," she begged at the maid's ankles. "I must see him."

"Are you finished?" she asked, tugging the plate out of the girl's hands.

"Please!" she begged as the woman pulled the plate from her. "Agatha," she clung to the bottom of the woman's leg. "Don't leave me here."

"Guard!" Agatha called as she glared down at the

innocent girl. A large man grabbed the girl by the collar of her dress and threw her back against the stone wall. An edge of the stone hit her spine as she fell to the floor. While she was down, Agatha took her exit. The girl darted for the door before it could close.

"Please!" she shouted as the door shut. Her body hit the door and she banged her fists against it so much she thought, or hoped, it would fall off its hinges. "You can't leave me in here!" She forced all her weight against the door twice before giving up. "Let me speak to my father! Agatha!" The young girl cried as her body slid against the door from defeat. "Please! Father!"

LOST DAUGHTER

Anniversary Coming Soon

ACKNOWLEDGMENTS

To those who have read my work and continue to read my work I am forever grateful for each one of you. That look in a reader's eye, that curiosity, is what makes me want to create and share the stories I see in my head, the stories that keep me up at night. Keep reading, keep writing, and never forget what you create is magic.

Always,
Dylann

ABOUT THE AUTHOR

Dylann Rhea is a writer and illustrator originally from Bergen County, New Jersey. Rhea writes books with magic, imagination, and on occasion creatures that don't speak. A *Reader's Favorite* recipient of a Five Star review, Rhea continues to doodle, daydream, and create with magic in her head and passion in her heart.